**Two brand-new stories in every volume...
twice a month!**

Duets Vol. #71

Talented Liz Jarrett takes us to Texas for Part One of
the HOMETOWN HEARTTHROBS miniseries this
month. Leigh Barrett is so-o-o *tired* of her three
overprotective brothers! Her solution? Matchmake
and marry 'em off one by one! Liz always writes
"a passionate tale with delightful scenes and exciting
characters," says *Romantic Times*.

Duets Vol. #72

Twice voted storyteller of the Year by *Romantic Times*,
Silhouette writer Carol Finch never fails to "present her
fans with rollicking, wild adventures...and fun from
beginning to end." Jennifer Drew returns this month
with another fun-filled BAD BOY GROOMS story. This
writer "gives readers a top-notch reading experience
with vibrant characters, strong story development and
spicy tension," notes *Romantic Times*.

Be sure to pick up both Duets volumes today!

It was perfect

Megan knew Chase's kiss would be every bit as perfect as she'd imagined. Maybe even more so.

Chase finally opened his eyes and stared at her. "Uh. See...that kiss was what I thought it would be...don't get me wrong—it was a good kiss between friends—but there's no chemistry between us."

Huh? It took a second, but Megan knew what he was up to. "You're right. Now we know that kissing each other is like sucking on a dead fish."

Chase frowned. "A dead fish? Now hold on—"

Without waiting for him to follow her, Megan led the way to her front door. She opened it and stood back, watching him walk out. Her smile only grew as he passed by, muttering to himself.

Tonight Chase had kissed her. Really kissed her. And fireworks had happened, even if he wasn't ready to admit they'd been anything more than sparklers. She and Chase were perfect together. Just as she'd known they would be.

Things could only get better from here....

For more, turn to page 9

Give in to temptation?

No way. Hailey thought hard for a few minutes, when suddenly an idea occurred to her. "Whoever kisses the other first has to wash the other person's car."

Nathan looked openly dubious. "You think that's a strong enough incentive to keep us from kissing?"

"It's the best I can think of, unless you have a better idea," she replied.

"Afraid not. Okay, that will be our penalty." He gave her a big smile, then opened her apartment door to leave. "I'd better go on home. I'll talk to you tomorrow." He paused again and stared at her intently. "And just for the record, I have a feeling that before this summer is over, we'll both have the cleanest cars in the county."

Funny, 'cause Hailey was thinking the exact same thing.

For more, turn to page 197

HARLEQUIN DUETS

ISBN 0-373-44137-1

Copyright in the collection:
Copyright © 2002 by Harlequin Books S.A.

The publisher acknowledges the copyright holder
of the individual works as follows:

CATCHING CHASE
Copyright © 2002 by Mary E. Lounsbury

NABBING NATHAN
Copyright © 2002 by Mary E. Lounsbury

Printed in U.S.A.

Catching Chase

Liz
Jarrett

TORONTO • NEW YORK • LONDON
AMSTERDAM • PARIS • SYDNEY • HAMBURG
STOCKHOLM • ATHENS • TOKYO • MILAN • MADRID
PRAGUE • WARSAW • BUDAPEST • AUCKLAND

Dear Reader,

Aren't brothers and sisters great? They've shared
your past, they stand by you when times get tough
and most importantly, they love you for who you are.
Unfortunately, they also know all the embarrassing
things you did when you were young. Sometimes,
they also interfere a little too much in your life.

That's the problem facing Leigh Barrett. She's so-o-o
tired of her three brothers meddling in her life. She
figures the only way to get them to leave her alone
is to fix them up so they're too busy with their own
lives to bother with hers.

I really like Leigh. She knows what she wants
and goes after it. I hope you enjoy reading about
her and her brothers—Chase, Nathan and Trent—
in HOMETOWN HEARTTHROBS. Look for the
next miniseries installment in November when
Meant for Trent and *Leigh's for Me* is available!

All the best,

Liz Jarrett

Books by Liz Jarrett

HARLEQUIN DUETS
20—DARN NEAR PERFECT

HARLEQUIN TEMPTATION
827—TEMPTING TESS

To my husband, with love.
Thanks for so many wonderful years.

To my editor, Kathryn Lye.
Thanks for believing in these books.

1

AS SHE STUDIED HIM, standing near the entrance to the city council room, Megan Kendall couldn't help thinking what a heartbreaker Chase Barrett was. Everyone in the small town of Paxton, Texas, thought so as well. With his drop-dead gorgeous looks and his handsome-devil smile, women fell for him like pine trees knocked down by a powerful tornado. Even Megan couldn't claim to be immune. She and Chase had been good friends for over twenty years, and he still didn't know she was madly in love with him.

Yep, a heartbreaker all right.

"Picture him naked," Leigh Barrett whispered to Megan.

Stunned, Megan turned to stare at Chase's younger sister. "Excuse me?"

Thankfully Leigh nodded toward the front of the room instead of in her brother's direction. "The mayor. When you're giving your presentation, if you get nervous, picture him naked."

Megan slipped her glasses down her nose and studied Earl Guthrie, the seventy-three-year-old mayor of Paxton. When Earl caught her gaze, he gave Megan a benign, vague smile.

"I don't think so," Megan said to Leigh. "I prefer to think of Earl as fully clothed."

Leigh giggled. "Okay, maybe that wasn't such a hot idea after all. Let me see if I can find you someone else to think of naked."

"That's not necessary. I'm not nervous." Megan flipped through her index cards. Her argument was flawless, her plan foolproof. She had nothing to be nervous about. Besides as the head librarian of the Paxton Library, she knew every person in the room. This presentation would be a snap.

But with puppylike enthusiasm, Leigh had already stood and was looking around. She hadn't spotted her oldest brother yet, but Megan knew it was only a matter of time before she did.

"Leigh, I'm fine," Megan tried, but Leigh finally saw Chase and yelled at him to come over and join them.

Chase made his way through the crowded room. The city council meetings usually drew a big audience, but Megan was happy to see even more people than usual had turned out to listen to her presentation of fund-raiser ideas for new playground equipment.

When Chase got even with Megan and Leigh, he leaned across Megan to ruffle his sister's dark hair. Then he dropped into the folding chair next to Megan and winked at her. "Ladies, how are you tonight?"

Megan tried to keep her expression pleasant but it wasn't easy. Ever since she'd moved back to Paxton last year, pretending her feelings for Chase were platonic was proving harder and harder. At six-two, with deep black hair and even deeper blue eyes, he made her heart race and her palms sweat.

"Don't ruffle my hair, bozo," Leigh huffed on Megan's right, smoothing her hair. "I'm in college. I'm too old to have my hair ruffled."

On Megan's left, Chase chuckled. "Squirt, you're never going to be too old for me to ruffle your hair. When you're eighty, I'm going to totter up to you and do it."

"You and what orderly?" Leigh teased back. "And just for the record, I like Nathan and Trent much better than I like you."

"Oh, please." Megan rolled her eyes at that one. Leigh loved all of her brothers, but everyone knew Chase was her favorite. When she was home from college, she always stayed with Chase.

"I love you, too, squirt," Chase said, not rising to his sister's taunt. Instead he nudged Megan. "You okay?"

"I told her to imagine the mayor naked if she got nervous, but she doesn't want to do that," Leigh supplied.

"I can see why not," Chase said. "Earl's not exactly studmuffin material."

"Oooh, I know what she should do." Leigh practically bounced in her chair. "Megan, if you get nervous, picture Chase naked."

Megan froze and willed herself to stay calm. The absolute last thing she wanted to think about was Chase naked. Okay, maybe she *did* want to think of him naked, but not right now. Not right before she had to speak in front of a large portion of the entire town.

"I don't think so," Megan muttered, shooting a glare at Leigh. The younger woman knew how Megan felt about her brother, and this was simply one more not-so-subtle attempt to get the two of them together. In the past few months, Leigh's matchmaking maneuvers had grown more extreme.

"I don't think I'll need to picture anyone naked," Megan stated.

On her other side, Chase offered, "Well, if you get flustered and it will make things easier for you, you go ahead and think of me naked, Megan. Whatever I can do to help."

Megan knew Chase was teasing her, but suddenly she realized how many years she'd wasted waiting for him to take her seriously. She'd fallen for him when she'd moved to town at eight. Dreamed about him since she'd turned sixteen. And tried like the dickens to forget him when she'd been away at college and then later working at a library in Dallas for five years.

But nothing had helped. Not even seriously dating

a man in Dallas had helped. In her soul, Megan believed she and Chase were meant to be together.

If only she could get him to notice her.

"Hey there, Chase," a smooth, feline voice fairly purred over their shoulders. "You're looking yummy. Like an especially luscious dessert, and I positively love dessert."

Oh, great. Megan glanced behind her. Janet Defries. Just what she needed tonight.

Chase smiled at the woman half leaning on his chair. "Hey, Janet. Do you plan on helping Megan with her committee?"

From the look on Janet's face the only thing she planned on helping herself to was Chase, served on a platter. She leaned toward Chase, the position no doubt deliberate since a generous amount of cleavage was exposed. "Are *you* going to help with this committee, Chase? Because if you are, I might be able to pry free a few hours."

Yeah, right. Megan shared a glance with Leigh. They both knew Janet would no more help with the committee than dogs would sing.

"I'd like to help, but it's a busy time on the ranch," Chase said.

"Shame." Janet slipped into the chair directly behind him. "I think you and I should figure out a way to spend some quality time together."

Her message couldn't have been clearer if she'd plastered it on a billboard. Megan hated herself for wanting to know, but she couldn't *not* look. She turned to see what Chase's reaction was to the woman's blatant come-on.

Mild interest. Megan repressed a sigh. Of course. Janet was exactly the type of woman Chase favored. One with a high-octane body and zero interest in a lasting relationship.

"Maybe we'll figure it out one of these days," Chase said, and Megan felt her temperature climb.

Okay, so she didn't have a drawer at home full of D-cups, but Megan knew she could make Chase happy. She could make him believe in love again.

If the dimwit would give her the chance.

Janet placed one hand on Chase's arm and licked her lips. "Well, you hurry up, else I might decide to go after Nathan or Trent instead. You're not the only handsome devil in your family."

Chase chuckled as he faced forward in his chair once again. "I sure am being threatened with my brothers tonight. But I'd like to point out that neither of them stopped by to lend their support, and I'm sitting here like an angel."

Leigh snorted. "Angel? You? Give me a break. You could make the devil himself blush, Chase Barrett."

Chase's grin was pure male satisfaction. "I do my best."

As Megan knew only too well. She'd watched him beguile a large percentage of the females in this part of Texas. Darn him, why couldn't he throw a little of that wickedness her way? Just once, she'd like to show him how combustible they could be together. But even though she'd been back in Paxton for almost a year, the man still treated her like a teenager. She'd just celebrated her twenty-ninth birthday. She wasn't a sheltered virgin with fairy-tale dreams of romance. She was a flesh and blood woman who knew what she wanted out of life.

She wanted Chase.

After a great deal of commotion getting the microphone to the right level, the mayor finally started the meeting. Within a few minutes, it was time for her presentation. Megan stood, adjusting her glasses.

"Remember, picture Chase naked if you get nervous," Leigh whispered but not very softly.

Megan was in the process of scooting past Chase, who had stood to let her by. She froze, standing directly in front of the man who consumed her dreams and starred in her fantasies.

He grinned.

"You know, I think I just may do that," Megan said. "And if he gets nervous, he can picture me naked, too."

HAD TO BE THE HEAT, Chase decided as he settled back in the wobbly folding chair. Or maybe the water. Either way, something was weird because Megan Kendall had just flirted with him.

Leigh moved over to sit in the chair next to Chase. "You talk to Nathan or Trent today?"

Chase glanced at Megan, who was straightening

her notes, so he had a couple of seconds to answer his sister. "Nathan and all of his employees are working overtime trying to get that computer program done. Trent has a new officer who joined the force today, so he's busy, too. You're stuck with me."

Rather than looking upset, Leigh's expression was downright blissful. "Megan and I are thrilled you're here."

Through narrowed eyes, Chase studied his sister. She was up to something as sure as the sun rose in the East, and he'd bet his prize bull it had something to do with him breaking up her necking session with Billy Joe Tate last night.

"Whatever you're doing, stop it," Chase told her. "It won't work."

Leigh fluttered her eyelashes at him, feigning innocence. "Who me? I'm not up to anything. How could I be with you and Nathan and Trent on me every second of every day? I'm almost twenty-two, Chase."

"Spare me the melodrama. Just because I don't want my baby sister having wild sex in a Trans Am in front of my house doesn't make me a meddler."

Leigh snorted loud enough to make some of the ladies in the row in front of them turn to see what was happening. But Leigh, as usual, ignored everyone around her and barreled on.

"If it were up to my brothers, I'd still be a virgin," she actually hissed at him. "Thank goodness

I decided to go away for college. No one in Austin has ever heard of the Barrett brothers.''

Chase opened his mouth to say something, but ended up gaping at his sister like a dead fish. He was still formulating what to say to Leigh's pronouncement when Megan started her presentation. Good manners, drilled into him over the years, forced him to remain silent and listen to the speaker. But what in the blue bejesus was up with the women tonight? And why was he the lucky man who got to be trapped in the middle of it?

And since when wasn't Leigh a virgin? He glanced at his sister, who was nodding and smiling at Megan as she went over the reasons why the city park needed new playground equipment. He had to face facts. Their father had run off with a waitress when Leigh had been four. Their mother had died when Leigh had been eleven. She'd been raised by three older brothers who might have been strict with her but who did a fair amount of hell-raising on their own.

He should count his lucky stars that Leigh hadn't made him an uncle already.

But for crying out loud. He was all for liberated women, but did they all have to liberate themselves in front of him at the same time?

He turned away from Leigh, but not before making a mental note to talk to her once more about safe sex and nice boys.

Behind him, Chase could actually feel Janet Defries staring at the back of his head. No doubt she was planning all the things she could do to him if she had plastic wrap and an economy jar of mayonnaise.

And then there was Megan. Frowning, he looked at her. She was carefully explaining how the city could build a large wooden play castle like so many bigger cities had if they raised enough money and had enough volunteers. Her talk was going well, as expected, but Chase could tell she was nervous. They'd been friends for so long, he recognized the signs.

He gave her an encouraging smile.

And the look she gave back scorched him. Good Lord. She was picturing him naked.

Before he could stop himself, before he could even think about how downright stupid it was, he found himself picturing Megan naked, too.

And really, really liking what he pictured. Sure, a few times over the years, he'd turned the idea of Megan over in his mind. After all, she was attractive in a sedate sort of way. She had long ash-blond hair and pretty green eyes, and a slim body with just enough curves to keep a man interested. Sweet curves that would be soft to the touch, and silky to the taste and—

Whoa. What in the blazes was he doing? Megan Kendall was one of his best friends, not to mention, a woman who actually believed in things like love and marriage. He blinked, and mentally tossed a thick, woolen blanket over Megan's naked body.

That would be the end of that.

"I think Chase should cochair the committee with Megan," Leigh announced, bringing Chase's attention back to the meeting going on around him.

He glared at Leigh. "What? I don't have time to cochair a committee." He glanced at the city council, the mayor, and finally, at Megan. "Sorry. I'm too busy at the moment."

"Everyone is busy," Earl said. "But you make time for something as important as this." The mayor leaned forward. "Don't you want your children to have a nice park to play in someday, Chase?"

"I don't have any children, Earl, and I don't plan on having any."

He looked at Megan, whose expression could only be called sad. Great. Just great. Now he'd disappointed her by saying he wouldn't cochair the committee. Well at least he'd found a way to get her to stop picturing him naked.

"Hold on a minute here," Leigh said. "It's your turn to help, Chase Barrett. Trent's the chief of police, so he does a lot for this town. And Nathan's computer company supports practically everybody. I've volunteered at the senior center, and I'm coming back to town next fall to do my student teaching. It's your turn to do something to help."

A slow, steady throbbing sensation started somewhere in the back of Chase's brain. Leave it to his sister to put him in an awkward position. "I don't have the time right now, Leigh. I'll be happy to make a donation, though."

Megan's expression softened. She forgave him. He knew she forgave him. Naturally sweet Megan would understand.

Ah, hell. Now he felt lower than a rattlesnake's rump.

"What would it involve?" he half groaned, wanting to do whatever it took to get out of this room and away from these women.

"It wouldn't be much," Megan told him. "Just help with the carnival and the auction. I'd only need a couple hours of your time for the next few weeks."

Like he believed that. A carnival and an auction sounded like a lot of work. "Why do we have to have both?"

Leigh thwacked him on the arm. "Weren't you listening? Megan explained that the carnival will bring in the people, then the auction will bring in the big money."

Chase frowned at his sister. "Oh."

"I'll be willing to help on this committee if Chase is cochair," Janet said from over his shoulder.

The throbbing in the back of his head grew more intense as several other single women in the room also agreed to help on the committee, that is of course, if he did, too."

"See there, Chase, you're a popular guy. Lots of

folks want to help out if you join in," Earl said. He glanced at the members of the city council. "I think this sounds like a great plan. Let's take a vote."

Chase wasn't surprised the council agreed with the mayor. What wasn't to like? Everyone was happy except for him.

"I never agreed to help," he pointed out to Leigh after Megan gathered her things and headed back to sit down.

"Oh, let it go, Chase. You're like a neutered hound dog, going on about something that's over," Leigh said.

A soft, sexy, feminine laugh floated around him, raising his body temperature. Who in the world... He turned, bumping right into Megan. The smile she gave him was so very unlike the Megan he'd known for years and years.

Her smile was pure seduction.

"Trust me, Chase is nothing like a neutered hound dog," she said softly.

The water. Something was definitely wrong with the water in this town.

CHASE WAS UPSET WITH HER, but Megan couldn't muster the guilt to feel badly about how things had turned out. Chase was cochairing the committee with her, and she couldn't be happier.

Turning her compact car onto the long gravel driveway leading to Chase's house, Megan found herself humming. Last night couldn't have gone better if she'd choreographed it. Everyone had taken it for granted that Chase was the cochair. Then Leigh had invited her to join the family for the traditional Sunday barbecue, and Megan had quickly accepted, leaving the meeting before Chase could finagle his way out of helping.

Now all she had to do was take advantage of this opportunity that Leigh and the citizens of Paxton had inadvertently given her. Well, maybe that the citizens of Paxton had inadvertently given her. Megan was fairly certain Leigh had pushed her together with Chase on purpose.

Either way, it didn't matter. She had a chance to make Chase notice her, and she planned on using that chance. Last night, she'd stayed up late skimming two of the recent additions to the Paxton Library: *Squash the Wimp Within* and the sequel, *Do It or Die Sorry.* According to the books, many women didn't go after what they wanted in life. They had been raised to be polite, to not rock the boat. Megan knew that up until now, she had been one of those women. But no more. She'd tried being subtle, and Chase hadn't caught on.

Drastic action became her only recourse.

Getting Chase interested wouldn't be easy. With a string of broken relationships behind him, the man didn't believe in love. He'd once told her he had a better chance of Santa shimming down his chimney than of finding a woman to love forever.

But even with his attitude, Megan would never

forgive herself if she didn't at least try. In her heart, she knew Chase was the right man for her. Sure, he could be mule-headed at times, but as everyone knew, the course of true love never did flow smoothly.

Megan parked her car next to Nathan's expensive sedan and Trent's squad car and climbed out. As she headed up the steps to the front door of the white, two-story house, the Texas sun was warm on her back, even though it was only late March. But thankfully, her new cotton dress was cool.

And bright. A bright, vibrant emerald-green. After a great deal of thought, she'd decided to further shake up Chase by changing her style. Not so much her clothing choices, but rather their colors. Traditionally Megan favored flowing dresses in calming pastels. Instinctively she knew the best way to get Chase to notice her wasn't to suddenly appear wearing a sequined bustier and spandex shorts. That kind of radical change would signal Chase that something was up, and he'd be on guard.

But if instead she made small, subtle changes, then he'd notice her without knowing why he was noticing. She understood Chase needed time to adjust to the change in their relationship, so she wouldn't rush him. But she had hope. Lots of hope.

Because at least once last night, she knew for a fact he'd pictured her naked.

What a wonderful way to set a plan in motion. Smoothing the skirt of her sundress, Megan started to knock. Abruptly the door flew open, Leigh grabbed her arm, then tugged her inside.

"Don't let him wiggle out of this," Leigh whispered with a grin. "He's trying. But you stand firm."

Megan's spirits sank a tad. "Is he unhappy?"

Leigh huffed. "He's fine. Now head on out back. He's barbecuing dinner. Flatter his fragile male ego. I know, tell him how much you appreciate him helping, and that you think he's a great guy."

"I do. Very much. I really think this playground will be terrific for the children of Paxton. Did you know the equipment there is almost forty years old? I couldn't—"

Leigh rolled her eyes. "You're preaching to the choir, Megan. And don't worry about Chase. Working on this carnival will be good for him. He'll spend some time away from the ranch, which he needs, and he'll do something terrific for the kids of this town." She nudged Megan farther inside the house. "Now no wavering. Go outside and ask him if he needs any help with the grill."

As Megan was about to head toward the back of the house, Leigh grabbed her arm once again.

"Oh, and don't ask for any water. He keeps muttering about there being something wrong with it."

Perplexed, Megan simply nodded, then followed Leigh through the living room, past the kitchen and into the family room. Funny, there was nothing wrong with her water.

Nathan, Trent, and a red-haired woman Megan didn't recognize sat watching a basketball game on the wide-screen TV. When Leigh and Megan walked in, the conversation floundered to a halt.

"Megan, you know my brothers. And this is Sandi, with an *i*," Leigh said hurriedly. "Trent's date."

Megan moved forward to shake Sandi's hand. The young woman was very pretty, but all Trent's dates were pretty.

"Nice to meet you, Sandi," she said.

Sandi grinned. "Thanks. I'm really glad to be here."

Megan decided she liked Sandi with an *i* even if she knew she'd only meet her this once. Trent's girlfriends didn't last as long as a gallon of milk.

"Hi, Nathan. Trent." Megan said.

Nathan stood. "Hello, Megan. It's good to see you again. You're looking lovely today."

Megan smiled. Nathan was a natural-born charmer. He could convince birds to give up their feathers in the dead of winter. "It's good to see you, too, Nathan. I hope you don't mind me being here."

Nathan grinned, making his handsome face even more appealing. Like all the Barrett men, he had black hair and the most amazing blue eyes. Unlike his brothers, though, Nathan's hair was styled, giving him a more polished, sophisticated look. "Not at all. I'm happy you can join us."

Trent also stood, and the grin he flashed Megan

was pure flirt. "Hey, Megan. Like Nathan said, you look good today."

The way he said *good* dripped with innuendo, but since she'd grown up around Trent, Megan didn't take his flirting seriously. She merely shook her head at him.

"Cut it out, you dweebs," Leigh said. She gave Megan a little push toward the door leading to the back porch. "Ignore them. Go say hello to Chase. You two need to start planning for the carnival. That's going to take a lot of work."

"I understand you're going to have an auction as well," Nathan said. "Barrett Software will be happy to donate a computer system."

"Thanks, I really appre—"

Leigh grabbed Megan's arm once more and started dragging her toward the door leading out to the patio.

"Yeah, yeah. Nathan's the salt of the earth," Leigh said. "Now go talk to Chase."

Megan refused to budge. "Leigh, give me a second here." When she looked back at Trent and Nathan, they both had knowing expressions on their faces.

They smelled a plot.

Trent was the first to break the silence.

"Oh, yeah, Megan, why don't you go say hi to Chase? I know he'll be happy to see you."

"I agree. Great idea," Nathan said, his expression way too innocent to be believable.

Megan rolled her eyes. "It's not what you think."

But since it was exactly what they thought, she didn't see the point in saying anything else. Megan realized that everyone in the room now knew with utter certainty why Chase had been coerced into co-chairing the playground committee.

Okay, so maybe Sandi didn't know. Yet. But she probably would before dinner was over. Eventually everyone would know.

Except with any luck, not Chase. Megan wanted to find a way to get the message across to him on her own. Slowly. So he'd have time to adjust to the idea of them becoming more than friends. With care and finesse and—

"Now I get it," Sandi announced loudly. "She has the hots for your older brother, right?"

Megan groaned. Or more than likely, he'd know in about a minute and a half.

2

CHASE FIDDLED WITH the steaks on the barbecue grill. Dinner would be ready soon, and judging from the commotion he could hear going on in the family room, Megan had arrived.

Good. He needed to talk to her. He'd come to a few decisions last night, not the least of which was that he didn't have time to cochair any committee, even one she was running. Megan would have to accept his decision.

Once he cleared up that misunderstanding, they next needed to talk about had happened between them. He wanted to make certain she'd been kidding last night when she'd openly flirted with him. Megan of all people knew how he felt about love and romance. She also knew how he felt about her. They were friends. Good friends. And even though they'd both changed a lot during those years when she'd been away at college and then working in Dallas, they'd remained friends.

Just as they'd been since that day when she'd been eight and was being tormented by a bully for being the new kid. He'd stepped in to help her, and they'd been friends ever since. Even though he was five years older than she was, Megan had always understood him without getting all sappy and girlie.

So he knew they could clear up last night's misunderstanding without any problems. There wasn't anything the two of them couldn't talk about. Even if she had developed a little crush on him, they could work through it. He'd help her see that what she thought was love was only her hormones acting up. Naturally they couldn't do anything about those hormones, because having sex would ruin their friendship. But at least she'd know he cared.

After that, they'd simply ignore this bump in the road of their friendship. Then in a few weeks, everything would go back to normal.

When he heard the door behind him open, he glanced over his shoulder. It was Megan, so he turned toward her. "Hey."

"Hi, Chase." She sat in one of the wrought-iron patio chairs near the grill. "How are you?"

Okay. So far, so good. She wasn't flirting. "I'm fine," he said carefully, still uncertain of the waters. "And you?"

She smiled up at him, and he couldn't help noticing that her dress did really remarkable things to her eyes. Since she wasn't wearing the glasses she wore when reading, he could see her eyes clearly. They looked deep green, and so incredibly inviting.

Whoa. Rein that horse in. What in the world was he doing? He didn't care if her eyes looked really green. That wasn't what they needed to talk about.

He returned his focus to the problem at hand. "Look, Megan, about last night—"

"Thanks again for volunteering to help," she said, crossing her legs. The mild spring breeze fluttered her skirt around her calves, and Chase's gaze strayed and stayed. Megan had really great legs. Long, slender. Sexy.

Oh, for crying out loud. He blew out a disgusted breath, and Megan frowned at him.

"What's wrong with you today?" she asked.

"What's wrong with *me?*"

"Yes. You." She smiled. "Are you truly upset about last night? I know you got railroaded into helping. But I do appreciate it, and I'll make certain you're not asked to do too much."

The sizzle of the steaks caught his attention for a moment, so Chase turned to flip them over, then he looked back at Megan. "Okay, we'll talk about that first."

She opened her eyes wide, and once again he was struck by how exceptionally green they looked today. "First? You have a lot on your mind, do you?"

"Yeah, you could say that." Knowing he needed to handle this conversation carefully so he didn't hurt her feelings, he squatted next to her chair, putting him at eye level with her. "I'm not really the carnival type."

"I wasn't expecting you to perform tricks with barnyard animals."

Ignoring the radiant smile she gave him, he tried

again. "No, what I mean is I'm not the type to help on a committee. Just like I'm not the type for a lot of things."

He said the last sentence with meaning in his voice so she would know what he was talking about.

Megan laughed and placed her hand on his forehead. "Are you feeling all right? You're not sick are you?"

He brushed her hand away and stood, partially because he was annoyed she hadn't caught on to his message, and well, partially because he'd really liked the sensation of her touching him.

"I'm fine."

She came over to stand next to him. "Are you sure? Maybe you breathed in too much of Janet's perfume last night and are having an allergic reaction. I read in a new book the library got last week, *Why Life Stinks,* that many people are allergic to certain scents. And just like some scents can make you feel warm or loved or sexy, others can make you violently ill. Maybe Janet's perfume did that to you."

Chase patiently waited for her to finish, then he said, "I'm not allergic to Janet's perfume, and I feel fine. I want to talk about last night."

Megan settled back in her chair. "Okay. What's up?"

This was more like it. "First, I'd rather not cochair the committee. I'm too busy right now."

"You don't think the playground is a good idea?"

"Well sure. It's a great idea."

She nodded slowly. "Just not one you're willing to help make happen."

"It's not that I don't wish you every success. And you know I'll help. In some smaller way."

"Then maybe I shouldn't try to do this, either. I'm really busy at the library right now, too. You may have a good point."

Ah, hell. At times like this, he couldn't help wondering if his parents had been cousins.

Determined to find a way out of the hole he'd dug for himself, he said carefully, "Of course you should do it. You've told me lots of times how much building that playground means to you. It's one of your dreams. Ever since you were a kid you always said if you had enough money, you'd build this great playground for everyone to enjoy. Well, now you've got a way to make that happen," he encouraged.

Megan's expression was thoughtful. "So I should make my dream come true, but without the help of my best friend, is that right?"

Dang it all. He hadn't seen that one coming. This hole he'd dug for himself kept getting bigger and bigger. Megan knew he firmly believed that friends helped each other make their dreams come true. She'd neatly nailed him with his own code of ethics. But why did it have to be a carnival?

Scrubbing one hand over his face, he looked at

Megan. "Let's talk about something else for a minute."

She smiled at him again. "Okay."

Since he couldn't think of an easy way to say this, he just said it. "All the picturing each other naked stuff got out of hand last night."

Megan continued to smile at him. "Really? In what way?"

"You and I are friends, Megan. We've been friends most of our lives. We shouldn't go around picturing each other naked." There. He couldn't be much clearer than that.

"I see. But you said it was okay for me to picture you naked if I got nervous," she pointed out.

"I was kidding."

"I see. So instead, we should picture other people naked, not each other. For instance, you can picture Janet naked if you want to, right?"

Chase ran a hand through his hair. "Uh, well I don't know about that because—"

"And since I'm not close friends with either Nathan or Trent, I can picture one of them naked if I get nervous, right?"

She looked very pleased with herself, and Chase frowned. "You know that isn't what I meant."

"I guess then I'm not exactly sure what you do mean, Chase. I don't see what's wrong with picturing your brothers naked. I'm sure if I concentrated, I could imagine—"

Chase placed one hand over her mouth. He didn't

know when aliens had swooped down and stolen the real Megan, but he knew it had happened. The Megan he knew and had known for years didn't act this way.

Her soft lips pressed against the palm of his hand, and even though she didn't move a muscle, Chase felt as if a bolt of lightning shot straight through his body. He dropped his hand and moved away from her as if he'd caught on fire.

"What is *with* you?" he demanded, annoyed at what was happening with her, and even more annoyed at what was happening with him. When he'd felt her lips against his skin, desire had surged through his body, making his heart pound heavy in his chest.

He did *not* want to want Megan. No, make that he *refused* to want Megan. They were friends, dammit, and friends didn't lust after each other.

Megan moved closer to him. "Nothing is with me, Chase. But if it makes you feel any better, I promise I'll no longer picture you naked. And since it bothers you so much, I won't picture your brothers naked, either. If I feel the uncontrollable desire to picture anyone naked, I'll picture some other man. Does that make you feel better?"

Hell no, it didn't make him feel better. "Megan, don't go around picturing anyone naked." Narrowing his eyes, he added, "You're spending way too much time with Leigh. She's a bad influence on you."

Megan laughed, then turned and walked back toward the house. "You're losing it, cowboy."

Yeah, well, tell him something he didn't know.

"Megan, we're not through yet," he told her as she reached out to open the door.

Megan turned and looked at him. For several seconds, she didn't say a word, merely studied him. Then she gave him a tiny smile that was one of the most seductive things Chase had ever seen in his life.

"Oh, I know we're not through yet. Not by a long shot."

"YOU ROCK," LEIGH SAID to Megan when she came into the kitchen. "I think Chase is wrapped up tighter than a Christmas present right now."

Megan drew several deep, soothing breaths into her lungs, willing herself to calm down. Her conversation with Chase had left her rattled and flushed.

"You could hear us?" she asked Leigh.

"No. Not all of it, anyway. But I did catch the part about picturing people naked." She frowned. "By the way, I agree with Chase. I don't think you should go around picturing Nathan and Trent naked. That seems kind of gross considering how you feel about Chase."

Megan frowned back at Leigh. "I'm not going to picture anyone naked. For the record, though, you started all this, with your comment last night."

"Hey, and it worked, too." Leigh opened the refrigerator and pulled out a pitcher of iced tea. "You didn't seem a bit nervous last night."

"Well, I was. And I wouldn't have been if you hadn't made that crack about Chase."

A slow, calculating smile crossed Leigh's face. "Really cinched your girdle, did it, thinking about Chase that way? It's about time you took some action. Chase is too thickheaded to see what's smack in front of his face, but you're a smart lady. I thought you'd never come to your senses."

Megan felt the heat of a blush climb from her neck to her face. "I'm not even sure myself how to handle this with Chase. You need to let the two of us work things through on our own."

Leigh leaned against the kitchen island and seemed to consider what Megan had said. After a moment, though, she shook her head. "Nah. No can do. If I leave this completely up to you guys, you'll probably mess it up."

Megan realized Chase's sister was serious. She really did intend to keep on meddling. But this plan to make Chase change his mind about her was difficult enough without having Leigh doing crazy things.

"You may scare him off," Megan warned. "Chase and I need to settle this ourselves."

Once again, Leigh tipped her head as if considering what Megan had said. After a couple of seconds, she told Megan, "I'll make you a deal. Since this seems so important to you, I'll back off."

Megan smiled, but before she could relax, Leigh held up one hand.

"*But* if I see you making a real mess of things, or if I see Chase acting like an idiot about the situation, then all promises are off," Leigh pronounced.

Megan glanced around. Once she was certain no one could hear them, she said, "Leigh, that's not fair. This is none of your business."

"Of course it is. He's my brother. You're my friend. I have a duty to help."

This wasn't at all how she wanted to handle this situation. Megan preferred to carefully outline any plan she had, and if possible, detail it on index cards. Although she knew she couldn't script what she wanted to happen with Chase, she also wasn't happy leaving it up to Leigh's dubious devices.

"I don't want your help," she told Leigh. "It's sweet of you to offer, but this is something I need to do myself."

"I know you do, Meggie." Leigh blew out a loud breath, which ruffled the row of bangs across her forehead. "Oh, okay. I'll try to butt out. I really will. It's just that I'm so excited about the thought of Chase finally getting a life. He'll become an old fuddy-duddy if he doesn't break out of his habits soon. He needs a wife and a family."

Something about the way Leigh delivered this speech made Megan suspicious. The younger woman had obviously given this topic a great deal of thought.

"So you're doing this out of love for your brother?" Megan asked.

Leigh grinned. "Oh, yeah. Love for my brother. You two will be perfect together. I know it. You know it. All we have to do is get him to know it."

"And what's in it for you if this works?"

Leigh blinked. "Why, nothing."

As if Megan believed that. She hadn't been born yesterday. "Let's try this again. What's in it for you?"

Leigh made a big production out of retossing an already tossed salad. "For me? Why, nothing's in it for me except knowing I helped two fellow human beings find love."

"Bunk." Megan turned the question over in her mind, then suddenly saw the light. "You want Chase to butt out of your life, so that's why you're butting into his, right? You think if he gets involved with me, he'll leave you alone."

"Okay, well maybe. I mean, every blasted time I'm home from college, he's always spoiling my fun. I figure if he's busy having a little fun of his own, then maybe I can finally be left alone. I'm moving back here this summer, and next fall I start student teaching at the high school. I'll have no fun in my life at all if Chase has anything to say about it."

Megan knew by *no fun in her life,* Leigh actually

meant no guys. "But even if Chase does get distracted, you'll still have Nathan and Trent to deal with."

"Yeah, I know." Leigh circled the kitchen island to come stand by Megan. "But don't you honestly think you're meant to be with Chase? Don't you think the two of you could be truly happy?"

A slow warmth crept through Megan at just the thought of spending her life with Chase. "Yes, I honestly believe we could be very happy. That's why I've decided to try to get him to think of me in a whole new light."

Leigh smiled. "I think so, too. You're the only woman he's let be part of his life for more than a few months. The two of you have been friends forever. He trusts you, and he doesn't trust many people. If anyone can show him love really does exist, it's you. That's why I'm meddling. And that's why I'll keep meddling if you royally mess up."

Megan couldn't help smiling at Leigh's last sentiment. "Thanks for the vote of confidence."

"Some things are too important to be left to chance."

CHASE TOSSED THE BASKETBALL to Nathan. "Throw it in."

Nathan caught the ball with an exaggerated "oomph." Then he shot a grin at Trent. "Looks to me like someone's in a bad mood."

Trent laughed. "Yeah, I wonder why."

Chase glared at his younger brothers. "You know, for a couple of deadbeats who just ate *my* food in *my* house, you're real comedians. Now play."

Nathan started dribbling the basketball down their makeshift court in back of the garage. Chase tried to stay focused on the game, but it wasn't easy. Dinner tonight had been a disaster. The conversation had been stilted, that is when someone wasn't snickering for no apparent reason. Through it all, Megan had acted like nothing was happening, Sandi with an *i* had gone on and on about shoes, and Leigh had looked like the proverbial cat who had eaten a canary.

Chase's nerves were raw, and he wanted to let off some steam. As soon as Megan had driven off, he'd dragged his brothers outside to play basketball. Out here at least, he could stop thinking about women in general, and Megan in particular.

When Nathan got even with Chase, he veered off to the right before Chase could steal the ball away.

"Sandi seems nice," Nathan said to Trent.

Trent lunged for the ball, snagging it away from Nathan with no trouble. "Yeah. She's great." He headed in and easily made a basket. After a short and stupid victory dance, he tossed the ball to Chase. "Plus, she can tie a cherry stem into a knot using only her tongue."

Nathan and Chase froze and stared at him.

When he finally recovered, Chase headed toward

the basket. "I can see this is another of your deep, meaningful relationships."

Trent chuckled. "Hey, what's wrong with having a little fun?"

"Sooner or later, you have to grow up and be responsible." Nathan recovered the ball after Chase made a basket.

"I'm the chief of police of this town. If that's not responsible, I don't know what is," Trent said.

"You're responsible in your work, but not in your personal life," Chase felt obligated to point out. "Sandi, just like the rest of your girlfriends, thinks you may get serious about her."

Trent grabbed the ball away from Nathan and stopped the game. "Okay, if we're going to critique each other's lives, why don't we start with you, Chase, since you're the oldest."

Chase shook his head. The last thing he needed or wanted right now was to get into this kind of discussion with his brothers. All he wanted to do was blow off some tension.

"Forget it. I shouldn't have said anything."

"No way," Trent said. "We're not going to forget it because that's what this is all about. You're freaking out because Megan might actually have feelings for you, and you're making us pay for it." He grinned at Nathan. "I just love this, don't you?"

Nathan nodded. "Yeah, it is fun."

Chase ignored their teasing. "So you noticed it, too? She's acting strangely."

"No, she's not. She's acting like a woman who is interested in you." Nathan slapped Chase on the back. "Face it, big brother, she wants you bad."

Chase groaned as his brothers dissolved into laughter. Great. Just great. When they finally caught their breath, he said, "Not to spoil your fun, but did it ever occur to you that Megan's going to get hurt if she doesn't cut this out? Love doesn't last, and she's kidding herself if she thinks we can ever have anything together."

"What if you're the one who's wrong?" Nathan asked.

"I'm not. But I bet she's acting this way because she'll be thirty soon." Chase nodded to himself, turning the idea over in his mind. "She probably decided since I'm the only guy in her life at the moment, she'd see if she could make something happen. If I leave things alone for a while, everything will go back to normal."

Trent and Nathan looked at each other, then dissolved into laughter once again.

"What is with you clowns? I'm asking your opinion on how to handle this so I don't end up hurting Megan and destroying our friendship. You could help a little. Jeez." He grabbed the ball away from Nathan and shot another basket.

After a few seconds, his brothers trotted over to stand next to him.

"Okay, you want help. We'll help," Trent said. "The way I see it, you're probably right. Megan's feeling restless, and you're around. If you want to discourage her from having romantic thoughts about you, go on the defensive.''

Chase opened his mouth to argue, but then realized his brother had a good point. ''I'm listening.''

''You need to come on to her,'' Nathan said. ''When she flirts with you, flirt back. Or better yet, you flirt first. Knowing Megan, she'll come to her senses, realize what a mistake this is, and go back to being your friend.''

''But what if she takes my flirting seriously? That will make things worse. She'll start thinking we're going to live happily ever after.''

Trent shook his head. ''Naw, she won't. Because worse case, you kiss her a couple of times, show her there's no sexual chemistry between the two of you, and wham! She'll be out looking for a different guy. Someone who can—''

''Tie cherry stems with his tongue,'' Nathan supplied.

He and Trent both laughed once again.

Chase frowned. ''Stop it.'' For several long moments, he stared at his brothers, debating whether they were right. He'd already tried the direct approach with Megan. Or at least, he'd *tried* to try the direct approach with her. Maybe this was the best way to solve the problem. A little harmless flirtation. A kiss or two. She'd quickly see there was nothing sexual between them.

A picture of her naked slammed into his mind.

Okay, maybe this wasn't such a good idea after all. Maybe he should simply avoid her. For a few days. Or weeks. Or surely a couple of years would solve this problem.

"I don't know," he admitted. "I don't want Megan to end up getting hurt."

"Which is why you're such a nice guy," Nathan said. "But trust us, this is the kindest way to handle the situation. It lets Megan make the final decision. And what can go wrong? It's not like the two of you would burn up the sheets if you ever did have sex, right? I mean, if you were overcome with animal lust for her, you would have done something about it before now."

Chase wasn't a hundred percent sure about that. He'd noticed before that Megan was attractive. Beautiful, even, especially when she was excited about something. Her face lit up, and her eyes seemed to sparkle, and her body came alive.

More than a few times over the years, he'd found himself thinking about Megan in a definitely unfriendlike manner. For instance, every time she came over to swim at the ranch. The woman was hot in a swimsuit, even if she did favor one-pieces that didn't show much. And he'd noticed her body whenever she stopped by to go riding and had on her favorite pair of old jeans that hugged her like a lover's hands.

The dull throbbing in the back of Chase's head returned. When he realized his brothers stood waiting for him to say something, the best he could manage was, "I guess."

"No guessing about it," Trent said. "If you two were wild for each other, you would have seduced her years ago in your pickup like you did half a dozen other girls."

The dull throbbing in his head became a stabbing pain. Being with Megan like that, in a hot-and-heavy session in his old truck, had never seemed right. And in the years since, when his lovemaking had moved from inside cars to inside his house, he'd never felt that he and Megan were meant to be lovers.

They were friends, and true friends were hard to find.

"Maybe. But I also never thought of her that way because Megan wants to get married and have children. Things I don't want. This playground idea of hers is because someday she wants her own children to be able to play in the park."

"Listen, Chase, don't worry about this so much," Nathan advised. "Try things our way. Help Megan with the carnival. Be a good friend to her. And if she keeps flirting with you, flirt a little back. Like we said, kiss her a couple of times. Everything will work out. You'll see."

Except Chase wasn't nearly as certain as Nathan and Trent seemed to be. "And what if we're all wrong? What if she takes me seriously, and I end up breaking her heart? What happens then?"

His brothers were silent for several long seconds,

then finally Nathan offered an answer. "If that happens, you'd need to be a good friend to her and help her put her heart back together. But at least you'd have let her find out for herself that you and love don't mix. I don't see any other way to handle the situation."

"Me, neither," Trent agreed. "You gotta let the lady figure out for herself that you're the wrong guy for her." He yanked the basketball out of Chase's arms.

"It really will work out," Nathan said.

Chase still wasn't sure. The only problem was, he didn't have a better plan than the one his brothers proposed. "I hope so."

They went back to playing basketball, with Chase winning by a wide margin. Had to be all his pent-up stress, because he rarely beat his brothers.

As they headed back inside the house, Trent grinned. "Oh, yeah, since you're so old you've probably forgotten how this works, remember that if you and Megan do decide to take up playing indoor sports, play safe."

Chase hung his head. The water. There was definitely something screwy with the water in this town.

3

MEGAN GLANCED AROUND HER crowded living room. As far as she could tell, almost every single or divorced woman in town had volunteered to help on the playground committee now that Chase was the cochair. All she could figure was that since Chase was always busy with his ranch, these ladies had decided if they wanted to get his attention, they needed to grab this opportunity.

Talk about filling your team with competition. But Megan refused to worry about it. If Chase decided he was interested in one of the other women, she'd simply have to accept it. Might take a while, but she'd accept it. At least then she'd know where she stood with him and would've tried to make this work.

"Rather than waiting any longer, let's get started," Megan said.

"But honey, Chase isn't here yet," Janet said smoothly. "It would be inappropriate not to wait for him."

Speaking of inappropriate, that halter-top Janet had on was more than a little indecent. Megan opened her mouth to point this out when it occurred to her she was being catty, so she slammed her mouth shut. She would *not* turn into a name-calling shrew simply because she'd decided to show Chase how she felt about him.

"I think Megan is right," Amanda Newman said. As the wife of the minister and the only married woman in the room, Megan decided to sit next to her. If things got out of hand, Amanda could be the voice of reason.

"Oh, all right." Janet flounced over to the couch and sat. Immediately two of her best friends from high school, Tammy Holbrook and Caitlin Estes, sat on either side of her. Eventually the rest of the women found seats as well.

Megan began the meeting by recapping what she'd said to the city council. As she spoke, she quickly realized that only Amanda was paying the slightest bit of attention to her. Everyone else was listening for Chase to arrive.

Just great.

Amanda tugged gently on the sleeve of Megan's red dress. Megan leaned toward her, and the older woman said, "I think now would be a good time to make the assignments."

Baffled, Megan leaned back. Make the assignments? But no one was paying attention to her. If she made the assignments now…oh, yeah. Megan smiled. Excellent idea.

"So Janet, you and Tammy will head up refreshments, right? You'll need to arrange for plenty of sodas and food.''

From across the room, Janet nodded vaguely, her gaze still on Megan's front door. "Sure, whatever. Just put my name down.''

Megan bit back a smile. This was going to be much easier than she'd expected. In fact, during the next ten minutes, she made almost all of the assignments, and no one raised a finger to stop her.

She'd just finished filling in Caitlin's name for the job of finding prizes to give out to the winners of the carnival games when the sound of a pickup pulling up silenced the group.

"Show time,'' Amanda murmured with a smile.

Megan didn't have the chance to let Chase into the house because before she could even stand, three women were by the door, welcoming him. Chase looked startled when he walked in, but within a couple of seconds, he looked practically horrified.

"Am I the only man here?'' he growled to Megan when he finally made it across the room.

"I'm afraid so. But don't worry. We have plenty of volunteers,'' she said.

And each and every one of those volunteers—with the exception of Amanda—was looking at Chase as if he was a half-price silk blouse at a one-day-only sale. Megan knew even she was staring at him.

But who could blame them? Freshly showered and shaved, smelling like a clean healthy male and looking like a movie star, Chase Barrett was enough to get any female heart racing.

Not surprisingly he was offered almost any and every chair in the room. Janet even offered to let him have her seat, and of course, she'd be happy to sit in his lap. But Chase just said thanks and sat on the ottoman by Megan's chair. A silly, schoolgirl thrill ran through her when he chose to be near her, and Megan mentally berated herself on being so petty. This wasn't a game she was playing. Unlike most of the women in the room, she wasn't interested in having wild, crazy sex with Chase simply so she could brag to her friends.

She was interested in love, and commitment, and family. She glanced at him briefly, but when his dark blue gaze met her own, her pulse fluttered, her breathing grew shallow, and she forced herself to look away.

Okay, she wouldn't mind a *little* of that wild sex being thrown in as a bonus. But that wasn't her main goal. Her main goal was to show him she could make him happy. Truly happy. For life. Not just during one afternoon of frantic, yeehaw, ride-'em-cowboy sex.

Chase waved one hand in front of her face, and Megan jumped.

"You okay in there, Megan?" Chase teased. "You have a funny look on your face."

Oh, she'd just bet she did. "I'm fine," she said,

cringing when her voice came out way too breath-less and far too squeaky.

"So how's it going?" he asked.

Immediately several of the women launched into a description to bring Chase up-to-date. Almost all of them were surprised to learn that at some point, they'd volunteered to head up a particular task. But thankfully, they all took their job assignments in good stride. Even Janet said it wouldn't be the first time she couldn't remember what she'd promised to do.

"I promised my first husband I'd love him for-ever, and look how that turned out," she said with a laugh.

"Love needs care to make it flourish," Amanda said.

Pretty much everyone's expression made it clear they disagreed with Amanda, but since she was the minister's wife and a really nice lady in her own right, no one made a comment. Personally Megan thought Amanda was right. Love did need care and attention. But now was not the time, and this was not the crowd, to open the question up for debate.

"Anyway, we're now down to finding items for the auction," Megan said. "Earl has volunteered to let us use his big party tent to have the auction in. Nathan's donating a complete computer system. But we need a lot of other items as well so we can make enough money."

"I talked to my sister last night, and she's willing

to help," Amanda said. "She owns a bed-and-breakfast in San Antonio and is willing to donate a room for two for a weekend."

Megan smiled. "That's wonderful."

"If you're married," Janet said with a snort. "What if one of us single women wants to bid? What about tossing in someone to escort us on this trip if we win?" She scanned the room as if considering what to say next, but Megan knew without a doubt that Janet had this all planned out. "What about if the winning bidder so chooses, then Chase will be her escort for the weekend?"

Megan expected Amanda to protest, but instead, she seemed delighted by the idea. "I'm sure my sister will donate an extra room if that happens."

"Whoa, whoa. Hold on here a minute," Chase said. "I'm not going to be a gigolo prize in the auction."

"Of course not, dear," Amanda said. "The prize is the free hotel room near the River Walk in San Antonio. You'd only be the escort if the winner decides she wants one. And then naturally, you'd request the separate room. But this way, the lady could enjoy the trip in the company of a man she could trust."

It all sounded so tame and reasonable coming from Amanda, but the hot looks several of the women were directing at Chase made it clear the last thing they would want on the trip was a man they could trust.

"I still don't like it," Chase muttered. "But okay, just so long as everyone's clear about this up-front. I'm not a stud service." He glanced at Amanda. "Pardon my language."

She smiled. "No problem."

Megan bit back her own smile and made a mental note to check the latest balance on her savings account. There was no way she was going to let Janet Defries win that prize. If anyone was going away for a romantic weekend with Chase, it was going to be her.

CHASE WAS HALFWAY HOME when he pulled off to the side of the road, hooked a U-turn and headed back to Megan's house. This carnival-auction thing was getting out of hand. Now he was one of the prizes. And no way would he believe for a second that one of the single women in town wasn't going to win. He'd seen the way they'd looked at him. When one woman looked at you that way, it was nice. When ten looked at you with hunger in their eyes, it was downright scary.

Everyone was gone by the time he pulled back into Megan's driveway. No doubt they'd scattered as soon as he'd left.

After slamming his truck into Park, he sprinted to her front door and rapped loudly. A couple of seconds later, the light in the living room came on, and Megan opened the door.

"Don't you ask who it is before you fling open

your front door in the middle of the night..." His gaze dropped and scanned her body. "Wearing hardly any clothes," he barely managed to say.

Because she was wearing hardly any clothes, or at least, she looked that way. She had on a short pink nightie that clung to her every curve. Backlit as she was from the light inside the house, Chase now knew he wouldn't have to guess the next time he wanted to picture Megan naked.

"Oops." She dashed toward the back of the house.

Chase came inside and shut the door behind him. He could only hope Megan was putting on a thick, long, terry-cloth robe. But when she came back out from her bedroom, she actually had on a flowered, silky robe that came to the top of her knees. It wasn't a whole lot better than the nightie, but it was at least something.

"Why are you here?" she asked.

He'd been staring at her robe, his blood pounding hot and heavy through his body as he remembered what she'd looked like seconds ago, but at her question, he yanked his gaze back to her face. What had she asked? Oh, yeah, why was he here.

"I'm not having sex with those women so you can build a playground in the park," he told her.

Rather than being upset, Megan laughed and curled up on the couch. "No one is asking you to, Chase."

"Janet wants me to. And so do those other

women." He flopped down next to her on the couch, making certain he left plenty of room between them.

"All you have to say is no. And if you really don't want to go, I'll talk to Amanda, and we'll change the prize."

This was more like it. This was the sane, responsible Megan he knew. "Well, okay then."

She laughed again, and the soft sound floated around him. "You know, the easy solution is to have me place the winning bid on the weekend package," Megan said. "That way, you won't have to feel like a gigolo."

Her suggestion sounded reasonable enough, but it sure didn't feel that way to him. Going away to a bed-and-breakfast on the River Walk with Megan while all this flirting stuff was going on between them didn't feel reasonable at all.

It sounded hot. And dangerous.

"I'm not sure that would be a good idea," he said.

"Are you afraid I'll seduce you?"

"No." That wasn't the problem at all. At the moment, thinking about her in that nightie, he was afraid he'd try to seduce her. But the carnival was weeks away. Maybe by that time, Megan would come to her senses about them, and their friendship could return to normal.

She sat tucked in the corner of the couch, watching him. Waiting for him to say more.

He scrubbed his face with his hands, feeling as

cornered as a calf in a roping competition. "Okay, fine. If your committee insists on auctioning this weekend trip, then you'd better be the one to win it. I'll give you money so you—"

"I have money saved. I can pay for it myself."

The day he did that was the day he'd hang up his saddle and build himself a pine box. "No way are you paying, Megan. I am. I'll buy this trip to San Antonio."

"But don't you think Janet and the other women will be annoyed when they find out you bought the trip yourself?"

Boy, this was more complicated than figuring out a mutt's parentage. "Fine. I'll give *you* the money, and *you* buy the trip. Just make certain you don't lose."

Her smile was downright blissful. "Sounds like a great idea, and I promise, I won't lose."

"But we're going to have separate rooms. We're going as friends, because that's what we are and have always been. Say it with me...friends."

"Friends," she said the word slowly, but with a sexual overtone that made his heart race fast and furious.

Chase blew out an aggravated breath. He wanted whatever was going on here to stop. He wanted his life to get back to normal.

He wanted the old Megan back. He didn't want to picture her naked, didn't want to think about either of them seducing the other, didn't want to lose her friendship.

But he also was having no luck getting the image of her in that nightie out of his head.

"I want to talk to you about what's been going on," he finally said. "This whole thing with you and me. It can't work."

Her expression was innocent, but he could see the pulse beating wildly in her neck. She was far from calm.

"What thing would that be?" she asked.

Okay, so that was the way she planned on playing this. Fine.

"You've been flirting with me."

She blinked. "I have?"

"You know you have. You've never flirted with me before."

She nibbled on her bottom lip, and Chase barely bit back a groan. Did she know she was turning him on? Did she really mean to drive him wild?

Apparently, since she continued nibbling on her bottom lip for a good ten seconds. Finally he couldn't stand it anymore.

"Megan, do you want to have sex with me? Is that what this is about? You're lonely. I'm convenient."

Even in the muted light of the cozy living room, he could clearly see the blush that climbed her face. But she never looked away from him. She kept her gaze locked on his face.

"What would you do if I said yes?"

Chase felt like someone sucker-punched him in the gut. The breath in his lungs seemed to whoosh out of his body.

"You seriously want to have sex with me?" he finally managed to ask when he remembered how to talk. He hadn't expected her to be so blunt.

"Among other things." Her voice was even softer than before, and he had to strain to hear her clearly. "But not because I'm lonely. And not because you're convenient."

"I see." But he didn't at all. He didn't understand any of this. "Mind if I ask why now? Why after all these years? Is it because of your clock."

"Clock?"

He waved one hand. "You know. Your biological clock. Is this about having babies?"

She smiled at his comment. "No, my biological clock has nothing to do with this."

"Then what does? What's got you acting this way?"

She remained silent for so long that he wondered for a second if she intended on answering him. Finally she said, "Maybe I'm tired of not going after what I want in life." She drew in a deep breath, then added, "Going after the man I want in my life."

All sorts of emotions roared through Chase. For starters, he was flattered that he meant so much to her. Then he was annoyed that she was ruining the only successful relationship he'd ever had with a woman. And finally he was undeniably turned on.

But one conclusion was unavoidable. He needed to talk her out of this.

"We're good friends, Megan. Sex would ruin everything. Getting involved on any personal level would destroy the friendship we've had for twenty years."

"How do you know that? What if it makes everything better?"

How could she be so naive? She knew about his past, how his dad had bailed on the family one winter morning simply because he'd decided he was in love with a waitress from the local café. She knew about each and every one of his failed relationships, just as he knew about hers. They'd both tried several times to make love last, and it had disappeared quicker than a sinner on Sunday morning.

Those times, when what they thought was love turned out to be hormones, they'd moved on. Wiser. A little sadder. But not brokenhearted.

But this time, when the relationship ended, he'd lose his best friend. The woman he'd grown up with. The one true friend who had shared his life.

The price was just too damn high.

"It won't make everything better," he muttered. "You and I both know it won't. And then what will happen? Will we still be friends?"

"Of course."

"I can't help thinking you'll end up hating me."

He shifted closer to her on the couch. "I've tried, but love doesn't last. It didn't last for my parents. It doesn't last for me. You've had relationships, too. They didn't last."

Her green eyes sparkled with conviction when she said, "It could be different for us. We could be one of the lucky couples. One of the couples who finds true and lasting love."

Her soft voice enticed him to believe, but he couldn't let her fool herself this way. She deserved better. "It won't work, Megan."

"Because you're a heartbreaker."

Turning his head, he studied her. "Maybe. That's what the ladies in this town tell me."

She leaned toward him, the motion making the top of the robe open a tiny bit. Although Chase knew she didn't mean the action to be seductive, it was. He could now see just a sliver of her pink nightie. He stared at that small flash of cloth for a moment, trying not to think about the soft skin underneath. When his gaze finally met hers again, he felt the look clear to his soul.

"You don't always have to be a heartbreaker. You don't have to break my heart," she said.

Chase shut his eyes and leaned back against the couch. Megan was set on this, and it looked as if she was going to remain set on this until he proved her wrong.

Trent and Nathan's suggestion surfaced in his mind. Was that really the way to handle this situation? Should he prove her wrong, show her that the chemistry they shared would fade, as it always faded?

He tipped his head and looked at her. "Kiss me."

She blinked several times in rapid succession. "What?"

Okay, this was more like it. He'd thrown her. About time.

"I asked you to kiss me. You're telling me you want us to have sex. Well I figure we should start out with a kiss. Who knows, maybe the kiss will rank up there with catching the flu. Maybe after that, you'll find out you aren't so hot for me after all."

She laughed, her eyes dancing with humor. "Oh, I see. This is a test. You don't think I'll really kiss you."

"Oh, no, I believe you will. I'm just not sure you'll like it. We're friends, Megan. We probably have zip in the way of sexual chemistry. But hey, it you want to give it a try, then it's fine by me. Kiss me."

She narrowed her eyes. "I can't simply kiss you."

"Why not?"

She waved one hand as if searching for the words. "Because you lead up to a kiss. You share a romantic evening. You talk about your feelings. You don't just grab someone and kiss them."

"Why not?" he asked again.

"It's not romantic."

He shrugged. "I'm not a romantic guy. You know that."

Her expression softened. "Yes, you are. You're very romantic."

His heart seemed to lurch in his chest, but he refused to let her see this was getting to him. But it was. He was more than ready to show her anything she wanted.

But that was his hormones kicking in. It was late. She was practically naked and staring at him with desire in her eyes. He was a red-blooded, healthy male.

Of course his engine was racing.

But if Megan insisted on playing this game, then she had to be the one to lead it.

"If I'm such a romantic guy, then kiss me," he said.

He expected her to back down, but his request had the opposite effect. She gave him a look that let him know in no uncertain terms that she was on to his trick and wasn't about to fall for it. She slowly scooted forward until she was next to him on the couch. Holding his gaze, she leaned forward and lightly brushed her lips across his.

Chase was totally unprepared for the sensation. It felt like electricity skittered through his body at her touch. For a split second, they both froze. Then she pulled away from him.

"There. I kissed you," she said softly, her face mere inches from his own.

"Ah, now, Megan. That wasn't a kiss." He lightly touched her hair. "Old ladies kiss better than that. Guess I was right. We have no sexual chemistry," he lied.

Her eyes darkened, and she smiled at his obvious fib. "You think you're so smart, don't you?"

He couldn't prevent the grin that crossed his face. "Just pointing out the obvious."

She shoved his shoulder good-naturedly. "You figure you've got this all worked out. I know you. You think I'll chicken out and not give this kissing thing another try."

He chuckled, enjoying having Megan this close to him, even though he knew he shouldn't. "You? Chicken out? Couldn't happen."

She leaned even closer to him, the sweet scent of her citrus shampoo filling his lungs. "Well if you don't expect me to chicken out, then that means you figure if I give you a real kiss, fireworks won't go off. After that, I'll give up and forget the whole thing."

The lady knew him well, but he wasn't going to admit it. "Maybe."

"Maybe my foot." For a second, she assessed him. Then, her expression turned smug. "Okay, cowboy, hold on to your hat."

Chase figured he was prepared for anything she could dish out, but he hadn't counted on Megan half crawling into his lap, cupping his face in her small hands and kissing him hard.

She almost knocked him off balance with the impact, and out of necessity, he placed his hands on her waist to keep them from toppling over. But if Megan noticed their position, she made no comment. She was too busy kissing him.

And kissing him.

And kissing him.

It took every bit of his resolve to keep from kissing her back. He hadn't expected his body to respond to her the way it was, as if he'd been dying of thirst for a very long time and she was giving him sustenance.

But he knew she was wrong about this. So what if her kisses were setting his blood on fire. He'd been alone for some time, and Megan was soft and sweet.

"Kiss me back, Chase," she murmured against his lips. "Just this once. Kiss me back."

He shifted his head so his lips pressed against her cheek. "I don't think so."

Megan squirmed against him until he groaned and stopped her. Through the thinness of her robe, he could feel how soft and warm her body was. His experiment ranked right up there with Dr. Frankenstein's. He'd created a monster, and he had no idea how much longer he could hold out.

"Give me one real kiss, Chase," Megan whispered again. "If it doesn't drive us both wild, then I'll stop flirting with you. I promise."

At this point Chase figured the sooner they got

this experiment over with, the better. Finally, even though he knew he was making one humongous mistake, he relented.

"Fine," he said. "One kiss."

Megan rewarded him with a dimpled smile. "Thank you."

This time when she leaned forward and kissed him, he buried his hands in her hair, damned his own soul and kissed her back.

4

CHASE'S KISS WAS EVERY BIT as perfect as Megan had known it would be. Maybe even a little bit more perfect than expected, since his kiss alone was enough to shoot her libido sky-high. She'd never kissed anyone before who made her want to toss him to the ground and take wanton advantage of him.

But she sure wanted to with Chase.

Instead she settled for this kiss, this one chance to show Chase just how amazing they were together. Without waiting for him to take the initiative, Megan touched the tip of her tongue to his bottom lip. Joy rushed through her when he complied with her silent request by parting his lips. Now they were getting somewhere.

For long, languid minutes, they lost themselves in a kiss that was so much more than the mere meeting of lips. It was fireworks, shooting stars and magic all rolled into one. Megan was positive that Chase felt the electricity dance between them every bit as much as she did. How could he not? They were meant to be together.

With a loud groan, Chase finally broke the kiss. He opened his eyes and stared at her. He looked totally dazed, with maybe a touch of horrified thrown in, sort of like he'd just been kicked in the head by his favorite horse.

He was stunned. Good. Stunned she could work with. Megan smiled, offering him reassurance. She appreciated that their situation was new to Chase. He hadn't had a lot of time to adjust to the idea of being more than just friends. No doubt the incendiary nature of the kiss had been a surprise to him.

"That was something else," she said, caressing the side of his face with the gentlest of touches.

Chase leaned away from her hand. Then he cleared his throat. Twice. And blinked. Twice.

"Are you okay?" she asked.

He jerked his head in what she assumed was a nod. Then he made an incomprehensible response that sounded like "urpuft," and shifted her so she no longer straddled his lap. Once she was off him, he stood so quickly he almost seemed to shoot off the couch. "I gotta go."

Not exactly the reaction she'd hoped for, but certainly understandable.

"Okay." She gave him another encouraging smile.

He ran his hands through his hair and blew out a loud breath. Then he turned and stared at her, desire still heating his blue gaze. "Megan, about that kiss…"

Her heart rate quickened. She knew he was going to tell her how wonderful, how incredible, how miraculous the kiss had been. Maybe he'd ask her to kiss him again. "Yes?"

He cleared his throat again. "That kiss was what I thought it would be. Don't get me wrong—it was okay. A good kiss between friends. But like I said, there's no chemistry between us so it didn't exactly rock the world."

Openmouthed, Megan stared at him. *What?* The man had lost his mind. No chemistry? He knew that wasn't true.

Her gut reaction was to argue with him, to point out as nicely as possible that he was full of hooey. But her instincts warned her that was the wrong approach. She shut her mouth, understanding flowing through her. Chase needed time. She'd pushed him too hard, too fast. No wonder he was denying what was obvious.

She'd read a book last week that talked about this exact situation—*Fit to be Tied.* According to the author, even when a man was ready for a lasting relationship, old habits often died hard. These men lied about their feelings, even to themselves. Sometimes the lies were tiny. Sometimes they weren't.

In Chase's case, he was telling himself a whopper of a lie. A gargantuan lie. As his friend, it was her duty to help him face the truth. To do that, she needed to give him time to adjust to the inferno they'd generated when they'd kissed. Time for him to accept reality.

The best approach as far as she could tell was to go along with his cockamamy statement that the kiss had been nothing special. So to help him in the long run, she'd agree.

Unfolding herself from the couch, she stood. "You're right. The kiss wasn't a big deal. At least now we know that kissing each other is like sucking on a dead fish."

Chase frowned, but at least her statement seemed to snap him out of the daze he'd been in. "A dead fish? Hold on there, Megan. I didn't say it wasn't enjoyable. Just that it…you know, we're friends. It was a kiss between friends."

Megan bit back a smile at his defensive tone. Please. Friends only kissed that way if they were about to have wild and crazy sex. *Enjoyable* was the understatement of the year, but once again, she didn't argue.

"True. It was a simple little kiss between friends. I realize now how silly I was to expect fireworks between us. It was pleasant, but I've certainly had better."

That got him. Megan had never seen anyone manage to frown on top of an already existing frown, but Chase pulled it off. Megan resisted the impulse to tell him that his face might freeze like that. Instead she focused all of her attention on getting him to believe her ridiculous lie. Chase knew as well as she did that neither of them had ever experienced a kiss remotely as fantastic.

He folded his arms across his chest. "The kiss was a mite better than pleasant."

Keeping her tone light and casual, she said, "I

guess. A little bit, maybe.'' When he opened his mouth, presumably to argue with her, Megan hurriedly added, "Well, if you'll excuse me, I need to get my rest. Tomorrow is a busy day.''

"You're kicking me out?''

The smile she'd been holding back broke free. She ended up grinning like a schoolgirl. "You need to go home now. Have a nice night.''

Without waiting for him to follow her, she led the way to her front door. Opening it, she watched him walk out, her smile only growing as he passed by her muttering about women and the water and the world in general.

"Drive safely,'' she told Chase, feeling positively delighted with how the evening had turned out. Tonight, Chase had kissed her. Really kissed her. And fireworks had happened, even if he wasn't ready to admit they'd been anything more than sparklers.

She and Chase were perfect together. Just as she'd known they would be.

Things could only get better from here.

THIS WAS A DISASTER. A full-fledged, the-barn's-on-fire disaster. Chase sat in his truck, still parked outside Megan's house. He watched her turn off the lights in the living room. She was going to bed, and he hated the fact that he wanted to join her in that bed.

He really, *really* wanted to join her in that bed.

But it couldn't—make that wouldn't—happen. He

rubbed his forehead as frustration crept up his spine and crouched in his neck muscles.

Damn. Why had he agreed to that kiss? He was smarter than that. He'd stepped right into that trap like a blind fool. Now his life was even more catawampus than it had been before, and he had no one to blame but himself.

But come on, how was he supposed to know a simple kiss from Megan would shake him right down to his boots? That heat and desire and good-old want would flare to the point that he felt as if he'd literally caught on fire?

And what had she meant with that crack about having had better kisses? That was physically impossible. No one had *ever* had a better kiss than the one they'd shared.

Maybe it had been a fluke. He'd been Megan's friend for a long, long time. If they truly did have that kind of amazing chemistry between them, he would have felt it before now, right? So the kiss had to be a fluke.

But even knowing the combustible kiss had been a fluke didn't change the simple fact that he needed to be reasonable about this. They had to ignore this aberration in their friendship. His brothers had been wrong. Dead wrong. He needed to squash this attraction he felt toward Megan like a big old barn spider. No evasion. No hesitation.

He started his truck and backed out of Megan's driveway. When he'd put a couple of miles between them, he felt much better. Now, with the sizzle from the kiss gone, he was positive it had been a fluke. So with a little effort, he could put it behind him.

By tomorrow, he and Megan would be back to their usual friendship, and this kissing nonsense would be over. They'd once again be pals, hanging around together, sharing jokes, kidding each other.

But no more kissing. From this point on, the two of them were going to keep their lips to themselves.

MEGAN GLANCED OVER THE NEW books she needed to catalog. Two romances, a mystery, an assortment of children's books and three new self-help books. Two of them dealt with child rearing, something she currently had no use for, but with any luck, would someday soon.

The last book caught her eye—*Browbeating for the Naturally Shy*. Now there was something she could use. Not that she intended on browbeating Chase, but she did need to be more assertive, especially now. No doubt Chase intended on avoiding any more physical contact with her, which of course, would make getting him to kiss her again a bit of a challenge. But she needed him to kiss her again so he could see that the fire of the first kiss hadn't been a one-time wonder.

She opened her desk drawer and pulled out a stack of index cards. What she needed was a plan.

"You're handling him all wrong," Leigh said as she breezed into the office.

Megan glanced up. The younger woman stood just inside the doorway with her hands on her hips, a frown on her pretty face. Seems like all Megan did these days was cause members of the Barrett family to frown at her.

"What are you talking about?" Megan asked.

Leigh dropped into the chair facing Megan's desk. "Chase. You're handling him all wrong."

"I'm not *handling* him at all," she told Leigh.

"Sure you arc. You're trying to trap him—"

"No, I'm not."

Leigh groaned. "Fine. You're trying to lure him—"

Megan was the one to groan this time. "Leigh, I'm not trying to handle, trap, or lure your brother into anything."

Leaning forward, Leigh said, "Call it whatever you want, but you want to make my brother fall in love with you. Right?"

An unsettling feeling lodged in Megan's stomach. She sincerely didn't want to trick Chase into anything. She believed in being forthright and honest at all times. She'd never try something so completely underhanded.

She glanced at the blank index cards sitting in front of her and inwardly cringed. But those cards were for a plan, and a plan was different than a trap, right? Just because she wanted to think of ways to make Chase notice her as a woman didn't mean she was trapping him.

Did it?

She looked at Leigh. "I'm not trying to make your brother fall in love with me. I'm hoping that our friendship and affection for each other can grow naturally into something deeper and more profound.''

For a moment, Leigh stared at her. Then she made a snorting noise and said, ''Pig slop.''

''It is not pig slop. It's how I feel.''

''Megan, hon, I love you like a sister, but there's a couple of things wrong with what you said. First up, you got Chase on your committee so you could try to get him to fall for you.''

Megan sat up straighter in her chair. ''Excuse me, Leigh, but *I* didn't get Chase on my committee, you did. You backed him into a corner so he had no choice but to agree to help.''

Leigh waved one hand. ''Semantics. You. Me. It doesn't really matter. All that matters is that he was forced onto your committee.''

Megan sighed. Leigh was…well, Leigh. The woman could make a tornado seem tame by comparison. And to be completely honest, regardless of who had gotten him on the committee, Megan was thrilled he'd ended up there. Moreover, Leigh was right. She did intend on using the committee as a way to spend more time with him.

But that didn't mean she was luring, trapping, or tricking the man. She was simply giving him lots of opportunities to realize his feelings for her.

Megan frowned. Maybe she wasn't being quite as forthright with Chase as she thought. But she wasn't handling him. Images of last night flashed in her brain. Okay, she'd *handled* him somewhat last night, but not in the way Leigh meant.

With another sigh, this time directed at herself, Megan looked at her friend. "Why are you here?"

Leigh chuckled. "Got you tangled up, huh?" When Megan didn't respond, she continued, "I'm here because Chase is being a colossal pain today. Whatever you did to him last night has got him stomping around muttering about you."

That didn't sound good. "Muttering about me? Is he angry?"

"Can't tell. I've never seen him like this. He's jumpy and snarly. Chase is the most easygoing guy in the world. Usually I have to hold a mirror in front of his face to make sure he's still alive. But not today. Today he's more jittery than a werewolf in a silver-bullet factory."

Megan turned this information over in her mind. Jumpy and snarly and jittery didn't sound like Chase. Not at all. Maybe this was a good sign. Maybe the kiss had thrown him for a loop, and he didn't know what to make of it.

Maybe this was the first step in Chase coming to terms with his feelings for her. This could be a very good sign.

Then again, maybe it was the first step in him deciding to never see her again. Maybe he was so mad at her that he'd never want to see her again.

Uh-oh. This could be a really bad, bad sign.

Leigh sat staring at her, obviously expecting her to say something. Unclear what the younger woman wanted to hear, Megan settled for, "Sorry he's grumpy."

"Grumpy? He's a lot more than grumpy. He told me this morning that we have too many *toothpicks* in the house. Toothpicks, Megan. He's talking about toothpicks."

"And that means?" Megan asked, trying to understand what could possibly have bothered Chase about toothpicks.

Leigh rolled her eyes. "Heck if I know. He's not himself. At first I thought you'd managed to shake him up, and that he'd finally get a clue about how he feels about you. Now I'm not so sure. Chase can be stubborn. He may ricochet the other way and decide the safest approach is not to have anything to do with you."

Megan felt as if her heart dropped to her shoes. Surely Leigh wasn't right. "He'll probably calm down soon."

Leigh leaned forward. "Just in case he doesn't, let me give you a hand in getting him to fall for you."

No way. Leigh was a walking, talking, trouble magnet. Her interference would only upset the precarious balance Megan had created with Chase. These things needed to be handled delicately, and the word delicate wasn't in Leigh's vocabulary.

"I appreciate your offer, but I want to handle this myself," Megan told her. "I realize I may have confused your brother, but I still believe if he's given enough time, he'll come to see we're meant to be together."

Leigh tipped her head and studied Megan. "You honestly believe that, don't you?"

"I certainly do. I think Chase will respond best if I approach him with honesty and compassion."

Leigh bobbed her head, but Megan suspected she wasn't really listening. The younger woman simply waited until Megan finished speaking, then blurted, "I'll tell you what Chase will respond to. You call him up, tell him you need to talk to him about the fund-raiser, then you show up at the ranch wearing racy undies and holding a can of whipped cream. The boy will come around real quick after that." Leigh's smile turned devilish. "If he doesn't keel over from a heart attack, he'll be yours for life."

Megan's mouth dropped open about halfway through Leigh's suggestion and refused to shut no matter how hard she tried. Racy underwear? Whipped cream?

"I could never do something like that," Megan finally managed to squeak out when Leigh stopped speaking. "I'd feel like a..."

"Tramp?" Leigh winked. "But it would take his mind off the toothpick problem, I can guarantee you that."

For one second, the image Leigh had created slithered through Megan's mind. She could almost see Chase's expression when he opened the door to find her standing there in racy undies. She'd give him her sexiest smile, squirt a dollop of whipped cream on one finger, then slip it into his mouth and...

Oh, my.

Megan took a deep breath, trying to mentally quell her libido and throw a bucket of ice water on the image she'd created in her mind. Whatever else she did over the next few weeks, she most certainly wasn't going to show up on Chase's doorstep barely dressed.

This was about love. Not sex.

Thinking that Megan's silence meant she'd found a convert, Leigh warmed to her subject. "If you don't like whipped cream, there's always strawberry jam. Or chili. Chase likes chili."

Megan's mouth tried to drop open again, but she stopped it. *Chili?* What in the world would she do with chili? Megan refused to even think about that one.

"I'm not seducing your brother. I'm not showing up at the ranch in racy undies. And I'm not bringing food of any sort with me," Megan maintained firmly. "Chase and I will sort this out on our own without tricks."

Leigh sighed and stood. "I figured you'd be unreasonable. Fine. Do it your way. But just so you know, I'm not going to spend the next few weeks living with a man who complains about how many toothpicks we have in the house. Something's going to give, and it won't be me."

With that as her parting shot, Leigh walked out.

Megan fiddled with the index cards on her desk.

This situation with Chase was confusing enough without having Leigh interfering.

She picked up the book on her desk. Did she really want to browbeat Chase? She knew in her heart that she didn't. She wanted Chase to love her because...well, because he did. She didn't want to trick him into caring.

She pushed the book aside and slipped the index cards back into her desk drawer. She'd rather give up than feel as if she'd deceived Chase.

Besides, as long as he continued to work on the committee with her, she would have plenty of time to get him to notice her as more than a friend. Plenty of time.

CHASE PULLED HIS TRUCK UP in front of the library and turned off the engine. He glanced at the darkened front door and couldn't help wishing he'd missed Megan. He was as nervous as a fifteen-year-old about to ask out a girl for the first time.

"Get a grip, Barrett," he muttered to himself. He threw open the truck door and climbed out. He wasn't going to get weird about one little kiss. Now that he'd had a day to think about it, he was positive the kiss hadn't been a big deal. Sure, it had been a good kiss, maybe even a great kiss, but that was it. Nothing special. Nothing unusual.

Nothing he couldn't handle.

Determined, he headed toward the library's front door, rapping loudly on the glass. After a couple of seconds, Megan appeared and waved to him. She signaled him to wait, then headed back in the direction of her office.

Chase shifted his weight from one leg to the other. He wasn't looking forward to this conversation. In fact, if he'd had his way, he would have avoided Megan for a couple of days. Just until things between them settled down. But Megan had called, saying she needed him to stop by and pick up some papers having to do with the committee.

That was another thing. He sure wished he could think of a way to get off this committee, especially now that he and Megan were so jumpy around each other. But he couldn't do that to her. He was already hurting her by making her face reality when it came to this attraction between them. He couldn't also bail on her committee.

He watched as Megan hurried to the door, twisting the lock.

"Hi," she said, her voice slightly breathless as he walked by her and into the library. He could only hope she was breathless because she'd been scurrying around not because he was near her.

"Hey." He glanced around the library. They were alone, just as he'd feared.

"Where are Carl and Debbie tonight?" he asked, hoping the other employees of the Paxton City Library were simply hiding somewhere and hadn't left for the day.

"They've already gone home." She gave him a nervous smile, then headed toward her office.

Silently cursing himself, Chase followed. He

should have known better than to let her talk him into that kissing nonsense last night. Now Megan was uncomfortable around him. No two ways around it, they needed to forget about all this sexual stuff.

Without intending to, his gaze dropped and he watched the gentle sway of Megan's hips as she walked. Damn, she was one nice-looking lady. Her dark blue slacks hugged her curves, and he couldn't help wondering what would happen if he—

What in the sweet name of sanity was he doing? He yanked his gaze away and ran his hands through his hair. Twice.

A grip. He needed to get a grip. He once again cursed himself.

Megan turned toward him. "What did you just say?"

Beat the hell out of him. He hadn't realized he'd spoken aloud. "Nothing," he tried, but the look she gave him made it clear she wasn't buying that.

She crossed her arms and studied him. "It sounded suspiciously like you called me a name."

The way she was standing drew his attention to her breasts. He remembered all too well what those breasts had looked like last night in that pink nightie she'd had on.

"Yoo-hoo. Chase. Are you all right?"

He pulled his gaze back up to her face, then groaned. What was happening to him? He was losing his mind. Or worse, turning into some sort of degenerate. All he seemed to be doing was staring at parts of Megan that he had no business staring at.

"I wasn't talking to you. I was talking to myself. I called myself a name," he explained, and she had no idea how much he meant it. He was sorry. A sorry son-of-a-horse-trader. "I think maybe we should postpone this meeting."

She took a step toward him. "Aren't you feeling well?"

He debated what to say. He didn't want her to worry that he was sick, but he could hardly tell her what was really bothering him. This was all the fault of that blasted kiss. His gaze landed on her lips. She wasn't wearing lipstick. Her mouth looked soft, and sweet, and oh-so-kissable. He remembered all too well what her lips had felt like pressed against his, her breath mixing with his own, her tongue in his mouth.

He blew out a disgusted breath and hung his head. He was dumber than a box of rocks.

"Are you feeling dizzy?" she asked.

He raised his head. "No, I'm not dizzy. And I'm not sick. I'm..." The word horny popped into his brain, but he refused to say it.

She had on her glasses, which she now nudged up her small nose. "Are you confused, because of what happened last night?"

Grabbing that excuse like a drowning man lunging for a life preserver, he said, "Yeah. That's it. The kiss last night is bothering me, Megan."

She smiled. "It got me all bothered, too."

"No. I don't mean *bothered* as in hot and bothered. I mean *bothered* in the sense that I'm worried you may have gotten the wrong idea last night."

"The wrong idea?"

Although her voice was steady and she didn't move a muscle, Chase knew she'd tensed.

He took a couple of steps forward until he stood directly in front of her. He started to put one hand on her shoulder for comfort, but quickly decided he'd be much better off if he didn't touch Megan right now.

"I'm worried you got the wrong idea about that kiss," he said gently.

She shrugged. "I thought we agreed last night it wasn't much of a kiss anyway."

He wasn't going to get into that whole fish-sucking thing right now because both of them knew it wasn't true. The kiss had been hot. Damn hot.

"Megan, I'm sorry about last night. It shouldn't have happened."

Rather than appearing upset, she nodded thoughtfully. "No problem. Now if you want to come to my office, I'll get those papers for the carnival. Thanks for stopping by. Saves me coming out to your ranch. Anyway, these are lists of local companies, churches and organizations that may be interested in having booths at the carnival. I thought you and I could split the list and call around to see who wants to help."

She seemed so calm, so relaxed, but Chase knew she had to feel the sexual pull between them. Attraction crackled around them, and every time he looked into her wide green eyes, he had the almost overwhelming desire to do something unbelievably stupid. But hey, if she wanted to ignore what was happening, fine by him. He'd already done enough stupid things to last him a month. His gaze dropped to her lips. No, make that a year.

"Sure. Give me the list. I'll call around," he said, anxious to get out of here.

She rewarded him with a smile. "Thank you." She headed to her office, but Chase waited where he was. No way was he going into that small room. He'd be all alone with Megan in a room that had a door and a wide, firm desk that would be perfect for making love on.

This cowboy was staying right where he was. After a minute or so, she came back carrying a handful of papers.

"Here you go," Megan said.

Chase took the lists and moved away from her, away from temptation. "Thanks. I'll let you know how I do."

She took two deliberate steps forward until she once again stood directly next to him. Then she patted his arm and said in a soothing voice, "It's going to be okay, Chase. Really it is."

He looked at her hand, resting on his arm. He could imagine that same small hand wandering across his chest, her fingers caressing his skin. With effort, he swallowed past the knot in his throat.

"Don't worry so much," she said softly.

Then before he could do a single thing to stop her, she leaned up and placed a warm kiss on the side of his face. Every hormone in his body screamed for him to pull her into his arms and kiss her back, but he flat out wouldn't do it. He wasn't having sex with her no matter what she—and his own traitorous body—wanted.

Dag-nab-it, he still had some scruples left. Granted, his supply was running low. But he still had a couple kicking around. And those scruples were going to see him through this debacle.

He gazed down into her wide green eyes, all set to tell her that he wasn't going to play, when she smiled at him. One of those purely feminine smiles that made a man's blood run hot and his IQ drop to that of fungus.

Damn. He only prayed that those couple of scruples he had left were going to be enough.

5

"MAN, THIS PLACE MAKES HELL look like a tropical vacation spot," Chase muttered.

Megan glanced around the Paxton City Park and sighed. Chase was right. The two acres devoted to the children were barren and forlorn. As far as she could tell, the founding fathers of Paxton had picked the ugliest piece of land to devote to the park.

In fact, even though most of Paxton had lovely shade trees, this park was noticeably devoid of any trees. Well, there was one tired looking pine that leaned at a precarious angle near the far corner of the park, but other than that, nothing. She couldn't help feeling sorry for the tree. And even sorrier for what passed as playground equipment.

"The kids would be safer if they threw rocks at each other," Chase observed.

"It is rather bleak," she admitted. The few pieces of playground equipment that weren't broken were covered in a thick layer of dirt and rust.

"Bleak?" Chase walked farther into the park. "This place is pitiful. Downright pitiful. I didn't realize it was this bad."

Megan was glad he felt that way. She wanted

Chase to get as emotionally involved in this project as she was. Mostly for selfish reasons. Despite its appearance, this place meant a great deal to her. After her parents had died and she'd come to live with Aunt Florene in Paxton, she'd spent many afternoons at the park. Florene hadn't wanted her around the house, and since she was new in town she didn't have any friends. So she'd hung around the park. And one fateful day, she'd met Chase Barrett here.

Tommy Whitman had started picking on her, shoving her and teasing her about not having parents. Then suddenly, Chase had appeared. Now as an adult she knew he hadn't been the superhero she'd thought him to be that day, but to her, he'd always be a hero. Chase hadn't given an inch. He'd stood up to Tommy, something no one else in town wanted to do. Tommy had ended up backing down simply based on the look Chase had given him. It had proven to be one heck of a look, since to this day, Tommy still showed her respect whenever he saw her.

From the moment he'd stood up for her, Megan had been in love with Chase Barrett. And she still loved this park, but the children of this town deserved better. No matter what it took, she was going to make certain they got a great place to play.

She watched Chase head over to the playground equipment. Boy, it was good to see him. After their meeting at the library last week, Chase had avoided her, which wasn't an easy task considering how small Paxton was. But Chase had pulled it off, which was one more indication of how rattled he was.

But now he'd had a couple of days to calm down. Hopefully he'd found a way to accept what had happened and had given up fussing about toothpicks.

"Megan, look at this." Chase shook one of the support poles for the swing set. The metal wobbled and let out an ominous creak. "This place is an ER room's nightmare. I think we need to call the city council tonight and tell them we're tearing this monster down right away."

Muttering and fussing, he moved over to the teeter-totter. When he pushed it, part of the seat came off in his hand. He turned to Megan, his expression dumbfounded. "I cannot believe this place."

"Now you see why I want to buy new equipment." She moved closer to him, drawn despite her promise to herself not to push him about their relationship. But how could she resist? He looked scrumptious today in jeans and a deep burgundy T-shirt.

Trying to keep hold of her racing heart, she said, "I'll call Earl, although I know what he's going to say—the city doesn't have the manpower to take down this equipment."

Chase turned toward her, and for the first time since he'd arrived, he looked directly at her. His deep blue gaze made tingles skitter across her skin.

"I have the manpower," he said. "I'll get my

brothers over here tomorrow to tear this junk apart. I can use my truck to haul it to the dump.''

''I can help, too.''

He shook his head, causing a lock of his black hair to droop across his forehead. With an impatient gesture, he pushed it back in place. ''Best not. If you're here, we can't cuss, and judging from what I see, this job will involve a lot of cussing.''

She laughed. ''I think I can stand a few choice words.''

For long moments, he looked at her. She felt the same heat she always felt dance between them. Then Chase muttered something about scruples and not only looked away from her, but he also walked away from her.

Well she wasn't going to let him get away so easily. She quickly caught up with him. ''You're so nice,'' she told him. ''This means a lot to the kids.''

Her comment caused him to stop. He spun on his boot heel and faced her. Darn it all, he was frowning again.

''I'm not nice, Megan. Not at all.''

''Sure you are. You're concerned about children getting hurt on the playground.''

He shook his head. ''No. I'm worried about the city getting sued.''

''Like I believe that. Admit it. You're worried about the children.''

For a second, she thought he was going to argue with her, but then he sighed, the sound loud and heartfelt. "Let's walk this off and see how much space you have for new equipment."

Megan fell into step with him, knowing without a doubt what he was doing. Chase didn't want her complimenting him. He was obviously still upset by the kiss they'd shared.

That was a good sign, right?

Grabbing a pencil and notepad from her purse, she jotted down the rough measurements she and Chase came up with. There should be enough room to build a decent-size wooden play castle. The kids were going to go nuts when they saw it.

"At least you've got a flat piece of land. Should make it easier." Chase turned and headed over to the lone pine tree. "You going to cut this down?"

Horrified, Megan came to stand next to him. "Of course not. I wouldn't dream of hurting that poor tree." She patted the trunk. "It's earned the right to be part of the new park."

Chase chuckled. "Megan, it's a tree, not a war veteran. All it did was avoid tornadoes and snotty-nosed kids." He pointed toward a carving near the lower branches. "Looks like it didn't avoid all of those kids."

Megan moved to the side and studied the faded carving. A pair of initials surrounded by a heart. "That's so sweet."

"Bet the tree doesn't think so," Chase said dryly.

Turning, she studied him. "Probably not, but I think it's romantic that a couple was so in love that they carved their initials in the tree for everyone to see.''

Chase made a snorting noise. ''You can't be serious. This isn't about true love, Megan. Some horny, teenaged boy did that carving cause he was hoping to get lucky.''

For one second, Megan wondered if Chase had been the wayward youth. She quickly rechecked the tree, happy to see the initials weren't his.

Good. She didn't know what she would have done if the tree had been a testimony of Chase's love— or even lust—for another woman.

''I still think it's romantic,'' she maintained. ''I think it would be wonderful to have someone so in love with me that he'd make that sort of public declaration. Imagine how special you'd feel, how treasured.''

Chase moved closer, stopping when he stood only a few inches from her. Megan wished she knew what he was thinking, what he felt for her. He sure was frowning, so whatever he was thinking, he wasn't too happy about it.

Finally he said, ''You've always been special, Megan. I know maybe Florene didn't make you feel wanted, but the people of Paxton care for you.''

She had to smile at the vagueness of his comment. ''The people care? What about you, Chase? Do you care? Am I special to you?''

''You know you are.'' He blew out a loud breath, and again, his gaze met hers. Attraction arced and sparkled between them, and even though she knew he wasn't a bit pleased about it, she also knew he could feel it. And he was fighting it.

"Dang it, Megan. This is all Leigh's fault. We were fine until she started all that naked business," he muttered.

Deciding she'd long since passed the point of pretending with Chase, she admitted, "It's not Leigh's fault. I've pictured you that way many times in my life. I've wanted you for a long time."

He groaned. "Someone must be putting pheromones in this town's water. That's all I've got to say."

"Why can't you accept what's happening between us?" she whispered. "Why can't you believe we can be much more than friends?"

They stood only a couple of inches apart, but now Chase closed that slim distance between them. He placed one hand under her chin, and tilted her head so her gaze was locked with his. "I don't want to lose you in my life, Megan. That's how special you are to me." His deep blue gaze scanned her face. "Don't you see that?"

"No," she said on a sigh. "Because the fact is you may lose me anyway. I can't help how I feel about you." When he opened his mouth to argue, she hurriedly added, "And it has nothing to do with Leigh. I've felt this way about you since the day you defended me against Tommy Whitman in this very park."

When the hand he'd used to tip her chin slid up the side of her face to caress her cheek, Megan pushed her advantage.

"Come on, cowboy. It won't kill you to admit you feel a little something for me," she teased, anxious to hear his response.

He studied her face for a heartbeat, then said, "Damn the scruples."

Before she could do much more than suck a startled breath into her lungs, he wrapped his arms around her, pulled her body flush against his own, and kissed her.

CHASE KNEW HE SHOULDN'T be kissing Megan. Hell, that was the last thing he should be doing. Right now, he should be explaining how much her friendship meant to him. Barring that, he should be telling her how she'd always be a special part of his life.

He should be doing about any old blasted thing other than kissing Megan. But that's what he was doing—kissing her. And not just a nice little peck between friends. No, he was kissing her as if his life depended on it. One of those wild, wet, warm kisses that seemed to only lead to more kisses. Hungry kisses that spoke of lust and want and desire.

And Megan, bless her soul, was kissing him back with equal ferocity. He intended on breaking off the kiss. He really did. His brain kept sending signals to his lips to cut it out. But when she made a little mewing noise and wrapped herself even tighter around him, he cupped her face in his hands and deepened the kiss even more. At this point, he figured he'd already sunk the ship. He might as well capsize the dinghy, too.

So he gave in to the need he felt and kissed her. And kissed her. And kissed her.

The sound of a car backfiring somewhere nearby made reality crash back into him. His brain finally won the tug-of-war, and he tore his mouth free from Megan's.

He struggled to regain control, sucking deep breaths into his lungs. Of all the pea-brained moves. He was standing in the middle of a city park, in plain view of anyone who happened to drive by, kissing Megan. And not just kissing Megan, practically devouring her.

Way to solve the problem, Einstein. What had happened to his plan to once again calmly and rationally explain how they could never be more than friends? He'd decided over the past few days that if he explained his concerns to her often enough, she'd eventually come over to his way of thinking.

Of course, he might have had a better chance of convincing her of that little fact if he hadn't been busy exploring her mouth with his tongue. And what about his scruples? Plankton had more scruples than he did.

He slowly backed away from Megan. "About that kiss—"

After giving him a completely feminine smile that

looked a little too complacent for his peace of mind, she held up one hand. "Don't tell me, it was a mistake and it will never happen again."

Okay. At least she was being reasonable. "That's right."

"Got it. Well you take care, Chase. I'll see you around."

With a flirty little wave, she walked away, leaving him standing in the middle of the park, dumbfounded. She couldn't seriously be okay with this, could she? Sure, he didn't want to hurt her. And sure, he knew sex would ruin their friendship, but how could she calmly walk away when two seconds ago they'd been sharing a kiss that had caught them both on fire?

He narrowed his gaze and watched her climb into her car. As she drove off, reality hit him in the face like a wet sock. She wasn't unaffected, she just wanted him to think she was. Megan didn't want to fight about the kiss, so she'd gone on the defensive and cut off any chance he had of starting a fight.

Smart lady. He couldn't help admiring the neat way she'd outmaneuvered him like a roper chasing a calf. Still, she might have avoided a fight today, but sooner or later, this mess was going to boil over. Megan still thought they had a romantic future, but they didn't.

Okay after the two kisses they'd shared, he'd admit they shared more chemistry than he'd originally counted on. But chemistry could be ignored or even changed if you tried hard enough.

He blew out a disgusted breath and headed across the park to his truck. One way or the other, he needed to get her to face facts about their relationship.

"You stupid cowpoke, why don't you stop kissing her for starters," he muttered as he climbed in the cab of his truck.

Yeah, that would go a long way toward cooling things off.

"THE COWARD'S HIDING FROM YOU," Leigh said, then tossed a piece of popcorn into the air and caught it neatly in her mouth. "You need to stop him."

Megan scanned the carnival grounds, looking for Chase. Leigh was right. Chase was back to avoiding her. He'd done a lot of amazing footwork in the past few weeks to keep his distance, and she had no reason to expect him to change today.

His behavior was a direct result of their last kiss. She understood it had rattled him. It had rattled her, too. Heck, there was a fairly good chance it had registered on the Richter scale.

But rattled or not, she hadn't let the kiss distract her from the carnival and thankfully, neither had Chase. He'd simply used his brothers as a human shield.

The day after their last kiss when she'd swung by

the park to help dismantle the old playground equipment at the appointed time of eight in the morning, she'd found Trent and Nathan standing in front of a neatly stacked pile of old rusty metal. They'd told her Chase had a conflict, so he and his brothers had started at six in the morning and were already done.

And gee, no one had thought to call her.

Then when she'd needed additional help lining up sponsors for the booths, Chase had done the calling but Nathan had dropped the forms off at the library.

And when she'd run into trouble getting Earl to commit resources to assemble the tent, Chase had taken care of that as well. This time, though, Trent had been the one to drop off the final paperwork at the library.

She sighed. Nothing like running a committee with stand-ins.

"I still think you should give my idea a twirl," Leigh offered. "Whipped cream has brought many a man into line."

Megan continued to scan the crowd, still finding no sign of Chase. Disappointment washed over her, but she pushed it away. Today, she wasn't going to mope about Chase. The weather had turned out gorgeous, and the carnival had attracted a huge crowd. Not only did it appear most of Paxton was crammed into the small city park, but quite a few out-of-towners had come as well.

"Are you sure Chase is here?" Megan asked

Leigh, standing on her tiptoes to get a better look.
"I need to talk to him about the auction."

"Yeah, he's here. Lurking around."

Well that didn't make her feel any better. It hurt
that Chase was avoiding her. She didn't enjoy feeling like day-old liver at a Sunday brunch.

Giving up, she turned and headed toward the tent
where the auction would start in a few minutes.
She'd just slipped inside the darkened interior when
two of the men running some of the carnival games
cornered her. As she'd feared, the bigger turnout
was taking a toll on the homemade booths. They
needed help making a few quick repairs.

Before Megan could even open her mouth, Chase
spoke from behind her.

"I'll pitch in. Let me just grab my brothers, and
I'll meet you over there."

After the men walked away, Megan turned to look
at Chase. As usual, the sight of him made her heart
beat faster.

"Hi," he said, moving a little closer when a large
group of people came through the door.

Megan drank in the sight of him. He looked so
handsome today in his jeans and plain white shirt.
The simplicity of his clothes only served to show-
case his gorgeous face and amazing blue eyes. Of
course she'd never tell him that. Chase Barrett was
the least vain man she'd ever met. She knew his
choice of clothing was based on practicality not on
impression. But she was impressed, and she knew

without even looking that the other women in the tent were impressed, too.

Slowly she let her gaze wander over him. Her confidence soared when he took his time looking her over, too. She'd given a great deal of thought to her appearance, and the simple white sundress with the blue and green flowers made her feel pretty.

Chase seemed to agree because when he said, "You look nice," his voice had a husky overtone to it.

"Thanks. You look nice, too."

The goofy look Chase gave her made her laugh, and when he smiled in return, she felt her gloomy mood evaporate. Things were going to be fine. At least she hadn't lost her best friend. Not completely at least.

"I haven't seen you in forever," she said, even though she'd promised herself this morning that she wouldn't mention his absence. But how could she not? He really had been avoiding her.

"Yeah, sorry about that. I've been busy. But you got everything done you needed, right?"

She took a step closer to him. "Yes, but I still would've liked to have seen you."

"Couldn't be helped," was all he said.

"Really?" When he didn't elaborate, she pushed on. "Problems on the ranch?"

"Yes. No. Well, you know. Ranch stuff."

She smiled. "Ranch stuff?"

His shrug was self-conscious. "Horses, cows, ranch stuff."

Before Megan could question him further, Janet entered the tent, her red lips forming a wide smile at the sight of Chase. She was wearing her trademark flashy halter-top, this time in the exact same shade of heart-attack red as her lipstick.

"Chase Barrett, you're harder to find than my ex-husband when he owes me alimony. I thought when I joined this committee that we'd spend time together. Maybe get to know each other."

Megan leaned forward and told the other woman, "Chase has been busy with ranch stuff."

Janet raised one thin brow. "Ranch stuff?"

Megan nodded and adopted her most sage voice. "Yes. You know, horses, cows, ranch stuff."

With a knowing nod, Janet said, "I see."

Megan bit back a giggle, and almost lost it completely when Chase groaned. "If you ladies will excuse me, I've got to go help fix a couple of the booths."

"Wait." Janet grabbed Chase's arm. "I just wanted you to know I plan on bidding on the trip to San Antonio. And if I win, I'll definitely need an escort."

With that, and a quick wink, Janet wandered farther into the tent, eventually sitting near the front with her girlfriends.

"Damn, I'd forgotten all about that stupid trip."

Chase moved closer to Megan. "Listen, you've got to make certain you come in with the winning bid."

"I will. I can go as high as five hundred dollars," she told him.

Chase frowned. "We already agreed to use my money, so I'll be the one to go as high as five hundred dollars."

Megan didn't want to argue with him, especially not in front of a large portion of Paxton, so she merely nodded. Besides, if things got rough—and with Janet involved, they very well could—she could add her five hundred to his five hundred. There was no way Janet would bid more than a thousand dollars. Even she wasn't that crazy.

"Don't worry, I won't lose," Megan assured him.

His gaze locked with hers. "Truthfully I'm not sure what worries me more—you losing or you winning."

While Megan turned his comment over in her mind, a commotion near the front of the room drew her attention. The mayor was about to begin the auction. As much as she hated walking away from Chase when she'd finally gotten to see him, she had to go help with the auction.

"I have to go, but can I convince you not to disappear after the carnival is over?" Drat. She sounded as if she was pleading with him, which in a way, she was.

"I won't disappear," Chase assured her. "Besides, I have to find out who won the trip."

With that, he turned and left the tent. Megan felt like the energy had left as well. But before she could even miss him, Earl called her to the podium.

Public speaking had never been her strong suit, but Megan figured after the past few weeks, she was definitely getting better at it. She made a few introductions, gave a lot of thanks and a couple of reminders, then stepped aside and let Earl start the auction.

Megan sat in a small chair next to Leigh and settled back to watch the action. The first few items were small, a suitcase and a silk flower arrangement. They attracted only a hundred dollars each. But as each minute ticked by, the items became more expensive. The computer system Nathan had donated generated a lot of bids, eventually selling for more than it would have if bought at retail.

"Jeez, this crowd is like a school of sharks smelling blood. Earl has whipped them into a frenzy," Leigh said.

Leigh was right. Earl had obviously missed his calling. The seventy-three-year-old mayor was teasing and cajoling the crowd out of money like an old pro. This could be bad. Very bad. Earl might very well convince the ladies of Paxton that a trip with Chase was worth big bucks.

Megan glanced toward the back of the tent, hoping she'd spot Chase, but he wasn't there.

"Okay, next up is a trip to a bed-and-breakfast in San Antonio." Earl peered at the crowd over the top of his glasses. "Now in case you folks don't know this, San Antonio isn't just famous for the Alamo. It's also one of the world's most romantic cities. And I understand that if a single lady bids, she can decide to ask Chase Barrett to come along with her for company. I want everyone here to picture yourself on the River Walk. Soft music. Fine wine. A full moon." After a long, long silence, he grinned a devil's grin. "May just have to bid on this myself and take Mrs. Guthrie there for our anniversary. This old house still has a fire burning in the hearth, if you know what I mean."

The crowd laughed, then Earl started the bidding at a hundred dollars. Before Megan could even raise her hand, the bid shot up to two-fifty.

"Oh, no, go find Chase," she whispered to Leigh.

Leigh glanced at her. "What's wrong?"

The bid went up to six hundred.

"Leigh, I only have a thousand dollars to bid on this. I promised Chase I'd make the winning bid."

The bid went to eleven hundred.

"Hurry," Megan told Leigh.

"I have fifteen hundred. Do I hear sixteen?" Earl asked.

"Wow, you'd think Chase was a professional gigolo the way these ladies are bidding," Leigh pointed out.

Megan felt her heart drop to her shoes. This bidding was out of control. By now, the only bidders were single women. All of the couples had long since dropped out. Megan grabbed Leigh's arm. "Seriously, you have to go get him."

"Two thousand dollars. I have two thousand dollars from Janet Defries," Earl said. "Come on, let's keep going. This is starting to get interesting."

Megan felt her heart sputter. Oh, no. She stared at Leigh, who merely shrugged.

"Going once…"

"Going twice…."

Leigh shot to her feet. "Stop!"

The tent fell silent. Everyone stared at Leigh, who in turn stared at Megan. Leigh's expression clearly asked "What do I do now?" but Megan had no answer for her.

"What's the problem?" Janet demanded. "I want to be declared the winner."

After a nerve-wracking moment, Leigh turned toward Janet. "Tell me something, if you win, are you going to expect Chase to come with you on this trip?"

Janet's smile was feline. "I might like some company."

"Oh." Leigh looked at Megan, then turned toward Earl. "In that case, I think everyone here should know something."

"And what would that be, Leigh?" Earl asked patiently.

"Um, well…Janet can't win the trip because Chase can't go with her," Leigh said.

Megan frowned. Where was she going with this?

"Chase promised he would," Janet pointed out, her temper obviously at the breaking point.

Leigh grinned, a self-satisfied grin that Megan knew beyond a doubt boded trouble. She braced herself.

"Well, Janet, Chase made that promise a while ago," Leigh said. "Before he and Megan became engaged."

6

"CONGRATULATIONS, CHASE. Good for you."

Puzzled, Chase stopped hammering the side of the Go Fish booth back together and turned to look at the couple standing next to him. Edith and George Brown, owners of a neighboring ranch, both grinned at him.

"Um, thanks. But Megan arranged everything. I just did what she told me to do," Chase admitted, not wanting anyone to think he had anything to do with the success of the carnival and auction. Megan deserved all of the credit.

The Browns laughed, and George slapped him on the back. "Son, that's the best way to handle things. Just do what Megan tells you to do. You'll be a much happier man."

Still laughing, the elderly couple wandered away, leaving Chase frowning after them. What had George meant by that last comment?

Shaking his head, he went back to work, quickly fixing the booth and letting the juvenile fishers return to their fun.

Once he finished all the necessary repairs, he cut back toward the auction tent. Every few feet, someone stopped him with congratulations. After the third time, a bad feeling settled in his stomach. That feeling only intensified when he saw Leigh racing toward him, Nathan on her heels.

"Hey, Chase," Leigh said when she skidded to a stop in front of him.

Her expression screamed guilt.

"What did you do?" Chase asked, knowing he really didn't want to hear her answer.

"See, there was a bit of a problem during the auction." She fidgeted with her necklace that said: Kiss Me, You Frog.

"I'll say," Nathan muttered. "Tell him, Leigh."

Chase put his hand on his sister's arm. "Yeah, tell me, Leigh. Right this second."

She let go of her necklace and put her hands on her hips. "Fine. But it's not a big deal. All that happened was I told some of the people at the auction that you and Megan are engaged."

Chase felt like all of his blood turned icy cold. For a minute, he only stared at his sister, unable to believe what she'd just told him. Then he got angry.

"Why in the blazes would you say something like that?" he demanded.

Leigh shrugged. "The bidding on that trip got out of hand, and Megan didn't have enough money. When it became obvious Janet Defries was going to win, I stopped the auction and said you couldn't go on the trip with Janet because you're engaged to Megan." She smiled brightly. "So now that you're up-to-date, I'm heading on over to the—"

Chase silenced her with a frown. Then he looked at Nathan. "Did you say anything to clear up this mess?

"Me?" Nathan shook his head slowly. "I didn't have a chance. Before I knew what had happened, Leigh said I'd donate the two thousand dollars the town would have made if Janet's bid had been accepted."

Unable to believe what she'd done, Chase stared at his sister. "You're like a one-person wrecking crew today."

Rather than appearing insulted, Leigh said, "Just trying to help."

"Help isn't the four-letter word I'd associate with you, Leigh," Chase muttered, heading toward the tent. As he grew nearer, more and more people congratulated him on his engagement to Megan. He'd have to set a lot of people straight later today, but right now, he had to see Megan.

He found her at the front of the auction tent, trying to talk to Earl and a couple of members of the city council. Not unexpectedly, no one was listening to her. They were too busy telling each other that they'd known all along that he and Megan were more than just friends.

When he stopped next to her, Megan looked up, relief immediately crossing her face. "I can't believe Leigh did this," she said. "Earl, Chase is here now. He and I want to explain that Leigh was wrong to—"

"Steal your thunder." Earl patted Megan's arm.

"I know. You and Chase probably wanted to wait before making an announcement. But don't worry, we won't push you for a wedding date. At least not right away."

"Still, they shouldn't wait too long if they want to reserve the church for the wedding." This came from Trent, who had come up to the group and now stood grinning at Megan and Chase like a court jester. "You two lovebirds don't want to let the grass grow beneath your feet. Seize the day, I say. You may want to give some thought to hightailing it to Las Vegas and getting hitched right away."

"Cute," Chase said to his younger brother. Turning back to the group, he said, "Could Megan and I have a minute with Earl, folks?"

The crowd agreed and after a few more congratulations, left them alone with the mayor.

Chase studied Megan's face, debating how to handle this fiasco. Although he knew she wanted their relationship to move into the romantic arena, he also knew she'd never push him into marriage. She didn't seem a bit more pleased about this bogus story than he was.

"Earl, about what Leigh said. She was wrong," Chase said, wanting to flatten this problem quickly.

His tone must have convinced Earl that he was serious. The mayor slipped his glasses down his nose and studied Chase and Megan closely. Finally he asked Megan, "Is that the truth? Is Leigh wrong?"

Megan didn't hesitate. "Yes, she's wrong."

"I see." Earl pushed his glasses back in place. "Well, I'm not sure I completely understand what the two of you are telling me. For instance, if you mean Leigh is wrong about you getting married anytime soon, I'd say that was your own business. But if, for instance of course, you were to tell me that you're not engaged after all, then we'd have a real problem on our hands. For starters, that would mean Janet is the rightful winner of the trip. And Chase did agree to go with the winner if asked, so we'd need him to take Janet to San Antonio. Then there would be the embarrassment factor. Not only would you two look like fools, but everyone might wonder if the auction was legit. Could cause the city problems."

Earl turned to Megan, his look intense. "I sure would hate to see a black cloud settle over this great carnival and auction you arranged. But if Leigh was wrong, then I guess, Leigh was wrong."

Chase heard Megan groan softly by his side, and he felt like kicking his family tree. Earl was right. If they turned around now and said Leigh had been joking, then Megan's hard work might fall under suspicion. Sure, they could explain, but some people would never believe them.

Megan took off her glasses. "Leigh was wrong about—"

"The wedding," Chase said. "We're not planning on getting married anytime soon. We want to have a long engagement."

She'd been all set to confess to the mayor, and

he couldn't let her do it. They could work this out with a little time. It wouldn't kill him to pretend to be engaged to Megan for a few weeks. Then, once things died down and her plans for the park were firm, they could tell everyone the engagement was off because they'd decided they made better friends than lovers. No one would be harmed by the deception, and the kids would still get their playground.

He looked at Megan, who was obviously confused by what he'd told Earl. "We're planning a long engagement. And don't try to change our minds about this. We both need time to think about our future."

As much as he hated lying to Earl, he knew he was doing the right thing for Megan and the town. He'd simply have to bide his time until they could straighten this out. But when he got home, he and Leigh were going to have a long, hard talk.

"Good. Good. Glad to hear that was what you wanted to tell me." Earl leaned forward and placed a kiss on Megan's cheek. "I'm really happy for you, honey. Despite his ornery tendencies, Chase here is a good man."

Beside him, Chase could feel how tense Megan was. Wanting to lighten the mood, he said to Earl, "Ornery tendencies? I don't have anything but pure sugar pumping through my veins."

Earl snorted. "You're a hoot, boy. A real hoot."

With that, he walked away, leaving Megan and Chase alone at the far end of the tent.

"Why didn't you tell him the truth?" Megan whispered.

Chase shrugged. "Because I don't want it to spoil the auction."

"But we're lying. We're not engaged."

That part bothered him, too. "Megan, will you marry me?"

She blinked. "What?"

"Now when people ask you if I really proposed, you can truthfully say yes," he pointed out.

Catching on quickly, Megan smiled. "I get it, and my answer is yes. Now you can tell everyone I accepted."

For a heartbeat, they shared a smile, two old friends who had figured out a solution to a major problem. Then worry gnawed at him. What if she'd misunderstood? "But you know this engagement is—"

"Relax, I'm not taking it seriously."

"Good. After the trip, we'll announce we've broken up."

"Are you sure you want to go on that trip together? I'll understand if you'd rather not."

Chase studied her, standing in front of him in her pretty white sundress, her hair fluffed around her face. She looked sexy and sweet at the same time. As far as he could tell, the two of them going away together on that trip was a lousy idea. But as Megan continued to look at him, the words dried up on his lips. He couldn't let the people in this town think he'd dumped her. And that's exactly what they'd think if he didn't go to San Antonio with Megan.

Concern for her feelings forced him to add, "But, Megan, we're going on this trip as friends. That's all."

"I understand." She drew an imaginary *X* across her chest. "I promise I won't kiss you. Nor will I picture you naked. I will be on my very best behavior."

Chase knew she meant that. Megan sincerely intended on being on her best behavior.

Now if only he could say the same thing about himself.

"I SHOULD HAVE GUESSED YOU and Chase were in love," Amanda Newman said the following Tuesday when she pushed her cart into line behind Megan at Palmer's Grocery. "The way you looked at each other the night of the meeting made it clear you both cared deeply."

Megan had been putting her groceries on the conveyor belt, but she stopped and turned to look at the minister's wife. Sure, there was a chance Amanda had seen something in her gaze as she'd looked at Chase. She was, after all, in love with the man. But Chase didn't love her. At least he didn't romantically love her.

Not yet anyway. But Megan still had hope. He had agreed to keep up their pretend engagement. A man didn't do that for just any woman who crossed his path.

"So you saw something in the way Chase looked at me?" Megan couldn't resist asking Amanda.

"Oh, yes. He looked at you the same way Conrad looks at me." Amanda's expression turned blissful. "Like you make him complete."

Megan liked the thought that in some way, Chase might feel she made him complete. "And he looked at me that way?"

Amanda laughed. "Of course he did, dear. Why else would he want to marry you?"

The comment felt like a bucket of ice dropped down the back of Megan's dress. That was the problem—their engagement wasn't real. Moreover, according to him, they would never be anything more than friends. Of course, friends didn't kiss the way she and Chase did.

"If you don't finish putting your groceries on the counter, I'm going to have to arrest you for loitering."

At Trent's voice, Megan spun around. He stood at the end of the counter, his grin wild and wicked. Holding up a head of lettuce, he asked, "You gonna make dinner for your loving fiancé?"

Megan shot Trent a reproachful look because he knew all too well that the engagement wasn't real. But her look only made him laugh.

He tossed the head of lettuce from hand to hand. "If you are, I should warn you that Chase is more of a meat and potatoes guy. He likes salads, but not as the main course." Nodding toward her cart, he added, "Why don't you give the rest of the folks standing in line a break and finish emptying your cart. I'll bag for you.''

Megan glanced behind her and realized with a start she really was holding up the line.

"Sorry," she said and quickly loaded her remaining food on the counter.

"She just got engaged," Amanda explained to the other customers in line. "It's to be expected that she'd be distracted. All those wedding plans to make."

"When's the big day?" Peggy Wylie, the cashier, asked.

"Yeah, Megan, when's the big day?" Trent winked. "I want to be certain I mark it on my calendar."

Megan felt the warmth of a blush climb her face. She hated lying with a passion, but she also agreed with Chase. The best way to handle this situation was to wait a few weeks, then tell everyone that she and Chase had decided they made better friends than lovers.

But she couldn't help wishing they really were engaged. Whenever someone asked her when the wedding was, her heart did a little flutter, almost as if she were really marrying Chase.

Everyone was looking at her, so Megan gave them the pat answer she and Chase had developed for when they were confronted with this question. "We want to have a long engagement, so we haven't set a date yet."

"Why a long engagement?" Amanda asked.

"You've known each other for most of your lives." Before Megan could respond, she pressed on. "If you want to have a June wedding, you need to hurry."

Megan grabbed onto that excuse with relief. "Yes. That's it. I want to have a June wedding, and since it's already May, I don't have time to put something together on such short notice. I want to wait until June of next year so I can have the wedding of my dreams."

Her answer must have sounded pretty good because Amanda's expression softened. "You do that. It's important that your wedding be exactly right."

Feeling satisfied that she'd handled this situation well, Megan paid the cashier and helped Trent finish bagging her groceries. Again, she couldn't help wishing her engagement were real. She really would like a June or a September wedding. While she was too late for June, she certainly could put together a wonderful ceremony before September. That is, naturally, if she could convince the groom to actually be a groom.

Just when Megan thought she was going to escape the store without future incidents, Trent said, "I don't think you should wait a whole year. What's important is you're getting married. You shouldn't care where or when the ceremony takes place."

Megan walked over to him and said softly, "Cut it out."

But Trent seemed to be warming to the topic. "Chase has been on his own for long enough. I bet the ladies of this town would be more than happy to help you come up with a beautiful wedding that could be pulled together quickly.''

"Oh, yes," Amanda said. "I'm sure Conrad would be able to find time for you. And if you want an outdoor ceremony, it's always lovely out at the lake. Or better yet, hold it at Chase's ranch. It would be wonderful by the pool."

Megan debated her answer and finally decided to use her groceries as an excuse to escape. "I'll keep all those ideas in mind. Thank you."

Then before anyone else could come up with suggestions for a wedding that realistically would never happen, Megan pushed her cart toward the parking lot. As she expected, Trent fell into step next to her.

"You're an evil man," she told him as soon as they were out of earshot of anyone else. "You shouldn't tease me like that. I don't want anyone to find out that the engagement isn't real."

Trent shrugged. "Maybe I wasn't teasing you. Maybe I don't think you and Chase should break your engagement, even if it is fake."

They had reached her car, so Megan turned to face him. She'd never had a serious conversation in her life with Chase's carefree younger brother. But his expression told her he was absolutely sincere today.

"You really feel that way?" she asked.

"Sure," Trent said. "I think you're good for Chase. You always have been. Marriage would probably suit him."

Megan stared at Trent, stunned that he could feel that way. She thought he, of all people, would discourage his oldest brother from marriage. She'd never figured him for an ally.

"You're teasing me again, right?" she asked, deciding this was simply another one of his pranks.

Trent shook his head. "No. Dead serious this time. I love Chase. I want what's best for him, even if sometimes he's too dense to know what that might be. Sure, at first it was a joke, but now that I've thought about it, I think you two are perfect together."

Working on autopilot, Megan unlocked her car and loaded her groceries inside. Periodically she glanced at Trent, who was helping her. Trent thought she and Chase were perfect together? Would wonders never cease?

After her food was in the car, she faced Trent again. "I guess Leigh told you how I feel about Chase."

"Leigh didn't have to tell me. It's always been written all over you. Chase is the only one who never noticed," Trent said.

"I'm that obvious, huh?"

Trent pulled his sunglasses out of his shirt pocket and slipped them on. "Oh, yeah. You're like a neon sign. But hey, that's good. You should let people know how you feel about them. Life's too short to waste time playing games."

Megan laughed. "This from you? The master at playing games?"

"See, now that's where you're wrong. I'm always painfully honest with the ladies I date. They know up-front that we're only having fun."

Megan slipped her keys into the pocket of her slacks. "Thanks for telling me you'd think I'd be good for Chase. I think so, too. But he has to do what he feels is right for him. I can't force him to fall in love with me."

Trent leaned against her car, his expression thoughtful. "I don't agree. I think Chase needs encouragement. He's spent most of his life believing that love doesn't exist. You should take whatever drastic measures are necessary."

Uh-oh. She'd heard this sort of thing before. This could be dangerous. Especially to Chase. "What exactly do you mean by drastic measures?"

"You've got resources on your side, Megan. You should use them."

Totally baffled, she asked, "What resources?"

"Leigh. Me. Nathan. We can work on Chase from the inside while you work on him from the outside."

Oh, no. The thought of Trent, Leigh, and Nathan ganging up on Chase was positively scary.

"Chase needs to make this decision on his own," Megan said firmly. "I appreciate your offer, but this is between the two of us."

For a few seconds, Trent simply looked at her. Then he grinned. "Megan, I have an idea. Get yourself some racy undies. Maybe in red. Then drive out to the ranch, knock on the door, and when Chase answers—"

Megan groaned. Did all these Barretts think alike? "I know, flash him my scanty undies and a couple of cans of whipped cream and tell him I'm dessert. Leigh already suggested that one."

Trent seemed puzzled. "Wow, Megan, I wasn't going to say anything like that. The racy undies were to go under your clothes, of course. They would give you self-confidence when you went to talk to Chase about making this engagement real. I saw a show on TV where the lady said she always felt like she could conquer the world when she wore her sexiest underwear under her suit." He gave her his best chief of police look. "You and Leigh sure come up with some wild stuff. Whipped cream. Yow."

Closing her eyes, Megan willed herself not to blush but failed. She felt warmth climb her face. When she finally looked at Trent again, he was grinning.

"Thank you for the suggestion," she said stiffly. "I'll consider it."

"Not that Chase wouldn't like the whipped cream thing. I'm sure he would." He tipped his head and studied her. "You wouldn't by any chance be able to tie a cherry stem into a knot using only your tongue would you?"

Her voice was strangled when she said, "Um, I'm pretty sure that's a talent I lack."

Trent seemed unaware of her discomfort. "Oh, it's real easy. You just need to practice. First, you get yourself some maraschino cherries. Then you—''

Megan held up one hand to silence him. "Thanks, but I'm not really interested in learning how to tie cherry stems with my tongue."

"Too bad. Because if you did that whipped cream thing and could also tie a cherry stem, I'm pretty sure Chase would follow you straight to the altar without making a single protest."

Shaking her head at Trent's nonsense, Megan opened her car door. "I'll keep the suggestion in mind. But please, let me work this out with Chase myself."

With a shrug, Trent said, "You bet. I won't interfere. Not a bit. Just wanted you to know you've got friends on your side."

Because she knew in his own way, Trent's offer of help was sincere, Megan said, "Thanks."

"No problem..." His voice drifted away as Lucy Marshall, a recent divorcée, walked by carrying a tiny bag of groceries. She gave Trent a flirty smile.

"Hey there, Trent," Lucy said.

Trent moved forward. "Hey, Lucy. Let me give you a hand carrying those groceries." He took two more steps forward before stopping and glancing back at Megan. "We're done, right?"

Megan bit back a smile. Trent was in full wolf mode. "Yes, we're done. See you around."

Trent nodded, but his attention was already riveted on Lucy. As Megan climbed into her car, she watched Trent flirt with the other woman. And Lucy flirted back. Outrageously. Now why couldn't she be like those two? Why couldn't she go after what she wanted with gusto? Sure, she'd been fairly direct with Chase the past few weeks, but still, it didn't seem to be enough. She needed to think of another way to get him to see her as the woman she really was, not just as a friend he'd known for twenty years.

Megan sat for a minute, watching Trent and Lucy until they walked away. Then with a sigh, she started her car and had just put it in Reverse when she stopped.

Drop by precious drop, her common sense left her. When it was completely gone, she carefully put the car back in Park, turned it off, climbed out and locked the door. Then she headed across the parking lot toward the entrance to the grocery store.

She suddenly had the urge to buy some cherries.

7

"I'M HAVING A WONDERFUL TIME. How about you?" Megan asked.

Chase gripped the steering wheel tighter. They were two hours into the drive to San Antonio with another hour plus left to go. Was he having a wonderful time? Was it possible to have a wonderful time while simultaneously feeling like a captain who knew in his bones that his ship was going to sink?

Wonderful wasn't exactly the word he'd choose to describe this afternoon. Uncomfortable as hell seemed to sum it up nicely. He could count on one hand the number of times he'd felt this uncomfortable. There was the night of his eighteenth birthday when his high school math teacher had made a pass at him. And the time he'd broken up with a woman only to serve as best man at her wedding three weeks later when she'd married a friend of his.

Neither of those times came close to being stuck in the tiny cab of his truck with Megan. Of course, she'd been nothing but nice and thoughtful. Megan specialized in nice and thoughtful. But she'd talked pretty much nonstop since he'd picked her up at two o'clock this afternoon. She'd talked about the weather, and the new playground equipment she'd ordered, and some recent acquisitions the library had made.

But she'd never mentioned their last kiss or the sham engagement, which was driving him nuts.

"Chase, you didn't answer me. Are you having a good time?"

"Yeah. Just swell." Noticing a billboard for a gas station at the next exit, he decided now would be a really good time for a break. "I need to get gas."

Not surprisingly, Megan agreed. "Sounds good."

After a few minutes, Chase pulled up next to a pump and turned off the engine. He looked over at Megan, who smiled at him. Damn. He felt like a jackass. Megan was being sweet, and he was as snarly as a bear woken up from his winter nap. But how else was he supposed to behave when he had to spend the weekend trying to resist Megan? After the two fiery kisses they'd shared, he knew it wasn't going to be easy.

"I'm going to go inside and buy a soda," Megan said. "Want anything?"

His sanity? His peace of mind? His old life back?

He shook his head. "No. I'm fine."

But as he filled the tank on his truck, he realized he hadn't been fine since that night at the city council meeting. Ever since then, he'd been fighting Megan and himself. And now, after the auction, he was fighting most of the town. Everywhere he went these days, people told him how perfect he and Megan were for each other.

Except for one tiny fact—she believed in love and marriage, and he knew those two concepts were a sham. He cared enough about Megan to refuse to be the man who broke her heart.

Megan still hadn't returned when he finished pumping the gas, so he headed inside the convenience store to make sure she was okay. He found her standing near the register and started toward her when he noticed she was talking to the man in line behind her.

No, she was *flirting* with the man in line behind her. Or at least, she wasn't doing a damn thing to stop the guy from flirting with her. And the man was flirting with Megan, at least he was when he wasn't too busy checking her out. The sight of the two of them smiling and laughing stopped Chase dead in his tracks.

As he watched, the yahoo leaned closer to Megan and asked, ''You live around here?''

Megan gave the man a vague smile and Chase's self-control snapped like a twig. What the blazes was she doing? She was an engaged woman, for crying out loud. She couldn't flirt with other men.

Struggling to keep a tight rein on his temper, Chase crossed the store at a clip and slipped one arm around Megan's waist.

''There you are, darlin','' he said, and with a

pointed look at the yahoo, dipped his head and kissed Megan soundly.

He'd only meant for the kiss to make his position clear, but once his lips touched Megan's, he got distracted. He deepened the kiss, and by the time he lifted his head, both of them were breathing hard.

Megan stared up at him and blinked. "Why did you do that?"

He didn't answer her because he wasn't sure what the answer was. Instead he turned his attention back to the man standing behind Megan. "My fiancée doesn't live around here. She lives in Paxton, with me."

That shut the yahoo up. Up close, Chase realized the other man was younger, maybe in his early twenties. But being young was no excuse for poaching on another man's woman. The kid took a couple of steps back, apparently catching on.

Satisfied that the situation was now clear, Chase looked at Megan. She continued staring at him as if he'd lost his mind, and it hit him like a kick in the head from an angry horse—he'd just acted like a real fiancé.

Ah, hell. Now he was getting as crazy as the rest of Paxton.

Megan was still staring at him as she paid for her soda, then led the way back to the truck. They both climbed in without comment, and Chase headed back toward the interstate. He knew Megan was waiting for him to say something, to offer some explanation for his behavior. But truthfully, he had none.

Finally he said, "Sorry about what happened back there."

"What exactly did happen back there? I'm a little confused."

Chase glanced at her, then returned his attention to the road. "I didn't like the way that man was treating you, so it seemed the easiest way to solve the problem."

Even to him, the explanation seemed lame. But hey, that was his story, and he was sticking to it.

Megan had turned toward him as much as her seat belt would let her. "He wasn't doing anything, Chase. Just being nice."

"Nice my as—" He cleared his throat, still struggling to understand why he was so upset. "That man was coming on to you because he wanted you. Who knows what would've happened if I hadn't come inside the store."

His outburst startled him. Whoa. He was acting like a jealous lover. What in the name of sweet sanity was wrong with him? Megan was his friend. If she wanted to flirt with yahoos, then that was her business.

The only problem was his mind might be convinced it wasn't his business, but he couldn't seem to get his emotions wrapped around the concept.

"Chase, were you jealous?" Megan asked softly.

When he cut his glance her way, she had a warm, sweet smile on her face.

Oh, for the love of Pete. He kept making this situation worse and worse.

"No, I wasn't *jealous.* Just concerned for your safety."

For a heartbeat, Megan simply studied him. Then an almost blissful expression crossed her face.

"Thank you for your concern," she said.

Chase felt like a man knitting his own noose. "Megan, I only said you were my fiancée because it was the easiest way to get the guy to back off." Some ornery part of his makeup compelled him to add, "Course it didn't help that you were flirting with him."

"Flirting? I wasn't flirting with him. He asked me how to get to San Antonio, and I gave him directions."

Chase snorted. "There are about thirty signs pointing the way to San Antonio. He needed directions about as much as I need to shave my legs."

She narrowed her eyes. "Be that as it may, that's what he asked me. I was merely being helpful. And he wasn't flirting with me."

Yeah, right, and cowboys don't love horses. "Don't be naive, Megan. That man was hot for you."

"How do you know?"

"Because of the way he looked at you," Chase

managed to say, still steaming at the thought of that guy checking out Megan when she wasn't looking. Not that Megan wasn't worth checking out. She looked especially pretty today in her jeans and pink T-shirt. The clothes showed off her trim figure, but were completely respectable.

Megan frowned at him. "How exactly did he look at me?"

Chase rolled his shoulders, trying to ease the knot forming in his muscles. "Like he was picturing you naked."

With a laugh, Megan placed one hand on his arm. "Oh, right. You're teasing me. For a second there I was worried you were really upset. I should have known better. You'd never get jealous of a man talking to me. Like you keep saying, we're friends, nothing more. What's to get jealous of?"

Nothing irked him more than having his own words tossed back at him, but Megan had a point. They were friends, and he had no cause to be jealous.

Reaching over, he turned on the CD player, making the music a tad louder than was really necessary. But the volume forced them to stop talking, which made him want to shout hallelujah. As far as he was concerned, he was through talking for today. Maybe for the rest of the trip.

Because it seemed whenever he opened his mouth these days, he got himself in trouble.

"YOU HAVE TO BE WRONG," Megan said, leaning farther over the counter. "Please check your computer again."

Judy Sullivan, Amanda Newman's sister and the owner of the B&B, shook her head. "I'm sorry about this mix-up, but I got a call yesterday from a woman saying she was Megan Kendall—saying she was you. She explained that she and Mr. Barrett were engaged and would only require one room. Since this is a busy time of year, I naturally was happy to have an additional room to rent out." She studied Megan. "My sister told me a couple of days ago about your engagement. Congratulations, by the way."

Megan forced herself to smile. "Thanks." Next to her, she could feel tension radiating from Chase. After Judy checked them in and gave them a key to their mutual room, Megan picked up her small suitcase and cosmetic case and finally gathered the courage to look at him.

"I don't know what happened," she told Chase. "I didn't call here."

"I know. Considering the way things have been going, we should have expected this. If I had to bet, I'd say this was another case of Leigh playing the two of us like a fiddle." He reached out and took Megan's suitcase, then nodded his head toward the stairs. "There doesn't seem to be anything we can do about it right now. Let's just hope this is a big room with two double beds."

Megan appreciated Chase being a good sport, but

she knew deep down he was upset. She was upset, too. She didn't want Chase to think she'd planned this as a way to seduce him. He'd been nice enough to help with the fund-raiser, and even though their personal relationship wasn't developing as she'd hoped, she also respected him enough not to trick him.

Of course, ever since the kiss at the gas station, she couldn't help wondering if Chase's feelings toward her were starting to change. He'd kissed her like a jealous man, and then he'd acted even more like a jealous man when they'd discussed it in the car. A friend wouldn't have cared that someone else was flirting with her.

But a man falling in love would care a lot.

Feeling infinitely better, Megan unlocked the door to the room and walked inside. A huge, king-size bed took up almost all of the room. The bed was gorgeous, covered with a delicate flowered spread that matched the drapes. Besides the bed, there was a small chair in the corner and a dresser. But mostly, the room was just bed.

"I don't believe this," Chase muttered over Megan's shoulder. "This is insane."

He set the suitcases down, then walked out of the room. Megan heard him heading back downstairs, and she didn't need to be clairvoyant to know he was trying to get them a different room. She couldn't blame him. Despite the sedate, refined decorations of the room, it did fairly scream sex. Okay, sedate, refined sex, but sex nonetheless. The bed was the focal point, and there was no way not to stare at it.

After a few minutes, a dejected Chase walked into the room. "I know this isn't going to be a surprise to you, but this room—which is the bridal suite, by the way—is the only room available tonight. Now who would have seen that coming?" Sarcasm dripped from his voice.

"I'm sorry," Megan said, meaning it.

Chase gave her a rueful smile. "Don't be. This isn't your fault. My sister did this, probably with the help of my brothers. When I get back to Paxton, I'm finding a new family."

"We can go to another hotel," she offered.

He sat in the small chair in the corner, then frowned at the bed. "No. That would hurt Amanda's feelings. We can stay here tonight. I'll sleep on the floor."

Megan glanced around. Since the bed was so big, there wasn't a lot of floor space to be had. But she didn't point this out to Chase. She also knew better than to argue with him as to which one of them slept on the bed.

She set her suitcase on the bed and opened it. Her pink nightie was folded neatly on top.

Chase groaned. "Megan, we have to have some rules if we're going to share this room tonight. For starters, I'm not going to have sex with you. Nothing personal, of course, but that's the way it's going to be."

Biting back her smile took a little effort. "I understand."

He waved at her suitcase. "Second, we're both sleeping in our clothes. You can't run around this room in your nightgown or your underwear or your robe. You must have clothes on at all times."

Containing her amusement was getting more and more difficult, but she knew Chase was serious, so she did her best to keep her expression neutral.

"Okay," she said. "I promise to keep my clothes on at all times." He looked so unhappy that she walked over and patted his shoulder. "I'll do whatever it takes so you can enjoy this trip. I'm not trying to trick or seduce you, Chase. I'll admit, I'd like our relationship to be different, but I know you don't feel the same way."

Even saying those words hurt, but she meant what she said. She wanted him to be happy, even if that meant he might never return her love.

Chase looked at her, his expression resigned. "Megan, I care enough about you not to want to see you hurt. But I'm having one hell of a time fighting you, my family, plus the entire town of Paxton. A man's only got so much self-control, and mine's running out."

Her heart fluttered a little at his confession. Chase wasn't immune to her; he was just worried about her. But he also felt the simmering sexuality dancing between them.

Still, Megan had no intention of using that knowledge against Chase. As much as she wanted them to be lovers, she accepted that he didn't.

"Let's get out of here," she suggested. "We'll go explore and have dinner somewhere."

For a second, Megan thought Chase was going to argue, but then with a sigh, he stood and nodded toward the door. "Lead on. The way my day is going, I'd probably choose a restaurant that only serves oysters."

CHASE HAD NEVER SLEPT on a bed of nails, but he'd be willing to bet his favorite bull that it was a damn sight more comfortable than the floor in their hotel room. For the hundredth time, he rolled over, trying to find a comfortable position. But it just didn't exist. The floor was tougher than the rockiest Texas ground.

"Why don't you come join me in this soft bed?" Megan's voice drifted down around Chase like a siren's song.

Oh, no, she wasn't tempting him now. Not with a soft bed and an even softer body. No sir. He'd withstood so much already. He could make it through the night without making love to her. He was strong.

Sort of.

"Thanks, but I'm fine down here," he lied. "You go on to sleep."

"I can't. I feel terrible that you're stuck on the floor. Here you were so nice to agree to come on this trip with the winner of the auction, and now you end up sleeping on the floor. The guilt is killing me. Besides, this is silly. We're mature adults. We can share a bed without having sex."

Chase didn't mean to laugh but he couldn't help himself. "No, I don't think we could."

Her voice was indignant when she said, "You really can trust me. Just because I…have feelings for you that are more than those of a friend doesn't mean you can't trust me. I promise I won't try to seduce you."

Yeah, but if he got in that bed, he'd have to resist two people—Megan and himself. Ticking him off big time was the fact that most of his body thought sleeping with Megan was a dandy idea. The only organ holding out on the plan was his brain. Okay, and maybe his heart. But that added up to slim defenses if his libido decided to get rowdy during the night.

No, the smart move was to remain where he was. On the blasted floor in this stupid room.

"Chase, you didn't answer me. I said I promise I won't seduce you. Please get off the floor and come to bed. I'll stay on my side. You won't even know I'm here."

"Yeah, I will."

"No. I promise. I won't come anywhere near you. I'll be good."

See now, that was the problem. Most of him didn't want her to be good. Most of him was rooting for her to be very, very bad. As far as he was concerned, there wasn't a bed in the world wide enough for the two of them to sleep in.

"Thanks, Megan, but I'm going to stay here." He rolled over onto his side and closed his eyes, praying for sleep.

After a couple of seconds, a soft shuffling sound made him turn onto his back. In the faint light drifting in from the partially opened drapes, Chase saw that to his horror, Megan was sliding off the side of the bed. He jackknifed into a sitting position.

"Dang, Megan, what are you doing?"

"It's not fair that you sleep on the floor. Since you won't sleep on the bed, I'm joining you on the floor," she said, dropping her pillow next to his. "Scoot over. The bed takes up so much space there's not much room here on the floor."

Chase felt as if he'd forgotten how to breathe. For a couple of seconds, he watched her, dumbfounded, while she fluffed her pillow and pulled the blanket off the bed.

"Now there, isn't this better?" she asked. "Come on. Stretch out and close your eyes. We need to go to sleep."

He finally recovered from his shock enough to tell her, "This isn't going to work. If I'm not willing to make love to you on the bed, I'm sure not going to make love to you on the floor.''

Although, as much as he hated himself for it, he really, really wanted to. She smelled wonderful and looked tempting as sin curled on the floor, smiling up at him.

"I already gave you my promise that I wouldn't seduce you. Now let's go to sleep.''

He sucked an unsteady breath into his lungs. "Get back up on the bed,'' he said, but was disappointed when rather than a stern command, the words came out more like a plea.

She merely laughed. "I will if you will.''

With a huff, he stretched out next to her, figuring the floor was probably so uncomfortable it would ward off any licentious thoughts he might have. But this close, he could smell her soft scent, part citrus shampoo, part warm woman.

"I never realized what a mean woman you are,'' he said after a couple of minutes.

"Thank you. I'm working on my mean side. Exercising it on a daily basis. I read a book recently, *Be a Bully,* that says to be truly happy, you have to do what you think is right, even if it upsets other people.''

"Well you'll be happy to know you're upsetting the hell out of me right now.''

"Sorry about that,'' she said, but he didn't believe for a second that she meant her apology.

Long minutes ticked by while the two of them lay

on the floor, side by side with only a ribbon of space separating their bodies. Chase tried to keep his mind on anything but the woman next to him. In his mind, he balanced the ranch's books, decided how much feed he needed to order when they got back to town, figured out what livestock he was going to enter in the state fair next year...

And wondered what color bra Megan had on. Maybe white, with lace. Or a pale pink, like her T-shirt.

Or maybe midnight-black. One of those that pushed everything up.

Chase groaned and jumped to his feet.

"Okay. You win." He grabbed his pillow and blanket off the floor and tossed them on the mattress. Then he turned on the lamp, sprawled on the bed, and told her, "I give up. I've been trying to be a decent guy, but for the past couple of months, I've been shanghaied, bamboozled and railroaded by everyone I know. I can't take it anymore. You want to have sex. Fine. Here I am. Have sex."

When Megan didn't say anything, he turned his head and looked at her. She stood next to the bed, her green eyes wide. He watched her debate her next action and felt the blood hum in his veins while he waited for her decision.

"Um, this isn't quite what I had in mind," she said. "I wanted it to be romantic."

"But sex isn't romantic," he pointed out, his emotions on a roller-coaster ride. He wanted her.

Really, really wanted her. But he also knew she'd end up getting hurt. "Sex is just sex, Megan. But hey, if that's what you want, then I'm willing to be a good friend and help you out."

She frowned. "Gee, thanks for the offer, but this isn't right, Chase. I'd feel like I was taking advantage of you," she said, although he noticed she put her pillow and blanket back on the bed. When she sat on the side of the mattress, he moved over to make room for her. "I can't have sex with you if you don't want to have sex with me."

"I'll survive." His heart raced in his chest, and he honestly didn't know what he wanted her to do. He couldn't stand anymore, so he was trying to prove a point. He could only be pushed so far before he'd snap. But now, looking at her, he couldn't help wishing she'd take him up on his offer. "I thought this was what you wanted."

She shook her head. "Not like this," she said softly, and he figured she was talking more to herself than to him.

Without saying anything else, she reached out and turned off the light. Then she moved over to the far left side of the bed and said, "Good night, Chase."

After a few minutes, he heard her breathing become soft and rhythmic. He figured it would be hours before he could fall asleep, but the bed really was comfortable and he was exhausted. Not ten minutes later, he felt himself drifting off.

Right before he fell asleep two things crossed his

mind—first, that Megan had managed to find a way to get him to share the bed with her after all.

And second, that he still couldn't help wondering what color bra she had on.

8

MEGAN TAPPED ON THE bathroom door. "Chase, are you all right? Has the swelling gone down yet?"

For at least a full minute there was no response. Then Chase threw open the bathroom door and frowned at her. "What did you say?"

He looked so yummy, standing there with only a towel wrapped around his waist, that Megan completely forgot what she'd said to him. Instead she was one hundred percent focused on his tanned chest.

"Up here, Megan," Chase said dryly. "My face is up here."

"Hmm?" Blinking, she pulled her attention away from his chest and forced it to stay on his face. He must have just finished shaving because a tiny spec of shaving cream rested in the slight indentation in his chin.

"Megan," he said impatiently. "Pay attention."

She blinked again. A couple of times. Then tapped down on her libido and concentrated on what she'd been saying.

"I asked if the swelling has gone down yet," she

said, not really surprised when her voice came out sounding more than a little breathless.

Again he frowned at her. ''I'm going to guess you're talking about the wasp bite and not something else. So yes, the wasp bite is better.''

''Good.'' She glanced over his torso again, this time telling herself she was only looking at all that tanned, gorgeous skin to see if he was okay. One large purple bruise darkened his left side. ''And the bruises? Do they still hurt?''

Chase sighed. ''I'm fine. Let me finish getting dressed, then we can talk.''

She looked back up at his face. ''And the bump on your head? Is that fine, too?''

''Yeah. I'm in dandy shape.''

With that, he closed the bathroom door again. Megan walked over and sat on the edge of the bed. Poor Chase. He was having a terrible day. It seemed the more things went right for her, the more they went wrong for him.

This morning she'd blissfully woken up in his arms. As much as she'd promised to stay on her side of the bed, she'd accidentally wandered over his way and wrapped herself around him like a vine. For several wonderful moments, she'd simply enjoyed being held by him. That was until he'd woken up, taken one look at her snuggled in his arms, and then jumped out of bed as if he'd caught on fire. Unfortunately his foot snagged in the blanket, and he ended up crashing onto the floor, giving himself a couple of good-size bruises.

Then at breakfast, she'd had a wonderful time because Chase had been his most charming. He'd told her he wanted the trip to be enjoyable for her, so he'd decided to stop being a grouch. He'd made good on his promise by telling her funny stories. At least he had until a distracted waitress had whacked him, rather hard, in the back of the head with a metal coffee carafe.

Finally, once Chase had been feeling better, they'd headed over to the Alamo. Exploring had been fun and educational, and several times during their tour, she'd caught Chase looking at her with a lot more than mere friendship in his eyes. One of those times, when his gaze had locked with hers, she'd winked at him. The gesture must have startled him, because he'd backed into a tree and ended up getting stung by a wasp.

But the absolute low point had come during their walk back to the hotel. A young man had hurried by them, bumping into Megan. When she'd started to lose her balance, Chase had grabbed her. Thanks to his quick thinking, she hadn't fallen in the water fountain they'd been walking by.

Unfortunately Chase had.

Altogether, the poor man had had quite a day. Well, at least she had good news for him now.

The door to the bathroom opened and Chase came out. Although he looked wonderful, Megan couldn't help regretting that an unbuttoned cotton shirt covered most of his gorgeous chest and jeans covered his sexy legs.

"You look better," she said brightly.

He nodded. "Hard not to look better since earlier I looked like a drowned rat."

Not exactly a rat, but he had taken quite a dunking.

Hoping to make him feel better, she held up a room key. "I convinced Judy to let me rent another room, so we won't have to share tonight. You can sleep in this bed all by yourself without worrying about me taking advantage of you."

He stared at the key for a moment. "Judy must have wondered why you wanted another room. I mean, she thinks we're a happily engaged couple."

"She was curious, so I told her that you and I never spend more than one night together."

His blue eyes studied her intently. "Run that one by me again."

Megan shrugged. "I tried every other explanation I could think of, and she didn't buy a single one." Ticking them off on her fingers, she said, "I told her you needed time alone after the bad day you'd had, and she said I should be supportive and nurturing. Then I told her that you were mad at me, and she said you seemed like a really nice guy and you'd cool down eventually. Finally I told her I was mad at you, but she said all I needed to do was tell you why I was upset, and she knew you'd do whatever it took to make the situation right."

Megan took a deep breath, then added, "At that point I had no idea what else to say so I told her we were superstitious and didn't want to spend more than one night together before the wedding."

Chase chuckled. "She must think we're odder than two alligators trying to ice skate."

"That's probably an understatement," she admitted, a smile tugging at her lips. "And I hate to think what she's going to tell Amanda. But I knew you'd be more comfortable if I moved to another room."

For several long seconds, Chase just looked at her, and Megan felt her heart race. *Say you want me to stay with you,* she chanted over and over in her mind. Unfortunately her telepathic abilities seemed to be on the fritz because what really came out of Chase's mouth was, "That'd probably be the best idea."

Drat. Oh well, it's not like she'd expected him to change his mind. That whack to the head he'd gotten hadn't been that hard.

Chase picked up his wallet and the room key. "I'll pay for the other room. And I'll be the one to move so you don't have to repack your things."

"Always the gentleman," she said, tracing the floral pattern on the bedspread with her index finger.

He sat down next to her. "I'm trying to be one, Megan. But like I said last night, I'm starting to run out of willpower."

As much as she hated herself for being thrilled to hear him admit that, she was. Thrilled beyond words. Losing his willpower implied that he found it difficult to resist her, which in turn meant he felt a lot more for her than mere friendship.

There was hope yet.

"Why don't we discuss this over dinner?" she asked, standing and heading for the door. "After the day you've had, you must be hungry."

He smiled. "Sure. Let me finish getting ready." He stood and buttoned his shirt. Megan watched him dressing, enjoying the feeling of intimacy caused by such an innocent action. Somehow watching Chase buttoning his shirt and tucking his wallet into his back pocket seemed very personal. This morning, he'd left the room while she'd gotten dressed, so she'd left the room when it had been his turn.

But watching him was exciting.

When he was done, he asked, "Ready?"

Mutely she nodded and picked up her purse.

He must have misunderstood her silence, because he said, "You know, I've had a lot worse days on the ranch, so stop worrying about a few bumps." He grinned and added, "But for your own safety, you might want to give me a wide berth."

That was the last thing she wanted to do. What she really wanted was for Chase to kiss her senseless. Unfortunately she knew that wasn't going to happen.

"Let's go," she said.

As they headed down the stairs, Chase asked, "Where do you want to eat?"

"Let's not tempt fate. Let's eat someplace away from the River Walk."

They asked Judy, who recommended a small barbecue restaurant just down the street from the B&B. Megan was worried that it would be a dark, intimate place, but instead it was rowdy and bright, with singing waitresses and food out of this world.

"This is a fun place," Chase observed, settling back in his chair.

Megan took a bite of her steak and felt as if she'd tasted heaven. "The food is wonderful."

When their waitress, Darla, stopped by again, she had a broad grin on her face and a couple of her co-workers in tow. "Judy from the B&B called. I understand you two just got engaged."

Oh, no. Megan subtly shook her head at Chase, but he seemed resigned to their fate.

"Something like that," he said.

Megan sensed what was coming and wanted to slip under the table, but no such luck. With a nudge to Chase, Darla said, "Well in that case, sweetie, you need to remember a few things if you're going to make a good husband."

With that, she and her two co-workers launched into the country song, "Any Man of Mine." As they detailed the many things Chase would need to do and say to make the woman in his life happy, Megan felt a blush flood her face. The poor, poor man.

What else could life do to him today? The entire restaurant was watching him and laughing.

Thankfully he took it well. He leaned back in his chair and nodded his head, as if he were trying to remember every warning the song gave. After Darla and company finished, he gave them a big tip and laughed.

"I guess that's better than getting hit in the head with a coffeepot," he said to Megan.

When he grinned at her, Megan smiled back. He was so wonderful. Not just his handsome devil looks, but his humor and kindness. How could she not be in love with him?

She took a sip of her lemonade, her gaze locking on the maraschino cherry floating on the top. "I guess we head back to Paxton in the morning," she said.

"I guess."

"Did you enjoy this trip at all?" She held her breath, waiting for his response, more than a little bit afraid he'd say he'd had a terrible time.

"Yeah. I enjoyed it." His gaze was intent, heated. Megan's heart beat furiously in her chest. She loved the way he was looking at her, with fire and want and lots of good old lust in his gaze. Leaning forward, he added, "I always enjoy being with you."

Megan tucked that comment close to her heart. Then she gathered her nerve and plucked the cherry out of her glass.

"Watch this," she said, holding Chase's gaze.

It took her a little bit of effort since she hadn't practiced nearly as much as she should have, but eventually, she managed to tie the cherry stem into a knot using only her tongue. She held out her handiwork for Chase to see.

"Ta Da," she said with a grin.

Chase looked as if he'd been struck by lightning. He made a mumbled, groaning sound as he first studied the knotted cherry stem, then glanced at her mouth.

"Party trick," she said softly.

"Come on." He stood and tossed money on the table. Then he wrapped his hand around hers, tugged her out of the restaurant and hustled her back to the hotel. It wasn't easy keeping up with him, but she managed.

When they reached the bridal suite, she waited while he unlocked the door, dreading what would happen next. One of them was going to pack up their things and move to a room father down the hall.

"Give me a moment to pack," she said, once they were inside the room.

As Chase tossed the key onto the dresser, Megan moved by him to get her suitcase. When she started to unzip it, he placed one hand on her wrist, stopping her.

"Hold on a moment."

His deep voice was husky, strained, and Megan moved closer to him. "Why?"

With a gentle touch, he brushed a strand of hair

off her forehead. "You remember I mentioned earlier that my willpower was draining away?"

She couldn't believe what was happening here, or at least, what she hoped was happening here. Trying to contain her excitement, she kept her voice even when she said, "Yes."

He seemed almost as if he were looking into her soul. "I'm afraid I'm on dead empty, Megan."

Then he bent his head and kissed her.

MEGAN DIDN'T GIVE HIM the chance to change his mind. As soon as he moved to kiss her, she rose up on her tiptoes and kissed him first. She threw herself at him with such gusto that he had to wrap his arms around her to keep them both from falling over.

"Whoa, whoa," he tore his mouth away from hers. "Sweetheart, let's not crash through the wall."

Megan kept kissing him. His cheek, his neck, his chin. "Kiss me," she murmured.

Oh, he intended on kissing her all right. He intended on doing a lot more than merely kissing her. But he also didn't want to end up in the hospital. Not now. Not when he'd finally decided to give in to the desire he felt for Megan.

He gave her another long, lingering kiss. Megan returned it with an enthusiasm that rocked him straight down to his boots. At the back of his mind, he still had a lot of reservations about making love with Megan. But he was only human, and he hadn't been kidding, his willpower had dried up quicker than rainwater in the Texas sun.

This time, one kiss led to another, then another. He couldn't seem to get enough of her. He was still busy kissing her when he felt her small hands undoing the buttons on his shirt. Although his hormones screamed *yes, yes,* reality smacked him in the face.

"Whoa."

She groaned and laid her head against his chest. "Stop saying whoa. Say giddy-up."

He chuckled. "I'll work on that. I only stopped this time because we've got a problem."

Before he could explain, she glanced down at the noticeable bulge in the front of his jeans.

"Everything seems to be working just fine," she said, moving closer to him.

When she pressed against him, he moaned, forgetting for a second what they'd been talking about. Then he remembered. "The problem is I don't have anything with me."

She tipped her head back and looked at him. "By anything, do you mean like handcuffs or feathered boas?"

"No, I don't think we're going to need any help having a good time." Slipping his arms around her, he pressed his body against hers, enjoying the feel of her soft curves. "I meant I don't have any condoms with me, and I can hardly call downstairs and ask Judy to send up a few."

Rather than looking disappointed, a grin lit Megan's face. "I have the situation covered—literally." She walked across the room and picked up her cosmetic case and opened it. She removed the tray containing her makeup, then pointed inside. "Will these do?"

Chase looked inside. There were half a dozen boxes of condoms in all styles and colors.

"What in the world? Megan, you must have fifty condoms in here. Expecting reinforcements?"

She giggled and nudged him. "No. I just wanted to be certain I got the right kind, and Mary said—"

That stopped him cold. Mary Monroe was the wife of Ted Monroe, the owner of the one drugstore in Paxton. "You bought all these condoms at Monroe's Drug Store?"

"Of course. At first I felt a little embarrassed, but I knew they wouldn't mind answering any questions I had. If I'd gone to a big store in a different town, they might not have been as helpful."

Megan was looking at him as if there wasn't anything unusual about buying condoms from the biggest gossip in a town that thrived on gossip. He looked at the boxes in the bottom on her makeup case. At least Mary would tell everyone he had a lot of stamina.

"So Mary told you to buy all of these?" he asked, picking up one of the boxes.

"Oh, no. She recommended the ones with the car on the front, but Lilah said—"

Chase groaned. "Lilah Pearson was there, too?"

"Well, yes. She thought the ones with the sunset would be better. And then Troy Everson said the ones with the arrow on the front were really good."

With effort, Chase tried to pull air into his lungs. Finally he managed, "Exactly how many people did you talk to about condoms?"

She shrugged. "Not that many. Four. Maybe five. And I didn't ask anyone's opinion. They noticed me looking and came over and made suggestions."

She squinched her eyes and admitted, "I guess I'd better tell you now that Nathan and Trent came into the store while I was there." She routed through the boxes, finally pulling out one with a picture of a shooting star on the front cover. "They told me to buy these."

Chase took the box his brothers had recommended and tossed it into the trash. "No offense, but considering everything that's happened, I don't think I'll trust my brothers."

With that, he snagged one of the other boxes and tossed it on the bed. Then he nibbled on Megan's neck. "The whole town thinks we're here having wild sex, and yet we're standing around talking."

She leaned toward him. "That does seem like a shame."

Holding her tightly, passion roared through his body. But before they put a dent in that healthy supply of condoms she'd brought, he needed to make certain she understood what tonight meant.

Leaning back, he held her gaze. "Megan, you know I won't change my feelings about love and marriage, right? You know that after this trip, I'm going to want to go back to being simply friends. Do you think you can do that?"

"I'll always be your friend, Chase," she assured him.

That wasn't exactly the response he'd been looking for, but when she pulled her navy T-shirt over her head and he saw her black bra, he decided her answer was good enough.

He kissed her again, long and hard and deep, until they both were hungry for each other. When she pressed against him, he reached behind her and flicked open her bra. Without hesitation, Megan slipped the slinky garment off, folded it and her T-shirt, and set them neatly on top of the dresser.

"You going to fold everything we take off tonight?" Chase asked with a smile as he explored the gorgeous curves she'd revealed. "This is a side of you I've never seen before."

The smile she gave him was pure seduction. "By side, do you mean my neatnick tendencies or do you mean..." Her gaze dropped to her naked breasts. "Do you mean this side?"

Chase chuckled. He'd never been as turned on as he was at the moment, and yet with Megan, everything seemed so natural, so easy. Wanting to feel her next to him, he quickly unbuttoned his shirt and set it on the dresser next to her bra. "And for the record, I'm not folding it."

"Fine, be a bad boy. See if I care." She slipped her arms around his waist and pressed herself against him. "I like reckless men."

Chase drew in a tight breath, and kissed her again. She tasted like lemonade and sweet, willing woman. Over the next few breathless moments, they managed to help each other out of the remainder of their clothes. Chase also managed to distract Megan to the point where she was no longer neatly folding her clothes but dropping them on the ground.

Once their clothes were off, she skimmed her hands across his chest and then down his body, exploring and tantalizing.

"You know, when I pictured you naked, I'm afraid my imagination underestimated and did you an injustice." She gave him a wicked grin. "Who knew?"

He couldn't help grinning back at her. "Glad I exceeded your imagination."

When they finally tumbled onto the bed, Chase couldn't believe he'd fought so hard against making love with Megan. It was outstanding, amazing. She was so responsive to him. When he kissed her, she mewed with pleasure. When he explored her body with his hands and his mouth, she sighed with need. And when he finally used one of the condoms she'd brought and joined their bodies, she gazed at him with red-hot desire.

"Chase," she murmured, touching his face with gentle fingers as he drove them relentlessly to ecstasy and beyond.

A long while later, after he'd managed to catch his breath and clean up, he gathered her in his arms. He flat-out couldn't remember ever feeling this happy.

"I take back every crack I ever made about us not having chemistry," he said, dropping a kiss on the top of her head. "We could create our own nuclear explosion without much effort at all."

Megan snuggled against him. "It was pretty terrific wasn't it? But still, I can't help feeling badly about what happened."

That was the last thing he'd expected her to say. He knew for a fact that she'd enjoyed herself, and she'd been the one so insistent that they have a physical relationship. Now she had regrets?

He leaned up so he could see her face. "You feel *bad?*"

"Not in the way you mean. It's just that I read several books just in case this situation ever happened, and yet when the time came, I didn't try any of the things I'd learned."

Still feeling muddled by the passion they'd shared, it took Chase a few seconds to follow what she'd said. Finally he asked, "You studied for this?"

"Yes."

Chase leaned back against the pillow, unable to contain the grin that crossed his face. "Were you expecting me to give you a quiz, 'cause I can probably come up with a question or two if I try."

His teasing brought a smile to her face. "That's okay. I meant I'd read up on the things I could do to you and for you that would make the experience better."

"Impossible," he assured her. "There is no way the experience could have been any better."

She leaned over and kissed his chest. "Not even if I'd done this?" Her tongue caressed one of his nipples before her mouth moved lower. "Nothing would have made it any better?"

"Yeah, maybe that would have helped," he barely managed to say.

She leaned up and kissed his lips. "I've learned all sorts of things recently."

"Like the cherry stem tying thing?"

With a flirtatious glance, she asked, "Did you like that?"

This conversation was revving his engine. He skimmed his hands down her silken body. "Yes, ma'am. I liked it very much."

"Well, if that's the case, you haven't seen anything yet. If you think you've got the stamina, I'll show you a few other things I learned from those books."

Chase was pretty sure he'd died and gone to heaven. "Bring it on, darlin'. Bring it on."

9

MEGAN STOOD ON HER FRONT porch, debating what to say to Chase. The drive back from San Antonio had been fairly silent, but not uncomfortable. They both seemed to be caught up in their emotions from last night. Just thinking about how wonderful it had been to make love with Chase brought a silly grin to her face.

But last night had been last night, and now it was time to pay the piper.

"Thanks again for everything," she said as Chase carried her suitcases into her house and set them on the living-room floor.

"Since I'm not exactly sure what you're thanking me for, I'm not going to say 'you're welcome.'" He turned to face her. "Besides, I didn't do anything that deserves your gratitude."

Okey dokey. That sounded like a man who had picked up a few regrets on his trip to San Antonio. As usual, Chase was being hard on himself. As the oldest in his family—who'd practically raised his siblings—he held himself to impossible standards and never cut himself any slack.

Determined to keep things light, she said, "Fine,

cowboy, have it your way. I had a great time. Glad you came with me."

He raised one dark eyebrow. "How do you mean that?"

Megan had to stop and think what she'd said, then she laughed. "I meant I'm glad you came with me on the trip, but you can take it the other way, too."

Her bluntness seemed to throw him for a moment. He shifted his weight, glanced around her living room, then cleared his throat. "Guess it's about time we talk about what happened."

Even though she was far from psychic, she knew what he was going to say next. He intended on apologizing, which was the last thing she wanted to hear. So to prevent him from saying he was sorry the best night of her life had happened, she said, "I love you."

That certainly shut him up. For a second, at least. Then he sighed.

Uh-oh. A sigh wasn't a good sign. Not at all. Again she hurried to prevent him from apologizing.

"Before you say last night was a huge mistake, I want to tell you something. I meant what I said. I love you. I've loved you for years as much more than a friend. And I think we can be happy together. But I also know you don't feel that way, and I accept that. I still want to be your friend. So let's forget about last night and get back to being just friends."

"Megan, last night was just lust. Nuclear lust, I

admit, but only lust. You can't let it convince you that you love me," he said softly.

She studied him for a moment, then said, "You know, sometimes you're one dumb cowboy."

"Excuse me?"

"I mean it. If you think for one second last night was about lust, then you're acting dumber than mud."

One corner of his mouth lifted and she could tell he was fighting back a smile. "For a lady who claims to be in love with me, you sure are calling me dumb a lot."

"Oh, I love you. I feel badly that you're avoiding happiness like it's a giant pothole, but I still love you."

He finally let his smile break free and gathered her close for a hug. "You don't hate me?"

His question tugged at her heart. "No. I could never hate you."

He rested his chin on top of her head and rocked them slowly. "Because you know, what you're feeling is infatuation. It will fade, trust me."

With a groan, she shoved out of his arms. "There you go, being dumb again. Of course it isn't infatuation, and of course my feelings for you won't change. Give me some credit here, cowboy. I know love when I'm standing in it."

"I just meant—"

Megan held up one hand. "I know. Well, here's the deal. Since you're so convinced what we shared is only lust, then last night should have slaked our appetite for each other. I mean we did about everything a couple can legally do in Texas.''

With a chuckle, Chase said, ''I'm not too sure about that last little idea you had. I can't believe you read about that in a book.''

''Books open new horizons,'' she said in her best librarian tone.

''Yeah, well it certainly taught me a thing or two.''

For a moment, they simply looked at each other, the memory of the previous night fresh and vivid between them. Then Chase broke eye contact.

Megan cleared her throat and forced herself to say the words she'd so carefully thought out during the ride home from San Antonio. ''Anyway, now that we've made love, your sexual interest in me should wane since you don't love me.''

He glanced back at her, the heat in his gaze still very real. But his response belied the look he was giving her. ''Guess so.''

''And in a few days, I'm sure we can go back to acting normal around each other.'' With effort, Megan pasted a bright smile on her face. What she was about to do was a calculated risk, but one she had to take. ''Let's avoid each other for a while and let things cool down. I know, the playground committee is set to meet a week from Tuesday. We can see each other then. We'll also use that as an opportu-

nity to tell everyone we've called off our engagement.''

For a moment, she thought Chase was going to
argue with her, and she couldn't help hoping he
would. She wanted him to say he couldn't stand the
thought of not seeing her for eight whole days. But
he didn't raise a single objection. Instead he nodded
his head.

He really was one dumb cowboy.

''Seems like the best idea.'' He shifted over to
the front door. ''Guess I'll see you at the meeting,
then. And Megan, I know you're going to find any
feelings you have for me will fade with time.''

She sighed, but she might as well argue with his
horse. Even after making love, Chase hadn't
changed his mind about them.

After he drove away, Megan looked out her front
window, surprised she didn't feel heartbroken. After
all, Chase still maintained he didn't return her feelings. But rather than feeling heartbroken, she felt
filled with expectation, like something wonderful
was going to happen to her very soon. No doubt the
sensation came from knowing that Chase loved her,
too. Oh sure, he didn't want to love her. And he was
going to fight it all the way. But she knew in her
soul that he loved her.

From now on, she wasn't going to push him anymore. She'd done what she promised herself she'd
do—she'd shown Chase how wonderful things
could be between them. He needed to take the final

step himself. He needed to decide if he wanted her in his life or not.

Smiling, she headed toward her bedroom to unpack. She had every confidence that sooner or later, things would work out. One way or the other.

"But if he does decide he loves me and wants to build a life together," she muttered to herself. "I only hope our children get his looks and my brains."

"WHAT DO YOU MEAN YOU DON'T want to talk about it?" Leigh crossed the family room and flopped onto the couch near Chase. "You have to talk about the trip. I've been dying to hear what happened."

"I'm not telling you a thing." He picked up his beer and took a long sip. Then he nailed his sister with a narrowed-eye look. "And by the way, you're grounded until you're eighty-six for that little stunt with the hotel rooms."

Rather than even attempting to appear innocent, Leigh grinned. "Liked that, did you? So what did you do? Sleep on the floor like a gentleman?"

"I already told you, I'm not saying a thing."

When Leigh finally realized he really wasn't going to give her any details, she threw her hands in the air and bolted from the couch. "I'm going to call Megan."

"She won't tell you anything, either," Chase warned.

Leigh stared at him, her expression mutinous.

"You can't do this. You owe it to the town to tell them what happened."

"You people need to get your own lives," he pointed out.

"I'm trying to, but since I'm grounded until I'm eighty-six, it may be a little difficult." She headed toward the kitchen, turning when she reached the doorway. "By the way, I'm too old to be grounded by you. It's a useless gesture."

"Fine, then I'll have Trent arrest you instead."

Leigh snorted. "You wish. I'm calling Megan."

After his sister flounced out of the room, Chase exhaled an exasperated breath. Women. They were driving him nuts. His original theory about the water still held true. The females in this town were acting weird.

Especially Megan. Why did she have to go and say she loved him? That's what he'd feared when he'd given into the lust he'd felt last night and made love with her. But he couldn't help himself. He'd never lost control like he had with her, but dang it, when she'd tied that cherry stem, he'd almost had a heart attack.

He really was one dumb cowboy. He sure had been last night, probably because all of the blood had rushed from his brain to other organs, leaving him with limited common sense.

"Hey, if it isn't one half of the town's most famous engaged couple," Nathan said, wandering into the family room.

Chase studied his brother. "How'd you get in here?"

"Came through the front door. I haven't quite mastered walking through walls yet. But I'm working on it."

"Very cute." Chase took another big swig of his beer. Although he rarely drank, he figured even a teetotaler would need a drink after the weekend he'd had. Heck, the way his life was going, the devil himself would be nervous. "I thought I'd locked the front door to keep undesirable people—like you—out."

Nathan sat in the chair facing him. "Leigh was leaving and let me in. She said she was going to go see Megan and uncover the juicy bits about your trip."

"Juicy bits? What if there weren't any juicy bits? Did you people ever consider that?"

Nathan pretended to think for a second, then said, "Nope. No one is going to believe nothing happened. Not after several of us witnessed Megan stocking up on condoms at Monroe's Drug Store."

Chase might not be the sharpest hook in the tackle box, but he knew bait when he smelled it. If he acknowledged he knew what Nathan was talking about, then his brother in turn would know he'd found out about condoms during the weekend.

He eyed his brother. "Megan bought condoms?"

Nathan chuckled. "You're good, but not good enough. I can tell from looking at you that you and

Megan did a lot more than sightsee in San Antonio.''

"Bull," Chase said.

"It's not bull. You've got that look about you." Grinning, Nathan stood. "But I'm going to take off now before you turn mean and decide to take out your frustration on me."

"If, like you say, I got lucky this weekend, then why would I be frustrated?" Chase figured he'd nailed Nathan's cage shut with that observation.

But Nathan only said, "You're frustrated because you want to be with her again, but you're fighting yourself because you think you're doing the right thing. You think you're protecting Megan, when in fact, you're hurting both of you."

"What in the blazes are you talking about?"

Nathan only shook his head. "Some things a man has to figure out for himself."

Before Chase could question him any further, Nathan left.

Of all the lamebrained comments to make. There was nothing to figure out. He'd made a mistake giving into his desire for Megan, but he wasn't going to make the situation worse by acting like some greenhorn just because they'd had great sex. He'd had great sex before in his life. Okay, maybe not nearly as great as what he'd shared with Megan last night, but close to it.

Sort of.

But it wasn't love, and the more people tried to

convince him he was in love, the more he knew he wasn't. Love was an illusion, like a magician sawing a lady in half. It wasn't real, and if you were foolish enough to believe, well sooner or later, you'd find yourself holding a big ol' bag of disappointment.

What he'd told Megan was the truth—the lust they'd felt for each other last night would fade in time. They'd taken the edge off the sexual hunger all that picturing each other naked business had created. And now, in a day or two, or certainly within a week, they'd be back to being friends. Only friends. More than likely, they'd laugh about what had happened.

And then, at last, his life could go back to normal. Close to it, anyway. Sure, it was going to take some doing to get the image of Megan naked unhooked from his brain. But he'd find a way to do it. He had to, for both their sakes.

"THERE ARE NO DETAILS to tell, so stop asking me," Megan told Leigh. "Besides, he's your brother."

Leigh sighed and dropped into the chair facing Megan's desk. For two days, the young woman had hounded Megan, trying to find out what did or did not happen in San Antonio. But since Chase had obviously told Leigh nothing, Megan wasn't going to tell her anything, either.

"Look, I'm not looking for specifics, because he is my brother and that would be too gross for words. All I want to know is if you managed to...you know, tiptoe through each other's tulips. If you did, then I figure I have a good chance of you becoming my sister-in-law.''

''Tiptoe through each other's tulips?'' Megan shook her head. ''Where do you get this stuff?''

''He's my brother. I can't get more specific than that without gagging. But you know exactly what I mean. Did you paddle his canoe? Dunk his cookies?''

''Wrap his Christmas presents?'' Megan suggested with a laugh.

''Exactly. Well, did you?''

All Megan said was, ''I can guarantee you that your brother and I never discussed Christmas on our trip.''

Leigh leaned back in her chair. ''Oh, perfect. Now I don't know if you mean the real Christmas or if you mean you two really didn't...stir each other's batter.''

Megan laughed again, glad to have the chance to do something other than miss Chase. Leigh certainly knew how to lighten her mood, and even though she wasn't going to tell the younger woman a thing, it felt good to laugh.

''What did Chase tell you?'' Megan asked.

''Not a blasted thing. The man's as silent as a mime, which ticks me off. But he's also getting grouchier by the day, which gives me hope. And yesterday, I caught him looking at the toothpicks again, which I'm absolutely certain is a good sign.''

Leigh leaned forward again. "I don't suppose you've given any thought to coming by the ranch soon with a couple of cans of whipped cream? You really need to give that some serious consideration."

"Not likely," Megan said, although she and Chase had done a lot of other things. But a promise was a promise, and she was going to honor the agreement they had. She was going to avoid seeing him until next week at the playground committee meeting. In the meantime, she'd simply have to settle for reliving in her mind what they'd shared.

"Ah, come on, Megan. Give it a try," Leigh pleaded.

"I'm not coming out to the ranch with whipped cream, so stop suggesting it." Megan picked up two books from her desk and stood. "Now if you'll excuse me, I'm reading to the toddlers this week, so shoo."

Leigh groaned and stood. "Jeez, you're as mean as Chase. And here I am, just trying to be nice and help you become my sister-in-law. You never even thanked me for arranging for you and Chase to share a room in San Antonio."

"I'm not going to thank you, Leigh, because that was a terrible thing you did," Megan said. "I've told you time and again, Chase and I have to work through our relationship ourselves without other people butting in. I can't force him to fall in love with me. He either does or he doesn't. If he doesn't, then I'll accept it."

As she said the words, Megan realized they were true. As much as she loved Chase, and as much as she wanted him to love her in return, maybe he'd never be able to admit to himself that he loved her.

And if that happened, she'd simply have to make new plans for her life. She wouldn't sit around dreaming that he'd one day change his mind. No, if Chase didn't tell her he loved her after the meeting next week, then Megan was going to move on.

"Love doesn't work that way," Leigh said. "You can't turn it off like a light switch."

"This from a woman who has never been in love," Megan pointed out.

Leigh shrugged. "You don't have to know how to swim to tell when another person is drowning."

Megan appreciated her friend's concern, but she couldn't make Chase do something he didn't want to do. "We'll just have to wait and see what happens. Patience, Leigh. We both need patience."

"I'd rather be rolled in tar and turned into a speed bump," Leigh said with another of her trademark snorts.

Megan patted her on the arm, then went to read to the toddlers. Truthfully, patience wasn't her strongest virtue, either. But she'd simply have to dig around and find some. Because there was no way she was going to rush Chase on this. And next week, regardless of what happened, she'd live with his decision.

"I WANT TO THANK EVERYONE for coming to the meeting tonight. The kids are going to be overjoyed by the new playground. Don't forget that the groundbreaking ceremony is two weeks from Saturday," Megan said.

From his position by the door, Chase watched several of the committee members jot down the date. He wouldn't forget it. Everything having to do with Megan stuck in his mind like a thorn these days.

He kept his gaze focused on her, although she avoided making eye contact with him all night. He knew she was waiting for him to announce to everyone that their engagement was off. The truth was, he wasn't willing to say that until he'd had a chance to talk to her.

Things in his life weren't back to normal. Not by a long shot. Over the past week, he'd expected his interest in Megan to wane. After all, the sexual pull between them should be satisfied.

But to his horror, his interest in her had become obsessive to the point where he'd been climbing the walls, wanting to see her, to be with her again.

Now, he was finally in the same room with her. If only this meeting would end. After what felt like a couple of eternities rolled into one, the ladies of the committee wandered out the front door, most of them flashing him smiles on their way by. He returned all of those smiles with a polite nod. Hey, as far as they knew, he was an engaged man. Didn't that mean anything to anyone anymore?

"Hey there, Chase," Janet said, coming over to stand close enough to see his DNA. "Rumor has it that you and Megan may be about to split up. No one's seen you together since you got back from San Antonio." She flicked one of the buttons on his shirt with a long, red fingernail. "If that's true, why don't you stop by later, and I'll help you mend your broken heart?"

Chase had seen vultures use more finesse. He took a step back from Janet, causing her hand to fall away. "Thanks for the offer, but I'm fine. Have a nice night."

With that, he shoved open Megan's front door and waited for Janet to leave. She narrowed her eyes but must have decided he wasn't kidding, because with a small shrug, she headed out. But as she passed him, she said, "You must be in love if you're turning me down."

Her comment caught him off guard. Unsure how to respond, he didn't say anything at all. Instead he turned his attention back to Megan.

The living room was empty except for the two of them. Chase closed the front door, then walked over to stand next to her. The blood hummed through his veins; his heart raced in his chest.

She was collecting the trash, but she stopped and glanced up at him. "Hi."

"Hi. Let me help."

As they gathered up the dirty dishes, he admitted, "I've missed you."

She gave him a sweet smile. "I've missed you, too."

"I've thought a lot about you."

"I've thought a lot about you, too."

"I think we should talk."

"I think we should talk, too."

He groaned. "Megan, if you keep echoing me, I'm going to start reciting dirty limericks."

With a laugh, she carefully placed the dirty cups back on the coffee table, then sat on the sofa. "Then I promise to stop echoing you, because I'm sure a cowboy like you knows some really dirty limericks."

"One or two," he agreed, sitting next to her. Now that he had her attention, he proceeded with caution, feeling like a jittery man in a nitroglycerin factory.

"I know you mentioned that after tonight we'd tell everyone we'd called off the engagement, but I was wondering what you thought about waiting for a while."

Her startled gaze met his. "Why?"

He saw no reason not to level with her. "Because I'd like to continue our relationship for a little bit longer."

"By relationship, do you mean our friendship?"

He held her gaze. "I mean our more recent relationship."

She frowned, obviously puzzled for a minute, then she said, "Oh, I see. You want to keep having sex."

When she put it that way, it sounded tacky. Hell, maybe it was tacky. But he couldn't stop thinking about the night they'd shared. Couldn't help wanting it to happen again even though he knew it wasn't fair to ask.

"So rather than friends, we'll be lovers?"

"No, we'll be friends, too."

"Friends who have sex."

"Really great sex." A dopey grin crossed his face just thinking about it, but when Megan shot him a dry look, he wiped away the smile.

"Do you love me?" she asked.

Chase had expected this question, and he wasn't going to lie to her. "You mean more to me than any woman I've ever met, which is why I want you in my life."

Megan's gaze held his as she asked, "Think you'll ever feel anything deeper for me?"

He had to be honest. "I don't believe in love. You know that. But I do believe that what we have is good. Hell, it's spectacular. I think we should appreciate what we have."

She closed her eyes, and for a second, he was afraid she was going to cry. But when she opened her eyes and looked at him, there wasn't a tear in sight.

"As tempting as your offer is, I'm going to have to pass. I realize it took a lot for you to admit you care for me, but you're never going to love me the way I love you. Cowboy, I'm not willing to settle for second best.''

''You'd never be that,'' he told her.

''Yes, I would. And I deserve better.'' She stood and headed toward the door. ''We want different things from life, Chase. I'm sorry, but it's best if you leave.''

Chase scrubbed his face with his hands. He'd be hard-pressed to think of a way tonight could have gone any worse. Damn, *this* was exactly what he'd been afraid of all along. His friendship with Megan had been destroyed because he'd let the boundaries in their relationship blur.

''I wish I could tell you this would work out. I wish I could give you the pretty words and the promises, but I can't lie about this. Especially not to you,'' he admitted, knowing he was breaking her heart. His own heart felt more than a little squashed at the moment.

He stood and walked over to her, wanting to offer her comfort. Wanting to soothe the injury as much as possible. But when he drew even with Megan, she didn't appear heartbroken in the least. In fact, she seemed remarkably calm. Resigned. He studied her face closely, looking for signs that she was putting on an act. But no, she seemed fine with what he was saying.

''Megan I know you're upset about this, but—''

She shook her head. ''I'm fine. You know, I read a book last week called *Build Your Own Sandcas-*

tle—*Don't Live in His*. And it said that I shouldn't hang my dreams on those of a man. That book is right. I want a man who will love me to distraction. That man isn't you, so I'll simply have to keep looking."

Chase frowned. "Keep looking?"

"Yes. Just because you didn't fall in love with me doesn't mean the next man won't." She opened her front door. "It shouldn't be too difficult to grab another man's attention. I learned a lot while I was trying to get you to notice me."

His blood ran cold. "You wouldn't."

"Why not?"

For one stupid second, he almost said she was engaged, but he caught himself in time. "You're not that type."

Her smile was wicked. "I am now. Thanks to you."

10

_____

"WHAT'S WRONG WITH YOU? If you get any meaner, you'll scare the bull," Trent said, tossing the basketball to Chase with enough force to almost knock the air out of his lungs.

"Nothing's wrong with me. I'm fine," Chase finally managed to say, although it was a lie. He was miserable. Not seeing Megan was killing him. But there was no sense telling his brothers that, so he headed toward the basket. Since his mind wasn't on the game, Nathan easily got the ball away from him.

Nathan made a basket, then turned to look at Chase. "Not only are you mean, you're not paying attention."

"I have things on my mind," Chase said.

Trent looked at Nathan, then they both looked at him.

"Megan," his brothers said in unison.

Chase grabbed the ball away from Nathan. He hated to think his brothers were right, but he knew they were. He'd spent the longest week of his life missing Megan, and now he couldn't think straight. He was going crazy, wanting to see her, to be with her.

"I don't want to talk about it," he said. "Let's play."

Nathan sat and leaned against the garage door. "No. I don't think so. You need to talk even if you don't think you do."

"Fine." Chase tossed the ball to Trent. "We'll play one-on-one."

Trent looked at Nathan, then at Chase, then back at Nathan. Finally he wandered over and sat next to Nathan. "I figure I have a better chance of living to a ripe old age by siding with Nathan on this one. You need to talk about what's happening with Megan. You're like a big ol' dam. You'll burst if you don't reduce some stress."

Chase glared at his brothers. This was the problem with family. They pushed when you wanted to be left alone. The last thing he needed right now was grief from his brothers. He was already feeling like a horse had tossed him. He didn't want to fight.

"I told you. I'm fine," he said. To prove his point, he grabbed the ball away from Trent and threw it. The ball soared, eventually hitting a tree nowhere near the hoop.

Nathan and Trent laughed. "Yeah, you seem just fine to me," Trent said. "But just in case, I think we should warn the birds."

Chase opened his mouth to argue, but realized there was no point. His brothers were right. He wasn't fine. Not at all.

He came over and sat on Trent's right. "Megan doesn't want to see me anymore."

Nathan leaned forward and looked at him. "She broke your engagement?"

"We were never engaged," Chase pointed out. "But we were…I mean we did become …let's just say our relationship has changed recently."

Trent nudged Nathan, and they both grinned at Chase.

"I knew you two boogied in San Antonio," Trent said.

Chase ran his hands through his hair. Maybe asking his brothers for help was a bad idea.

"Never mind. I've got work to do." Chase stood.

"Settle down. Don't go storming off. Trent and I will behave," Nathan said, but only after giving Trent a sharp look. "Now tell us what the problem is."

"I don't think so. The last time we discussed my personal life while playing basketball, you two dimwits gave me advice that blew my nice, orderly life all to hell. You told me to flirt with Megan, that a kiss or two would prove to her that we had no chemistry."

"But you had so much chemistry that things went kaboom, right?" Trent asked.

Chase wasn't about to discuss his sex life. All he was willing to say was, "Sort of."

Rather than appearing contrite, his brothers

grinned once again. Great. So much for finding a sympathetic ear around this place.

"You want to know what your problem is?" Nathan asked.

Chase glared at him. "No."

Without hesitating, Nathan said, "You never see what's standing directly in front of you. Megan has been in love with you for years, but you never saw it."

"We're friends. At least we were. I don't think we are anymore." Even saying the words hurt. Megan had been a great friend to him. He was going to miss her.

"You're a jackass," Trent said, standing and retrieving the ball. It went through the hoop with a whoosh. "Megan loves you. You love Megan. And if I'm understanding you right, the two of you howled at the moon in the bedroom. So that's that. Bing. Bang. Happy ending."

Nathan nodded. "Seems pretty easy to me as well."

"Megan wants love and forever. Let's face it. No one we know is happily married, and Megan already turned me down when I suggested we keep things casual."

Nathan stood and walked over to Chase. "Sometimes love does last. I can think of a lot of couples who are still going strong after twenty, thirty years."

"Name one of those couples," Chase challenged.

Just as he expected, Nathan couldn't. He shrugged. "Give me a moment."

Trent laughed. "I've got one. Conrad and Amanda Newman. They've been married forever."

Nathan nodded. "That's right. And the Monroes. They've been together a long time."

"And Earl and Fran. Married for years." Trent bounced the ball as he said, "Guess you're wrong, buddy boy. Lots of couples last."

Although his gut instinct was to dismiss what his brothers were saying, Chase had to admit, they were right. Those three couples had been together a long time and still were happy.

"I guess," he eventually conceded. "Maybe some people know the secret to making love last."

"I don't think there's a secret," Nathan said. "I think they work at it and don't take each other for granted.

"It's kind of like this ranch. You work hard to keep it going. I believe you'd work equally hard on keeping your marriage happy."

With effort, Chase swallowed past the lump in his throat. "Marriage? I'm not even sure I love her."

Trent shoved him. "Sure you love her. And you *should* be thinking about marriage. You can't take a woman like Megan away for a wild weekend of crazy sex and not ask her to marry you." He shook his head. "Damn, Chase, I thought you knew better than that."

Indignation filled Chase, more on Megan's behalf

than on his own. "I didn't say we had a wild weekend of crazy sex."

"Oh, give it up, Chase." This came from Leigh, who had walked out the kitchen door. "You're not fooling anyone. You and Megan made love. Everyone knows it. In fact, I was in Palmer's Grocery yesterday, and Betty Ann said she thought you and Megan had been fooling around for years."

"No, we haven't," Chase said.

"I don't think I believe you. I think Betty Ann may be right," Leigh countered.

"No, she's not. Megan and I never made love until—" He caught himself, but not in time. "Ah, hell. It doesn't matter."

"When you first made love doesn't matter," Nathan said, patting him on the arm. "But the fact that you're in love with Megan matters a great deal. You have to accept that you love her."

Trent bobbed his head. "Yep. It's either that, or you need to forget about her." His expression brightened. "Hey, if you're not interested in Megan, maybe I could—"

Chase silenced his brother with a glare. "Don't you dare say it. Not about Megan."

As soon as the words left his mouth, he realized their importance. The raging jealousy that had filled him at his brother's teasing crystallized his feelings. He loved Megan. Over the past few weeks, he'd seen both himself and Megan in a new light. He couldn't believe it had taken him so long to be ready to accept her as more than a friend.

He really was one dumb cowpoke.

But one fear still gnawed at him. "What if we can't make it work?" He scanned the faces of his brothers and his sister. "What if this doesn't last? I couldn't stand to see Megan hurt like that."

Nathan smiled and said with confidence. "You'll just have to make certain your love does last. Shouldn't be a problem. Your friendship has lasted for years."

So many questions roared through Chase. Could his siblings be right? Could he make the love he felt for Megan last a lifetime?

Leigh sighed. "Chase, answer me this—are you willing to never see Megan again?"

"No," he said without hesitation. "I couldn't take that."

"Are you willing to stand around while she marries someone else?" Leigh asked.

"No," he said firmly. Just the thought of her marrying someone else made him crazy.

"Then that's your answer," Nathan said. "It's like the old saying goes, sometimes you don't know what you've got until you lose it. Well, you've lost Megan. What are you going to do about it?"

"I might already be too late," Chase said.

"She didn't fall out of love with you this quickly. Convince her you mean business," Leigh said.

"How?"

Trent grinned, then looked at Nathan and Leigh. "Stick with us. We'll figure something out. Devious ideas come naturally to the Barretts."

"THIS PLAYGROUND IS GOING to be great," Earl Guthrie said as he came to stand next to Megan. "It's going to mean so much to the kids of Paxton."

Megan looked around the park. Yes, the playground was going to be great. At least one of her dreams had come true. Too bad the other one hadn't worked out.

"I appreciate all of your help," Megan said.

Earl grinned, "I didn't do anything but help nudge your idea along. You did all of the convincing yourself." He glanced around. "Big crowd here today, but I haven't seen Chase. Where are you hiding him?"

The crowd for the groundbreaking ceremony was large. Very large. But she knew for a fact that Chase wasn't here. She'd looked repeatedly for him.

"He hasn't arrived yet," she said.

Earl rocked back on his heals and peered at Megan over the top of his glasses. "Everything okay?"

Now was the time to tell him that the engagement was off, but Megan couldn't seem to form the words. "Fine."

He continued to study her. "Sure about that? You seem a bit pale. You feeling okay? Not pregnant, are you?"

Megan almost swallowed her tongue. "No, of course I'm not pregnant."

"Calm down. Seemed like the logical conclusion, what with you and Chase being so in love." He pointed at the lone tree in the far corner of the park. "I remember what young love is like. I was so crazy about Fran that I carved our initials in that tree over there. Now we have five children and eleven grandchildren. Falling in love's the most natural thing in the world."

Not the way she'd been going about it. There was nothing natural about how she'd tried to force Chase to fall in love with her. But she'd learned all the books were wrong. You can't make someone love you.

Apparently sensing her unhappiness, Earl patted her shoulder. "He'll come around. He's a good man, so don't worry. I took a while to come to my senses, too. But in the end, things with Fran and me worked out. The same will happen with you and Chase. I know it."

Earl was being so kind, Megan felt obligated to be honest with him. "About out engagement—"

Earl winked. "I didn't just tumble out of the cabbage patch yesterday, you know? But like I said, things will work out."

With that cryptic statement, the mayor walked away. Megan watched him go, wishing she could believe him. Wishing there was even a glimmer of hope that things would work out with Chase.

But how in the world could they?

"I told you to try the whipped cream," Leigh said as she came over to stand by Megan. "You look miserable, but it's your own fault. If you'd tried my whipped cream idea, you'd probably be locked in some tacky motel room with Chase right now doing things that would make a Kama Sutra scholar blush."

Megan felt the warmth of a blush climb her own cheeks. "Hello to you, too."

Leigh studied her face. "Seriously, are you okay? You look odd. Are you pregnant?"

Exasperated, Megan sighed. "Jeez, this town has a one-track mind. First Earl. Now you. No, I'm not pregnant. I'm just upset that Chase isn't here today."

Leigh shoved her sunglasses onto the top of her head. "That's what happens when you sleep with your friends. Things get confused."

"If memory serves me, you were all for me having a physical relationship with your brother."

Nodding, Leigh regarded her closely. "Oh, I was. I still am. I just think you didn't have enough of a physical relationship. You forgot the whipped cream. That would have cinched this deal."

Megan opened her mouth to argue with Leigh, but before she could say a word, the younger woman muttered something about being late and took off.

Left alone, Megan scanned the crowd, hoping against hope that Chase had decided to come to the ceremony. But there was no sign of him, so she sat in one of the folding chairs in the front row. She'd worked so hard to make this day happen, and now that it was here, she felt more than a little sad. She'd wanted Chase to share this moment with her. He should be here. Even though things had ended badly between them, he was the cochair of the committee. He should be at the groundbreaking.

After a few minutes, Leigh came and sat next to Megan. "I guess the speeches will start soon." She made a snoring noise. "Keep yours short, okay? I have a date this afternoon."

"I'll try," Megan assured her. She pulled her index cards out of her pocket. "I don't have a lot to say except thank you."

After a couple of minutes, Earl started the ceremony. First, he recapped the history of the project and how much money the carnival and auction had made. Then he smiled at Megan.

"Now here to say a few words is the lady who made all this happen—Megan Kendall."

Megan walked over to the podium, stacked her index cards neatly, then looked out at the crowd.

And froze. Chase stood directly in her line of sight, a lopsided grin on his handsome face. Megan's heart raced, joy rushing through her. He'd come to the ceremony after all.

As she looked at him, she realized she'd been kidding herself. No way could she walk away from this man. She'd told him she didn't want to continue their relationship if there was no love on his side, but now, looking at him, she realized that was hooey. In his way, she knew Chase loved her. He might not call it the same thing, but she felt his caring in his touch and in the heated looks he gave her.

She could see his love right now in his smile. The man cared for her and would never intentionally hurt her. She was the one hurting herself. Hurting both of them.

Well, that was a mistake that could quickly be remedied. After the ceremony, she'd tell him she was willing to continue being lovers. Anything. As long as they were together.

Feeling like a cartoon anvil had been lifted off her head, she smiled back at Chase.

"Remember what I told you last time," Leigh said, not even attempting to keep her voice down. "If you're nervous during your talk, picture Chase naked."

Megan laughed, as did most of the people sitting near Leigh. Megan's gaze met Chase's, and his grin only grew. He knew what she was picturing in her mind.

"Megan, honey, why don't you go ahead and give your speech, then you and Chase can go someplace quiet and stare at each other all day long if you want. I need to get home in time for supper," Earl said.

Megan blinked and looked at her cards. That was

love for you. She was standing in front of most of the town of Paxton making puppy eyes at Chase.

As quickly as possible, she ran through her speech. Thank goodness for her index cards. Without them, she would have forgotten everything she planned on saying. But she did remember to thank everyone who had helped with the fund-raiser. Finally she looked at Chase. "Of course, a big thank-you goes to Chase Barrett, for helping me when I needed him most. I couldn't have done it without you."

The crowd clapped loudly, and Earl stood, apparently ready to move on. But when Chase started walking toward the podium, silence fell over the crowd. Everyone swiveled their heads between Megan and Chase, watching the two of them closely.

"Mind if I say something?" Chase asked no one in particular. "I never made a secret of the fact that I wasn't keen on being on this committee. But I have to say, I'm glad I was. Not only so I could help the kids in this town get a sorely needed playground, but also because I learned a lot of things while helping out. I learned Earl never hears the word no, doesn't matter how loud you say it."

That comment brought a chuckle from the crowd. Chase continued walking toward Megan. "I learned that my brothers and sister might be a massive pain some of the time, but when it really counts and I need them, they stand by me."

Another chuckle rolled through the audience. "Finally, I learned the most important thing I've ever learned. I learned Megan Kendall loves me.''

Megan sucked in a tight breath, waiting anxiously for what he would say next.

''And I learned I love her back.''

Stunned, Megan stared at Chase. Had she really heard what she thought she'd heard? ''What did you say?'' she asked, her voice barely above a whisper.

But she could read the answer to her question on his face. Love lit his features and danced in his deep, blue eyes.

''Just so Megan never forgets how I feel, my family and I made a little something for the park.''

Nathan and Trent appeared at the back of the crowd. With a lot of jostling and teasing, they slowly made their way forward. They carried a large object wrapped in a thick striped blanket. When they were directly in front of Megan, they set the object next to Chase.

''Megan, I didn't want to hurt that poor tree, but I wanted a way to show you and the entire town of Paxton how I feel.''

With that, Chase pulled away the blanket. Underneath was a handcrafted wooden bench. Megan had never seen anything so beautiful. The workmanship was amazing.

But what amazed her most was the message carved into the back of the bench. It read: *Chase loves Megan.*

She felt the warmth of tears trickle down her face,

but she couldn't seem to stop them. For so very long, she'd dreamt of having this wonderful, caring, sexy man return her love. Now he finally did.

She took a step toward him, but before she could reach his side, he went down on one knee. More than a few of the citizens of Paxton were standing on their chairs to watch, but Megan didn't care. All she cared about was the man kneeling in front of her.

"Megan Kendall, will you marry me?" he asked.

Through her tears, Megan nodded, unable to get the words out. In her entire life, she'd never been at a loss for words, but she was now.

She rushed to Chase, and tugged him back up to his feet. Then she wrapped her arms around his neck and kissed him. A loud "ah" came from the crowd, but Megan just kept kissing Chase.

"You really love me?" Megan asked when they finally stopped kissing long enough to catch their breath.

"Yes. I'm sorry it took me so long to come to my senses." He cupped her face in his hands. "I can't believe I almost lost you."

She smiled, knowing their life together was going to be filled with love and laughter and many, many happy years. "You never even came close to losing me. I'd already decided I wasn't giving up yet." She kissed him again soundly, then explained, "See I still had one last trick I hadn't tried yet."

"And what would that be?"

"It involves showing up at the ranch wearing racy underwear and carrying a couple of cans of whipped cream. I was assured that you'd fall in love with me long before both cans were empty."

Chase grinned. "I like that idea. A lot."

Megan was kissing Chase again when Earl pointed out they needed to wrap up the ground-breaking ceremony. And as she stood next to the man she loved, she used her shovel to break ground on the playground she knew her own children would one day use.

"Ready to go home?" Chase asked, almost an hour later.

Megan anxiously nodded. Although she'd enjoyed the ceremony, she was dying to be alone with the man she loved.

"Want to come to my house or go to the ranch?" she asked.

"Let's go to your house. It's closer and I'm anxious to get you alone." They were almost to the parking lot when he added, "But I need to make a stop on the way."

"Where?"

His smile was wicked and downright wonderful. "Palmer's Grocery. I thought we'd pick up some whipped cream." With a wink he added, "And a couple of jars of maraschino cherries."

FREE GIFTS!

NO COST! NO OBLIGATION TO BUY!
NO PURCHASE NECESSARY!

PLAY THE
Lucky Key Game

Scratch gold area with a coin.
Then check below to see the books and gift you get!

311 HDL DH2X
111 HDL DH2P

YES! I have scratched off the gold area. Please send me the 2 Free books and gift for which I qualify. I understand I am under no obligation to purchase any books, as explained on the back and on the opposite page.

NAME   (PLEASE PRINT CLEARLY)

ADDRESS

APT.#   CITY

STATE/PROV.   ZIP/POSTAL CODE

2 free books plus a gift

2 free books

1 free book

Try Again!

Offer limited to one per household and not valid to current Harlequin Duets™ subscribers. All orders subject to approval.

(H-D-OS-03/02)

The Harlequin Reader Service® — Here's how it works:

Accepting your 2 free books and gift places you under no obligation to buy anything. You may keep the books and gift and return the shipping statement marked "cancel." If you do not cancel, about a month later we'll send you 2 additional books and bill you just $5.14 each in the U.S., or $6.14 each in Canada, plus 50¢ shipping & handling per book and applicable taxes if any.* That's the complete price and — compared to cover prices of $5.99 each in the U.S. and $6.99 each in Canada — it's quite a bargain! You may cancel at any time, but if you choose to continue, every month we'll send you 2 more books, which you may either purchase at the discount price or return to us and cancel your subscription.

*Terms and prices subject to change without notice. Sales tax applicable in N.Y. Canadian residents will be charged applicable provincial taxes and GST.

Nabbing Nathan

Liz
Jarrett

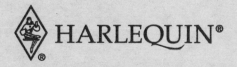

HARLEQUIN®

TORONTO • NEW YORK • LONDON
AMSTERDAM • PARIS • SYDNEY • HAMBURG
STOCKHOLM • ATHENS • TOKYO • MILAN • MADRID
PRAGUE • WARSAW • BUDAPEST • AUCKLAND

1

SOME MEN SHOULD NEVER WEAR a shirt, Hailey Montgomery decided as she watched Nathan Barrett shoot baskets on the sports court behind his house. The man was poetry in motion—a Shakespearian sonnet, a love poem by Keats.

He spun toward her and her gaze skittered down his muscled chest again.

Okay then, a really naughty limerick.

"You wait here," Leigh Barrett said from the passenger seat of Hailey's compact car. "I need to talk to Nathan for a second."

Now that didn't sound good. Not good at all. Hailey pulled her gaze away from Nathan and looked at his sister.

"You assured me that everything was set," Hailey pointed out.

Leigh bobbed her head, her short black hair brushing against her chin. "It is set, so stop worrying."

Not in the least reassured, Hailey asked, "Nathan knows I'm coming, right?"

Again, the head bob. "You bet."

"And he agreed that I could have the technical writing job?"

"Yep, that, too."

Still unable to shake the feeling that she'd stepped off the side of a mountain and was about to take one heck of a plunge, Hailey pressed on. "And he did agree that I could use his garage apartment this summer, right?"

"Everything is fine." Leigh shoved open the door to the car. "You're such a worrier, Hailey. No wonder you live on antacids. You need to relax. Take a few deep breaths. Find your center."

"My what?"

"You know. The child within. Your feminine side." With a grin, she added, "Feng shui yourself."

Hailey laughed and felt the tension level inside her slip down a notch or two. She should have known when push came to shove, Leigh wouldn't let her down. She knew how much Hailey needed this summer job.

"I promise to relax if you're certain everything is fine."

Leigh rolled her eyes. "Say it slowly with me: 'Ev…er…y thi…ng is fi…ne.'"

Hailey smiled. "Everything is fine."

Leigh glanced at her brother, then back at Hailey. "Very good. Now give me a head start. I just need to clarify one tiny detail with Nathan, then we can get you moved into the garage apartment."

There was something in the way Leigh said the words *one tiny detail* that made the feeling of dread rush right back into Hailey's stomach and settle down for a long stay. Something was rotten in Denmark, or rather in Paxton, Texas.

Hailey didn't want to ask. Not at all. Intuitively she knew she wasn't going to like the answer. But she had to know, so squinting in an attempt to lessen the expected blow, she asked, "What detail do you need to clarify with Nathan?"

"Oh, nothing special," Leigh said. "I just need to mention a few things." She swung her legs out of the car, then said in a rush, "Like that you're going to work for him at his software company for a few weeks while you live in the apartment over his garage. No biggee."

Hailey's mouth dropped open, but before she could say a word, Leigh sprinted away from the car. No biggee? This was a really *big* biggee. Nathan Barrett knew absolutely nothing about her plans.

Good grief. Fumbling in her purse, Hailey tugged out her roll of antacids and tossed a couple into her mouth. The familiar chalky taste brought her a tiny degree of comfort.

"You can do this," she muttered, willing the condors thrashing around in her stomach to chill. "You can handle this."

Even though she only half believed herself, she climbed out of her car. Leigh was already on the basketball court, talking with her brother.

"Darn her hide," Hailey muttered, slamming her car door. She should have known better than to trust her summer plans to Leigh Barrett. Leigh was funny and full of life and great to be around, but she was also kooky, and crazy, and often unreliable.

The last character trait was the one Hailey should have focused on when Leigh had brought up this idea about coming to Paxton. She should have checked and double-checked these plans like a bride planning a flawless wedding.

But she hadn't questioned a thing.

"You coward," she muttered to herself as she reached the outer corner of the sports court. She hadn't questioned Leigh simply because her friend had promised the solution to all of her problems. Leigh had assured Hailey that her brother needed a technical writer for a few weeks and that the pay would be great. And when Hailey had mentioned she'd need a place to stay, Leigh had had the answer to that one, too. Nathan had a nice apartment over his three-car garage.

What could be better? She'd be able to work on her dissertation in the evenings after she came home from Barrett Software. And she'd pick up some nice change to pay the never-ending college bills.

What a dummy. She might as well tattoo the word *sap* on her forehead. Just because she'd wanted this job to work out wasn't an excuse not to check her facts before leaving Austin and driving to Paxton with Leigh. Her superorganized father would be appalled that she hadn't verified the plans.

At the moment, jobless and homeless, she was pretty darn appalled, too.

As she approached Leigh and her brother, she

heard Leigh hastily explaining the situation while Nathan frowned. The man wasn't pleased. That much was obvious. He glanced in Hailey's direction, then walked over and grabbed a T-shirt off a bench and pulled it on.

"It's no big deal," Leigh was saying as Hailey drew even with them.

"It's a very big deal," Nathan shot back. He turned and looked at Hailey. "Hello."

Wow. Nathan was even better looking close up. Every female hormone in Hailey's body sat up and took notice, and for the briefest of moments, Hailey forgot her jobless/homeless problem and simply enjoyed looking at him.

"Nathan, this is my friend, Hailey Montgomery," Leigh said. "Hailey, this is Nathan, who will help me out, or I'll tell all of his secrets."

Nathan glanced at his sister. "What secrets? I don't have any secrets."

Leigh snorted, an unladylike sound that oddly fit her personality. "Oh, please, sell it to someone who's never met you. I know all the good things. Like that you cried for an hour the first time a girl kissed you—"

Nathan frowned. "I was six."

"Or the time when you had a crush on Lindsey Franklin, so you kept calling her up, but when she'd answer, you'd hang up—"

"I was eleven."

Leigh put her hands on her hips and said, "Best of all, how about the time in high school when Mary

Lou Delacourte's parents thought she was at a slumber party when actually she was with you and you two were—"

"Stop." Nathan tipped his head and looked at Hailey, humor gleaming in his amazing blue eyes. Despite being annoyed at his sister, there was a healthy dose of brotherly love obvious in his treatment of Leigh. He might not be happy with what she'd done, but he was being an exceptionally good sport about it. "Do you have any objections to being a material witness to a crime?"

Hailey laughed. "Under the circumstances, I completely understand."

"Ha, ha. Like you'd ever do anything to me." Leigh leaned up and gave her brother a loud, smacking kiss on his cheek. "Jeez, you're sweaty."

"I was shooting hoops and not expecting company," he said. His gaze returned to Hailey. "Sorry."

"I'm the one who's sorry. I had no idea this wasn't arranged." She frowned at Leigh. "I was under the impression you knew all about the plans. I guess I should head on back to Austin."

"Nathan Eric Barrett, how rude can you be?" Leigh scolded. "Look what you did."

"What *I* did? I haven't done anything to anyone," he said calmly. "Go inside, Leigh. I want to talk to Hailey alone."

"But if I'm not here—"

"Go inside," Nathan repeated.

Finally, muttering and fussing the whole way,

Leigh headed across the sports court and disappeared inside the large, brick house.

Left alone with Nathan, Hailey tried to keep her gaze firmly tacked on his face. Boy-oh-boy, it wasn't easy. His T-shirt hugged his muscles, but since she hated it when men talked to her chest, she imagined Nathan would hate it if she had a conversation with his pecs.

"So, if I'm following this, Leigh told you I had a job opening for a technical writer at Barrett Software," Nathan said.

Hailey nodded, hoping against hope that at least a little bit of Leigh's story had been true. She crossed her fingers. "Do you?"

His expression was kind. "I'm sorry, no."

"Oh." She swallowed past the nervous lump in her throat and struggled to maintain control.

Breathe, Hailey. Breathe.

She fumbled in her pocket, searching for her antacids, then remembered they were in her purse. That was okay. She could handle this. Sure, there weren't a lot of really great jobs lying around that would only last the summer. And sure, she'd been counting on this job to help pay off some bills. But she could manage. She hadn't made it all the way to the doctoral program at the University of Texas without becoming a pro at dealing with problems. This was only a setback. A big setback, granted, but one she could handle.

"I see," she managed to say when Nathan continued to give her a sympathetic look.

"I understand that Leigh also promised you could live in the apartment above my garage." This time, it was a statement, not a question.

The feeling of dread she'd been experiencing now took on monumental proportions. "Let me guess, you don't have an apartment over your garage, either."

"Yes, I do."

She nodded. "Of course you—you do?" Blinking, she tried to decide what that meant. Could this possibly be a tiny streak of good luck struggling to shine through the dark cloud?

"Yes, but it's my storage room, filled with old junk. Not really suitable to live in at the moment."

Ah, heck. Hailey blew out an exasperated breath. Great. Just great. No job. No place to live. Talk about with friends like Leigh, who needed enemies.

"Well, that's that. I guess I'd better go. Thank you for your time," she said.

Nathan grinned. "You give up too easily." He tossed her the basketball, which she just managed to catch. "Do you play?"

She looked at the ball in her hands. "What?"

"Sink it."

With a shrug, she turned, assessed her shot, and neatly sunk the ball. When she turned back to look at Nathan, he nodded.

"Nice shot."

"I played in high school," she told him. "Look, why don't I say goodbye to Leigh and head back—"

"Wait." Nathan wandered over and picked up the

basketball. He dribbled it as he came back over to stand next to her. She tried, really she did, to keep from staring at him, but how much was a woman supposed to resist? The man was gorgeous, absolutely gorgeous, and despite the disappointment flooding through her at the moment, she wasn't dead.

"Do you know why I sent Leigh inside?" he asked, a roguish gleam in his eyes.

Hailey considered the possibilities, finally settling on the most obvious. "Because you were afraid you'd do something terrible to her if you didn't?"

He chuckled, the sound warm and rich and electrifying as it danced across Hailey's skin. This man was like fudge ripple ice cream. Much, much too tempting.

"I sent Leigh inside so she could sweat for a little while. Even without looking, I know she's watching us through the kitchen window, wondering what we're talking about."

Hailey glanced toward the house and caught a glimpse of Leigh peering through the window before she disappeared. "You're right. She's there."

Nathan smiled. "I know. See she's about ninety-nine percent sure I'll save her. I always have in the past. But there's that one percent of uncertainty, the tiniest fragment of doubt, that's making her climb the walls. I figure the least I can do is make her squirm for a few minutes before I save her."

Hailey snagged onto what he'd said. He'd save Leigh? Did that mean she would get a job and a place to stay after all? Was it too soon to yell yahoo and dance around with joy?

She studied Nathan and tried not to let her optimism run away with her, but she couldn't help asking, "Are you saying you *do* have a job?"

"A couple. Neither of them is for a technical writer, though." His gaze skimmed her casual outfit of jean shorts and a green T-shirt, then nodded toward the basketball. "Want to try to make that shot again?"

At this point, Hailey would do just about anything to get a job. She didn't have time to waste going back to Austin and seeing if she could scrounge up something at the university. "Sure."

He tossed her the ball, and she sunk it.

"You're good." For a second, he studied her, and Hailey's pulse rate picked up. As much as she'd like to attribute the metabolic change to being nervous, she knew that was bunk. Her heart was racing because she was attracted to Nathan. Very attracted.

"Tell me about yourself," Nathan said.

This was hardly the place she would have picked for an interview, but at this point, she was willing to be interviewed in the middle of Interstate 20 if it meant she could get a job.

"I'm working on my doctorate in English at the University of Texas," she told him.

"That's where you met Leigh."

"Yes." She glanced toward the house, then added, "And up until a few minutes ago, we were great friends."

Nathan laughed again, and Hailey had to admit, that was a sound she could get used to without any trouble. "It's not that bad. Things will work out. My brothers and I are used to doing damage control when necessary to pull Leigh out of the fire."

"That doesn't upset you?"

Nathan snagged the ball again and easily made a shot. "Don't get me wrong. I don't approve of Leigh's methods. But she's just that way. Always has been. It's part of her personality...part of her charm."

"Being devious and conniving?"

His grin was devilish. "Yes. You'll get used to it."

Hailey sincerely doubted that. "Does that devious streak run in your family?"

Nathan's smile was oh-so enticing. "Me? I'm completely harmless."

Yeah, right, and she could wrestle crocodiles.

THIS TIME, LEIGH HAD REALLY taken the cake. Nathan glanced at the house and wondered not for the first time how pure mischief could flow through his sister's veins. Even for her, this was a bit much. Not only was she yanking him around, but she was also embroiling one of her friends in whatever this latest scheme was. A friend who was obviously upset.

He'd bet his new BMW that Leigh's motives were far from pure. If he had to guess, he'd bet his sister was up to something.

Leigh was always up to something.

And it didn't take a rocket scientist to figure out what. The data was pretty damn clear. Leigh had arranged for Hailey Montgomery to not only spend the summer working at Barrett Software, but she'd also managed to have Hailey living at his house. Hailey, who just so happened to be smart and gorgeous. Two traits he greatly admired in a woman, which Leigh knew. Could his sister be trying to fix him up? He knew she was tired of him interfering in her life. But tired enough that she'd go this far?

The concept was almost too diabolical to entertain. That would mean Leigh was willing to use her friend Hailey as bait. Could Leigh actually be that sneaky?

He sighed. Of course she could. He knew for a fact that she'd meddled in their brother Chase's life, fixing him up with the town librarian. Sure, Chase and Megan made a great couple, but he didn't want to be fixed up, especially not by Leigh.

He glanced back at Hailey. Did she realize she was a victim? Did she know her friend was setting her up? He wasn't picking up any flirtatious vibes from her, so he was fairly certain she truly was here simply for a job.

But when she smiled at him, Nathan felt his heart rate rev.

"Think we should stretch this out a little longer and make Leigh squirm some more?" he asked.

Hailey nodded. "Absolutely. Squirming is good for her."

Nathan couldn't help pointing out, "I see a little deviousness runs in your family, too."

"Apparently."

He looked at his house. Leigh stood at the kitchen window, watching them.

She was guilty all right.

He turned his attention back to Hailey. She had wavy auburn hair that hung to her shoulders. Auburn hair was his personal favorite. Or rather, it had become his favorite in the past few minutes. Hailey also had his favorite color eyes—hazel. Again, his propensity for hazel eyes was a recent discovery, but still, he really liked that shade. A lot.

Eyes like Hailey Montgomery's seemed to change color every few minutes. At the moment, they were a steely gray—sharp, intense, not missing a thing.

The back door to the house flew open and banged against the outside wall.

"I can't take it anymore, Nathan," Leigh hollered from the open door to the kitchen. "I swear if you send Hailey home, you'll no longer be my favorite brother."

Nathan grinned and winked at Hailey. "Is that a promise?"

"Ha, ha. Now stop tormenting us, and help unpack Hailey's car. You two have to go to work tomorrow. You can't stand around here all day yammering on the basketball court." Without waiting for his response, Leigh headed over to the small yellow compact car parked in his driveway.

"Guess she told us," Nathan said, waiting for Hailey to precede him to her car.

"You know, we don't have to do what she says," Hailey pointed out. "I mean, you don't have to give me a job...if you really don't want to."

Nathan knew that. Just because Leigh might have concocted some sort of scheme didn't mean he was going to fall for it. Oh sure, he'd let Hailey work at Barrett Software. He'd even let her live in the apartment once they got it straightened up. But that was all. He wasn't going to fall for Hailey Montgomery, no matter how hard his sister tried.

"It's no problem, Hailey," he assured her. "We'll work something out."

Feeling more in control of the situation, he headed toward the car to help. "Hey, Leigh, hold up. The garage apartment is full of junk. Hailey will have to stay in the house for a couple of nights."

Hailey had been walking along next to him, but now she stopped.

"I'm turning into a real inconvenience," she said. "I feel terrible about this."

They were close enough for Leigh to hear them, and his sister answered before he had the chance.

"Hailey, stop being so polite to Nathan. It will make him think even higher of himself than he does already, and none of us wants that. The whole town adores him. Everyone goes gaga over him, so don't puff up his ego anymore or he's apt to float away."

Nathan nudged his sister. "Hey, remember kiddo,

I'm helping you out. Don't bite the hand that's saving your tush.''

She rolled her eyes at him, looking more like a six-year-old than a young woman about to graduate from college.

''You know I love you,'' she said. ''But you also have more than your fair share of self-confidence. You don't need Hailey telling you how great you are.'' She fluttered her eyelashes. ''You've got the ladies of Paxton to do that.''

Hailey gave him an inquisitive look. ''You do?''

Before Nathan could make even a token effort to rescue his reputation, Leigh jumped back in.

''All the ladies in town are besotted with my brother. They chase him relentlessly.''

''No, they don't. Not exactly.'' He ruffled his sister's hair and grabbed a couple of suitcases out of the car.

Leigh turned to Hailey. ''Trust me. That's *exactly* what they do. They. Chase. Him.''

Nathan shook his head and headed toward the kitchen. There was no sense wasting his breath fighting with Leigh. When she got going, there was nothing to do but hang on for the ride. He could hear the women talking as they followed behind him. His sister discussing him was never a good thing, so he decided to change the subject.

''Hailey, you sure you don't want to take the summer off?'' Nathan asked. ''You could laze around on a beach somewhere.''

"I really do need a job this summer. If you don't think—"

"Nathan, you're upsetting Hailey," Leigh said. "Stop being rude and assure her that you have a job."

"I already told her I'd work something out." He set down the suitcases and stared at his sister. "In case you've forgotten, up until ten minutes ago, I didn't know you intended on bringing someone home with you. All you told me on the phone last night was that you'd caught a ride with a friend."

If he'd expected Leigh to look contrite, he would have been disappointed. She glared at him.

"Get over that, Nathan. Jeez. It's like ancient history. So I surprised you. Big woo. Now accept that Hailey is here and give her a job."

"Leigh, do you always push your brother around like this?" Hailey asked.

Nathan pinned Leigh with a direct look. "Yes. She does."

"Oh, you poor baby. I'm so mean to you." Leigh leaned over and gave him another kiss on the cheek. "You adore me, and you know it. If it weren't for me livening up your life, you'd fall into a big pile of computer codes and never come out. Admit it— you've been bored while I've been at UT, haven't you?"

He pretended to consider her question. "Bored? Have I been bored? My life has been restful while you've been gone."

"Your life will be restful when you're dead, too, but that doesn't make it a good thing."

Nathan laughed. Truthfully he was glad Leigh was home. Sure, she was a pain at times, but she also was a lot of fun.

"One of these days, I'm going to move and not give you the forwarding address," he teased as he picked the suitcases up and headed inside the house.

"Won't happen. Now figure out what you're going to do to help Hailey."

As he led the way inside the house, he debated which of the two open jobs to offer Hailey. One was in personnel, and Hailey struck him as the type who would be good with people. The other job was as his assistant. His current assistant was on maternity leave, and he was desperate.

"My assistant just had a baby, and I need someone to fill in for a few weeks. Barrett Software is working on an easily customized accounting package for small businesses that we're going to demo in Dallas in six weeks at BizExpo, one of the biggest computer shows in the country. The time frame is kind of tight and the program still has some problems, but if we make it, we'll get a lot of publicity. I really need help keeping everything moving. Sound like something you could do?"

"Of course Hailey can do it," Leigh said with a huff. "She's amazing. Unbelievable. Incredible."

Hailey sighed. "Leigh, so help me, if you say I can leap tall buildings in a single bound, I'm heading back to Austin."

"Har-de-har-har," Leigh said. "You two are just a couple of comedians. Here I've gone to all this trouble to help both of you, and you don't even seem to appreciate what I've done."

Nathan winked at Hailey. "Do you believe this? She's playing the martyr."

"Doing it well, too," Hailey said.

Nathan smiled at her, liking the auburn-haired beauty more and more. He was still looking at Hailey when Leigh snorted.

"Fine. Laugh all you want. But there's going to come a day when both of you will thank me for this. Trust me." With that, Leigh flounced up the stairs, carrying one of Hailey's suitcases with her.

Hailey had come to stand next to him. She smelled like flowers—rich, luxurious flowers, probably due to her shampoo rather than any perfume. The scent was too unintentional to be perfume.

But something about that scent tantalized him more than any expensive perfume ever could.

"Was that a promise or a threat?" Hailey asked.

"Sometimes with Leigh, it's hard to tell the difference," he admitted.

2

"WANT TO COME TO THE MOVIES with me tonight? It won't be any fun, but I guess you can come if you really want to," Leigh said from the doorway.

Hailey looked at her friend, who showed about as much enthusiasm as a dental patient right before a root canal. "Are you sure you want me to come? You don't seem too happy about the idea."

Leigh leaned against the doorjamb. "Like I said, it won't be fun. In fact, it will bore you to death, and you'll probably end up being mad at me for bringing you. But if you truly, truly want to come along, then it's okay with me."

Hailey laughed. "Wow, Leigh, that's *truly* one heck of an invitation."

A smile lurked around Leigh's mouth. "Yeah, I know. It *ttrrruuuly* sucked. And I don't mean it that way. You're my friend. I like spending time with you. I'm thrilled you're here."

Hailey sat on the comfy, queen-size bed in Nathan's guest room. Just from looking at Leigh, she could tell the younger woman was plotting and planning. Funny how she'd never noticed this side of her friend before, but Leigh did indeed have a wide devious streak in her makeup.

"What movie are you going to see?" Hailey asked, knowing she wasn't actually being invited along. But she couldn't help wishing the invitation were sincere. It would be fun to get out for a while and see the town. Nathan had headed into his office an hour ago, and frankly, Hailey would feel weird wandering around the man's house alone. After all, they had just met this afternoon.

Leigh broke eye contact and shrugged. "I'm not really sure. Something gross and gory."

Hailey laughed. "If the movie is gross, then why are you going?"

"My friend likes that sort of thing."

The pieces of this puzzle weren't fitting. "I thought you told Nathan you were going to the movies with someone named Sara," Hailey said. "Sara likes gory, gross movies?"

Leigh's attention fixed on the drapes behind Hailey. "Yeah, she's strange that way. But I know that's not the sort of thing you like, so my feelings won't be hurt if you say no."

By now, Hailey no more believed Leigh was going to the movies with a girlfriend named Sara than she believed in Santa Claus. She took a couple of T-shirts from her suitcase and put them in the dresser drawer. Then she faced Leigh. "Fess up, who are you going to the movies with? It's a guy, isn't it?"

It took a second or two, but finally Leigh laughed. "How did you possibly guess?"

"How could I possibly *not* guess? A rock could

have figured out what you're up to. You're a terrible actress," Hailey pointed out.

"Nathan believed me."

Hailey didn't think so. Nathan had raised one eyebrow and looked more than a little amused when Leigh had told him of her plans. But all he'd said was that Leigh should bring Hailey along since she was her guest. No doubt he'd figured Hailey's presence would put the kibosh on any romantic interlude Leigh had planned.

"What's his name?" Hailey asked.

"Jared Kendrick. He's great. I've known him for years, but we've never gone out before. I heard he was in town, so I called and asked him out." Her expression turned pleading. "Will you be too miserable if I leave you here alone? I'm an awful person, but I really want to go out with Jared. The man is serious eye candy."

Hailey laughed at Leigh's description. "Okay, so he's good-looking. But what kind of person is he?"

"A very good-looking person," Leigh said, then relented and added, "Relax, he won't do anything that I don't want him to, if that's what you're asking. But there isn't much most women don't want Jared to do."

As much as she wanted to pretend to be shocked, Hailey couldn't be so hypocritical. She was lusting after Nathan even though she'd only just met the man. Although her instincts told her he was a good guy, she knew almost nothing about him.

"I have no interest in standing in the way of true love," Hailey told Leigh. "Have a nice evening."

Leigh grinned. "Thanks, but it's not true love. Not at all. Tonight is about having fun."

"Should I tell Nathan you'll be home late?"

With a vehement shake of her head, Leigh said, "No. Don't say a word. You don't know how my brothers act. They watch me like hawks. If you hadn't been here, Nathan wouldn't have gone into the office. He would've stayed home and stared at me all night."

"I don't believe you," Hailey said. "Nathan seems like a man who has better things to do than baby-sit you."

Leigh sighed and sat on the corner of the dresser. "You would think so, wouldn't you? You would think those bozos would accept that I'm grown up and leave me alone. But *nooooo*. My brothers drive me crazy. Okay, maybe not Chase. Not anymore. But Nathan and Trent still do."

"Why did Chase stop?"

Leigh patted her chest over her heart. "Chase fell madly in love. He got married a couple of weeks ago, and he's currently away on his honeymoon. That's why I'm staying with Nathan. Normally I stay with Chase when I'm home from school, but I don't want to be anywhere near Chase's house when he and his bride, Megan, return home."

Intrigued despite herself, Hailey asked, "Why not? I'm sure they wouldn't mind having you around."

Leigh groaned. "Pu-lease, it's not them I'm worried about. It's me. I can only take so much lovey-dovey stuff before I go into sugar overload. Plus, it gets embarrassing. Everywhere I go, the two of them are fooling around." She shuddered. "He's my brother. Ick."

Hailey laughed. "I understand. So falling in love has put Chase out of the baby-sitter business. But Leigh, Nathan didn't seem too concerned about you going out tonight." She gave her friend a meaningful look. "Trust me, he didn't believe your story about Sara any more than I did. No one would believe your story."

"Yeah, well, he pretended to buy my story because he wanted to go into the office. You wait, when he gets home, the first thing he'll do is ask you if I went out with a guy. Then he'll get all huffy and macho and tell me off when I come home tonight." She grinned. "*If* I come home tonight."

Hailey wasn't comfortable with lying. "If he asks me where you are, I'm going to tell him the truth. I won't cover for you."

"Don't worry. You won't have to. This town is like gossip central. The CIA should come here to study espionage. I swear, two minutes after anyone spots Jared and me together, bam! Nathan's phone will ring over at Barrett Software. You can't get away with anything in Paxton. Nada. No one can. No wonder Trent rarely has to arrest anyone. Peer pressure keeps everyone in line. It's a terrible place to be when you have a burning desire to run amok."

Hailey would have to take Leigh's word on that one. Although she'd lived in lots of places while growing up, none of the towns had been small. They'd been huge cities, like L.A. or New York or Houston. She'd never had a problem disappearing into the crowd. Even though Austin wasn't as big as L.A., it was a good-size city. And the university was large, so she didn't stand out there, either. She had friends, but she'd never become the object of gossip just for going out on a date.

She couldn't help sympathizing with Leigh. Living in a fishbowl like Paxton with overprotective brothers couldn't be easy.

"Why don't you just level with your brothers?" Hailey suggested. "Tell them you don't like them meddling in your life. They love you, so I'm sure they'll take your feelings into consideration."

Leigh laughed, loud and long. "Hailey, no offense, but you don't know doodly about brothers, especially Texas brothers. Those boys won't back off no matter what I say. I'm their baby sister. They feel it's their duty to protect me, whether I like it or not. To them, it's a matter of honor."

"That's sexist."

"Naw. Not really. I feel it's my duty to protect them, too. For instance, if one of them hooked up with some bimbo and looked like he might let his hormones lead him down the aisle, I'd have to step in."

As an only child, Hailey simply couldn't relate. That kind of interference would bother her. A lot.

"Well if you feel you can butt into their lives, then I guess you can't complain when they butt into yours," Hailey said.

Leigh snorted. "If it was an *emergency,* I'd butt in. But not for any old reason in the world, which is what my brothers do. Butt in for absolutely no reason. Like my date tonight."

Hailey nodded, finally understanding Leigh's point. "I see. Tonight's date is no reason for your brothers to be alarmed."

When she turned toward Leigh for confirmation of her theory, the younger woman was clearly aghast at what Hailey had said.

"No reason? Yikes, I hope not. I've gone to a lot of trouble to go out with Jared. Shame on you for even suggesting such a thing."

Hailey laughed. "Sorry. Didn't mean to jinx your plans."

"That's okay. Nothing can ruin tonight."

When the doorbell rang, Leigh grinned at Hailey, her blue eyes dancing with excitement. "Wish me luck."

Although Hailey wasn't really sure wishing Leigh luck under these circumstances was a good thing, she still complied. "Good luck."

"Thanks. And sorry to jump ship on your first night in town. But Nathan should be home pretty soon. Then you can go back to staring at him like he rode up on a white horse."

Hailey felt like the air stuck in her throat. "What?"

Leigh raised one eyebrow, a gesture reminiscent of her brother. "I'm not the only one here who likes a little eye candy. Just keep in mind, Nathan's a natural charmer. Don't take him too seriously."

Before Hailey could say anything, Leigh waved and slipped out of the bedroom. Hailey wanted to sprint after Leigh and tell her she was all wrong, but what would be the point? She had stared at Nathan like he was a bowl full of chocolate bonbons and she was on a diet. She definitely deserved Leigh's warning.

Not wanting to risk bumping into Leigh and her date, Hailey took her time unpacking. She left most of what she'd brought in the suitcases on the chance she might be able to move into the garage apartment soon. Once she was done, she wandered around her room for a couple of minutes, until the silence in the house made her antsy.

Then she gathered up the research material she'd been reading and headed downstairs. The family room had caught her eye on the five-minute tour Leigh had given her of the place. With its cream leather furniture and paneled walls, the room tugged on Hailey's aesthetic side. Entering, she couldn't help thinking the dark blue throw pillows were the exact same shade as Nathan's eyes. Except Nathan's eyes were warm, and inviting, and... Oops. Enough of that. Hailey curled up in one of the over-stuffed chairs, and refused to think any more about throw pillows and Nathan's eyes. She had work to do, so she settled down with her pile of research material.

And promptly found herself thinking about Nathan again. Okay, this time wasn't really her fault. From this vantage point, she could see the mantel was lined with family pictures. Even though she told herself not to, the pictures pulled at her like a tractor beam, and before she knew it, she walked over to study them.

Leigh was in almost all the shots, as were three men. In each photo, Nathan was smiling at the camera. His smile invited her to smile back. The other two men were undeniably his brothers. Although they were equally handsome, Hailey couldn't stop looking at Nathan. There was something about him that made her mind almost shut down, something that made her want to get lost in his sexy smile and enticing gaze.

"Stop it," she muttered to herself, determined not to let Nathan distract her. She had a dissertation to write on the female character arc in nineteenth-century American literature. She wasn't going to waste time mooning over some man.

"The heck with you, Nathan Barrett," Hailey said, deliberately turning her back on the pictures. She picked up her research papers and started reading. No way was she going to let a handsome devil like Nathan muddle her brain. She shot a triumphant glance at the photos on the mantel. "Your plan won't work."

"What plan would that be?"

NATHAN STOOD IN THE DOORWAY to the family room, watching Hailey. She jumped and yelped a little when he spoke, obviously startled. How she hadn't known he was standing here was beyond him. He certainly hadn't tried to be quiet coming into the house.

But she had been surprised. Really surprised. She currently sat with one hand over her heart, her wide hazel eyes staring at him.

"Where in the world did you come from?" Her voice had a breathless overtone to it that he found very appealing.

Hoping to lighten the mood, he said, "My parents told me they found me under a cabbage leaf, but I never believed them." He wandered into the room and sat on the sofa facing her. "What do you think? Sounds like a suspicious story, doesn't it? I mean, I could understand if they'd found me in a haystack. Or maybe in a basket left on the doorstep by a stork. But come on? A cabbage patch seems a bit implausible."

Hailey was still staring at him, and as Nathan watched, a pale flush colored her pretty face. Now that was interesting. He'd love to know what had caused her to have that reaction.

"Where's Leigh?" he asked, already knowing the answer.

"Out. She went to the movies with her…friend, remember?"

Nathan settled back on the sofa. "Ah, that's right.

She went to the movies with Sara.'' He grinned at Hailey. ''Did you get to meet the lovely Sara?''

Hailey glanced away. ''No. I was unpacking when the doorbell rang.''

Nathan nodded, wondering just how far Hailey was willing to go to protect Leigh. ''Too bad. Sara's very nice. I'm sure you'll like her. So why didn't you go to the movies with them?''

''I had some reading to catch up on.''

''I see. So it wasn't the fact that you'd be in the way on Leigh's wild date that kept you home?''

Hailey met his gaze dead on. ''You knew?''

''Even before I left, I suspected her friend was going to be someone with a five-o'clock shadow and an Adam's apple who was named Mike or Keith or Horatio.''

A bubble of laughter escaped Hailey. ''Horatio? Hardly.''

''Yeah. I know.'' He watched her for a second, then said, ''His name's Jared. He's a rodeo rider. And I could skin Leigh alive for going out with him.''

Hailey set the stack of papers she'd been reading on the coffee table in front of her, then asked, ''Why do you care? Leigh's twenty-one. She's more than old enough to make her own decisions. You should let her choose her own friends.''

Nathan couldn't help smiling at Hailey's statement. ''You obviously didn't grow up around this area. Were you born in Texas?''

Hailey shook her head. ''No. I've only been in

Texas for five years. Before that, my mother and I moved fairly often.''

That explained a lot. "And if I had to guess, I'd say you're an only child."

"Right." She leaned forward, her expression intense. "None of that matters. No offense, but you shouldn't meddle in your sister's life. You may think you know what she should do, but it's her life and her choices."

There were very few things Nathan enjoyed more than a good argument with a worthy opponent. Hailey was definitely a worthy opponent.

"Leigh means the world to me. I don't want to see her hurt," he said simply.

"You need to trust her instincts."

He had to laugh at that one. "Really? Would those be the instincts that convinced her dying her hair bright green in high school was a terrific idea? Or the instincts that told her taking up motorcross racing would be a great way to meet guys but failed to mention that she could end up dead? Sorry, Hailey, but Leigh's got questionable instincts."

"Still, you should trust her."

For a second, he simply looked at Hailey, enjoying the quiet peace settling over them. Then, before he knew it, the atmosphere in the room seemed to suddenly shift. Awareness sparked, then danced between them. Not a good thing.

Since this little chat was becoming way too cozy, he suggested, "It's early yet. Want to take a walk? I can show you the sights of Paxton."

"Paxton has sights?"

He laughed. "Of course it has sights. Lots of them. How very big-city of you to think otherwise. You shouldn't miss this opportunity."

Hailey glanced at the papers on the coffee table. "As tempting as the idea of a walk sounds, I really should work."

Nathan decided to up his offer. "You sure I can't lure you away for just a while? Paxton is world-renowned for its fabulous ice cream. We could stop by the ice-cream parlor and get a double-scoop."

A smile slowly crossed her face. "Let me get this straight, you live in a small town that has a world-famous ice-cream parlor? Is this a Norman Rockwell picture or what?"

Nathan stood and extended his hand. "Why don't you come with me and find out?"

For a heartbeat, Hailey looked up at him. Then with a small sigh, she took his hand and stood. "All I want to know is if this ice-cream parlor is world-renowned, why haven't I even heard of it?"

Nathan reluctantly let go of her hand, then waited for Hailey to precede him out of the house. "I guess you've been hanging out in the wrong part of the world," he teased.

Hailey laughed, the sound was carefree and light. Nathan couldn't help smiling, enjoying himself for the first time in a long while. After they walked down the driveway, he headed them toward the center of town.

"I know you think you've distracted me, but you

haven't. Before we left the house, we were discussing Leigh.''

Nathan tipped his head and looked at her. ''We were?''

''Yes, we were. I firmly believe you should let her make her own decisions.'' Hailey's soft voice settled over him like a warm mist.

For the briefest of moments, Nathan allowed himself the luxury of simply looking at Hailey. Then he said, ''I don't think I could butt out of her life if I wanted to. Worrying about her is coded in my DNA.''

''Hi, Mr. Barrett.''

Nathan stopped and turned. The Maclusky twins were weeding in their garden. He smiled at the pre-teen girls, the daughters of one of his lead programmers. ''Hi, Debbie. Hi, Carrie. How are you ladies today?''

The girls giggled and blushed, although for the life of him, he didn't know why.

''We're excellent,'' said Debbie. ''Really excellent.'' She looked at Hailey and shyly said, ''Hi.''

Nathan quickly introduced Hailey to the girls, explaining that Hailey was going to work for Barrett Software.

''I'm going to work at Barrett Software after I get through college,'' Carrie said, dusting her hands off on her red shorts and leaving black marks. ''I'm going to be a programmer like Dad.''

''Me, too.'' Debbie smiled at him. ''I can't wait until I can work there.''

"It's great you two have your future mapped out," Hailey said. "When I was your age, I wanted to cure world hunger or be a rock star."

"That's because you didn't have Barrett Software as your third choice," Nathan teased.

"We've got it all planned," Carrie said. "It's going to be excellent."

And after a couple of minutes catching up, Nathan wished the girls a good evening, and he and Hailey headed on toward town.

"You have two not-so-secret admirers there," Hailey said after they'd walked half a block.

Nathan glanced at her. "They're a couple of great kids. That's all."

Hailey smiled. "I don't think so. I think they think you're *excellent.*"

Rather than answering, he put his hand on her arm, stopping her. "Hold on a second. You're going to step on Rufus if you're not careful."

"Rufus?"

Nathan nodded at the hound dog sprawled across the sidewalk up ahead. "Rufus."

Hailey let out a small gasp. "That's a dog?" She edged slowly closer, and as usual, Rufus didn't bother to move. "I caught it out of the corner of my eye, and I thought it was some kind of dog-shaped fungus growing on the sidewalk."

By now they were almost directly in front of the dog. When Hailey went to bend toward the mutt, Nathan stopped her again.

"Rufus doesn't like to be bothered. Just step over him."

Hailey blinked. "Does he bite?"

"No, he's just a gentleman who prefers his own company," Nathan explained, laughing at the incredulous expression on her face. He carefully stepped over Rufus, then turned and helped Hailey across.

"Is he sick? Shouldn't his owner take him to the vet?"

Nathan headed them down Main Street. "Rufus is as healthy as a horse. He's simply mellow and likes to snooze. The vet says it's his personality. Besides, he livens up when a car approaches."

"He chases cars?"

"No, not chases. But he barks at them," Nathan said. "Sometimes. When the mood strikes him."

Hailey shook her head. "Strange."

"That's Paxton for you. So tell me, how did you meet Leigh? No offense, but you don't seem to have a lot in common."

"Why not? Leigh's nice, and fun, and—"

"Crazy, and devious, and irresponsible at times."

When Hailey laughed, Nathan found himself looking at her lips and couldn't help wondering if they felt as soft as they appeared.

With effort, he pulled his gaze away from her lips and studied her face. "So, how'd you meet?"

"We both used to hang out in the library, and after a while, we started talking. Eventually we became friends."

That didn't sound like his sister at all. "The library? Leigh hung out in the library?"

"Yes, she was there quite a lot. I think you underestimate her. She takes her studies very seriously."

Although Leigh was getting decent grades in college, Nathan knew for a fact those grades came without a lot of time devoted to studying. She was a fast learner, and college came easily to her. Something didn't add up.

"Was she at the library at a certain time of day?" he asked.

Hailey frowned. "Why?"

"I'd be willing to bet there was a guy who worked there at the times that Leigh was around."

"You really are suspicious of her, aren't you?"

"I'm not suspicious. I'm a realist."

Apparently not buying his explanation, Hailey's frown deepened. "Are you suspicious of everyone or just Leigh?"

Oh, now this was getting fun. "Just Leigh. I trust most people."

They were outside Monroe's Drug Store. Out of habit and training, Nathan held the door for a local man, George Brown, who was coming out carrying several large bags.

"Hey there, Nathan," George said, shifting his packages and shaking Nathan's hand. Leaning close, he said, "I should tell you, I saw Leigh going into the movies with Jared Kendrick earlier tonight. You know 'bout that?"

Nathan nodded. "I know. How are you?"

George narrowed his gaze and for a second looked as if he was going to say more, but then he noticed Hailey. "Well, hello there. I don't think we've met."

Nathan quickly introduced them, and George shook Hailey's hand. "You're going to like working at Barrett Software. Great place." He slapped Nathan on the back. "The boy here has done good by this town. But we always knew he would. After he took the football team to State, we knew Paxton could count on him."

"We didn't win," Nathan felt compelled to point out.

"But you gave it your all, Nathan. That's what counts."

After helping George load his bags into his car, Nathan waved goodbye and started walking again. It took him a couple of seconds to realize Hailey wasn't walking with him.

"Everything okay?" he asked.

She slowly approached him, humor lurking in her eyes. "Tell me, does everyone in this town think you're the best thing since microwave popcorn or are we just running into the zealots?"

3

_____

"I HAVE FRIENDS IN PAXTON," Nathan admitted. "That's why I opened my business here."

"Friends? More like fans." She nodded toward the restored courthouse building that now housed Barrett Software. "You should be proud of what you've accomplished. It looks like your company keeps this town going."

Nathan idly kicked a stone on the sidewalk, not really comfortable with the conversation. "I've helped Paxton, sure, but this town was a great place long before I opened Barrett Software."

She smiled at him. "If you say so. But I can hardly wait to see who else we meet on our little stroll. I'm feeling pretty popular since I'm going for ice cream with the captain of the football team."

"_That_ was a long time ago," he said, looking at her. Wanting to talk about anything other than himself, he turned the tables. "You know way too much about me. Tell me about yourself instead."

For a second, she hesitated. Then she said, "Fine. We'll change the subject. We'll no longer discuss your glory days." She tipped her head and looked downright adorable. "Let's see. About me. Well, like I said, I'm working on my doctorate in English. End of story.''

Nathan chuckled. ''Ah. So you didn't start out as a baby, then grow up to be a teenager, and finally turn into a woman? You popped out of the womb a full-fledged Ph.D. candidate?''

Her smile was sassy. ''Wouldn't that have been a time saver? But you're right. I started out the boring, usual way.''

When she didn't expand on her answer, he teased, ''You're a chatty thing, aren't you? You keep on with these stories, and you'll burn my ears off.''

''Oh, fine, but if we're playing twenty questions here, you go first. Tell me about you. I already know you're adored in the town where you grew up and that you led the football team to State, which makes you a real hero around here. Tell me the rest.''

Nathan started them walking toward the ice-cream store again. ''The abridged version is I'm thirty-three with a master's in computer science from UT. I've never been married. My favorite food is lobster, but don't tell anyone around here because it should be steak since this is Texas. My favorite movie is *Die Hard.*'' At Hailey's smug look, he admitted, ''I know. What a male stereotype, but I like it. My favorite book is—''

Hailey held up one hand. ''Let me guess, *Catcher in the Rye.*''

''And yours is probably *Jane Eyre.*''

''*The Grapes of Wrath.*''

"Ah. I stand corrected. And your favorite movie is probably *Pretty Woman*."

She wrinkled her nose and ran one hand through her hair. "No."

"*Sleepless in Seattle?*"

"No. It's—"

"Let me guess." Determined to figure this out, Nathan scanned his brain for all the romantic movies he knew. Landing on one more, he asked, "*While You Were Sleeping?*"

She beamed. "Yes. Were you going to guess every chick flick you could think of until you got it right?"

"Of course. There was a principle at stake."

"What principle would that be?"

"The principle that says I'm never wrong," he told her.

She laughed again, and Nathan felt the simmering attraction between them heat up a couple more degrees. "Okay, what else do you want to know?"

He thought for a moment, then asked, "Tell me about your first crush."

She seemed surprised, but she didn't hesitate. "Donald Freed, when I was ten. I thought he was wonderful."

"Did you ever tell him?"

"No. And it was a good thing since I'd gotten over the crush by the time I was ten and a quarter. How about you? Who was your first crush on?"

"Sally Jean Myerson, fourth grade."

"Did you ever confess your love?"

"Nah, she liked another boy in class, and I didn't want to ruin their budding relationship."

"How noble."

Honesty forced him to admit, "Well her boyfriend was the size of two semis. He would have beat the stuffing out of me, so I decided to find someone else to like."

"Noble and wise. Good combination."

"So this Donald Freed, was he good-looking?" Nathan asked.

"Not really. Just predictable. Not into a lot of drama. I found that appealing. At least for one-quarter of a year."

"I take it you like ugly, boring men, then?"

Again, she ran one hand through her hair, and Nathan's gaze followed the gesture. He really did like the shade of her hair. The fading sun seemed to make it gleam.

"What can I tell you? I've got low standards," Hailey said.

"I'm pretty boring," Nathan found himself saying, then immediately wished he hadn't. He shouldn't be flirting with this woman. She was only in town for a few weeks. She was going to work for him.

And most importantly, whether she knew it or not, she was being used by Leigh as bait.

Fortunately Hailey didn't seem to read anything into his comment. She shook her head and said, "You may be boring, but you're not ugly. I'm afraid it won't work."

He snapped his fingers, still keeping the tone light and teasing. "Darn. Okay, so now tell me about your family."

"Well, my mom raised me."

"By herself?"

Hailey nodded. "Yes. She was a lot of fun. Big on adventures. She loved to pack up and move someplace new at a moment's notice just to see what life was like in a different sort of place. One day we'd live in the mountains, then we'd go live by the ocean for a few months. It was never boring around my mom." A soft smile lit her face. "She passed away a little over two years ago. I really miss her."

"She sounds like a great lady. What about your father?"

"He teaches at Wyneheart College, just west of Boston. I didn't get to spend a lot of time with him when I was growing up, but he always sent money and called frequently."

"He's the only family you have left?"

"Yes." She stopped to look in one of the store windows, then added, "But I'm finally going to get to spend time with him. He's arranged a teaching position for me at the college after I get my doctorate."

Happiness radiated off her. Nathan could tell how much this meant to her.

"Congratulations on the job and on getting to connect with your dad," he said. "I've heard of Wyneheart. It's a good college."

Hailey nodded. "It's wonderful. And I'll get to

focus on American Literature, which is my specialty." After a slight pause, she added, "I haven't told a soul this. Not even Leigh. But I'm really looking forward to living in the town of Wyneheart. It's wonderful. Small, but seeped in history. Very cozy."

Nathan completely understood the appeal. "Kind of like Paxton."

Hailey blinked and frowned at him. Slowly she looked around Main Street, then finally said, "Um. I guess."

He couldn't help laughing at her dumbfounded expression. "Okay. I know this may not look like Wyneheart, which was probably built by the Pilgrims, but Paxton has a lot of history. True Wild West history."

Her expression was openly dubious, but she still asked, "Such as?"

"Such as rumor has it that Wyatt Earp once ate at the local diner."

"Is that true?"

"Everyone says it is, and Wyatt's not around to argue, so we accept it as fact."

"What else?"

He thought for a second. "Bonnie and Clyde drove through town one time."

"Really?"

He had to bite back a smile. "Well, the car *was* moving very fast, but everyone was almost positive it was them."

She laughed. "Seems like the history of this town is a little shaky."

"Okay, here's a certifiable fact. For five years in the 1880s, Paxton housed more establishments for the entertainment of gentlemen than any other city in Texas, including the big cities."

It took only a fraction of a second for her to get his meaning. Then she laughed again. "You're kidding me, right?"

He solemnly shook his head. "Nope. It's true."

"Paxton had that many bordellos?"

"Yes, ma'am. It was called Heaven on Earth. But then settlers moved in and chased off the no-goods."

She rolled her eyes. "What a place."

"It suits me."

"So it seems. Tell me about Barrett Software."

Now that was his favorite subject. "We're doing well. Better than I'd hoped and growing each year. That accounting program I told you about should really put us on the map. That is, if we can get the bugs out in time to unveil it at the BizExpo, the Dallas computer show later this summer."

"The program is that good?"

"Got all the bells and whistles. We call it EZ-Books because it's easy to set up, easy to customize, and easy to use. It even can be voice-controlled."

"That's what I'll be helping with?"

"Yes. That's what everyone is working on. Mostly though, you'll be handling me."

She tipped her head. "Want to try that again."

He chuckled, although just the thought of her touching him was enough to get his blood pressure climbing.

"Since you'll be my assistant, you'll have to keep my schedule straight," he explained, trying to keep his wayward mind on track.

She nodded. "Gotcha. Don't worry. I'm very organized. When I need to be that is."

They had reached Estes Ice-Cream Parlor, so Nathan didn't ask for clarification on the last part of her statement. Instead he held the door open for her. As Hailey passed, her sweet scent taunted him again.

"Well if it isn't Nathan Barrett," Caitlin Estes, owner of the shop, said when she saw him. "It's about time you stopped by. You're harder to find than a mouse at a cat wedding."

"Hi, Caitlin." He nodded toward Hailey. "This is Hailey Montgomery. She's a friend of Leigh's who's going to work at Barrett Software for a few weeks."

The look Caitlin gave Hailey wasn't exactly cold, but Nathan wasn't obtuse enough to think the two women would become friends. Not that he was surprised. Caitlin had made it clear since she'd been head cheerleader in high school that she wanted to be a lot more than merely an acquaintance of his. It wasn't a sentiment he reciprocated.

"It's nice to meet you," Hailey said. Then she must have figured the ice cream was warmer than Caitlin, because she moved away and studied the flavors on display in the cases.

"Since you almost never come to see me, I'm going to have to find a way to visit you at your office," Caitlin said, flashing him a flirty smile.

Nathan was very careful to keep his expression neutral. "I appreciate the idea, Caitlin, but we're really busy right now."

Caitlin ran one finger under the thin strap of her T-shirt and winked. Now that was subtle. "Not too busy for a little fun I hope. I think we should spend some time together."

He didn't agree, but he also didn't want to hurt her feelings. "Normally I like having friends stop by the office, but I doubt if I'd have time to see you. Thanks anyway."

Caitlin pouted. "I'm not giving up that easily, Nathan Barrett. I guess I'll have to get creative." Her down mood didn't last long, because before she'd formed a really impressive pout, she brightened and asked, "Hey, did you hear that Leigh's out with Jared Kendrick? Did you know about that?"

"Yes, I know." Glancing toward Hailey, he found her watching him closely. Before he could say anything else to Caitlin, a crowd of young boys came in and snagged her attention. Relieved, Nathan moved over to join Hailey. She stood looking into one of the large display cases that contained a dazzling array of ice creams.

"Have you decided?" he asked.

She glanced up at him. "I'd like a single scoop of vanilla."

He laughed and nodded toward the ice-cream

case. "That's it? All these amazing choices and you want vanilla?"

Hailey shrugged. "Some of us know a good thing when we find it, and once our decision is made, we stick to it. I'm a vanilla purist." She waved her hand at the multitude of flavors. "Let me guess. You want something wild like—" She glanced in the ice-cream case again and said, "Loopy, Luscious Lemon? Or maybe Crazy, Cookey Coconut?"

Nathan smiled. "Not exactly."

Behind him, he heard Caitlin laugh. "Are you kidding? This guy is loyal to the end. It's vanilla all the way for him."

Nathan leaned against the display case, and smiled at Hailey. "I guess that makes two of us who stick with a good thing once we find it."

"THE FAX WORKS BETTER if you give it a good whack," Leigh said from the doorway to Hailey's office the next morning. "Here, let me show you."

Hailey had been carefully reading the instruction manual, but now she looked at Leigh and moved the fax out of the younger woman's reach. "Don't you dare hit it."

Leigh stopped midstride and grinned. "You're just like Nathan—sentimental. It's a machine, not a person. He should have gotten rid of that piece of junk years ago, but he keeps getting it fixed."

Hailey shifted the fax even further from Leigh's grasp, then leaned back in her chair. "I'm positive the fax can be fixed. It just sticks a little."

With a laugh, Leigh dropped into the chair facing Hailey's desk. "I can't believe you're defending a fax machine." She glanced around the office. "Any other equipment you've grown attached to already?"

Hailey relaxed for the first time this morning. She was really glad Leigh had dropped by. Her new job made her tense. Everyone at Barrett Software seemed tense. If the accounting program, EZBooks, wasn't error-free by the Dallas computer show, Barrett Software would miss a wonderful opportunity to introduce the product to the public. Building up a market would be so much more difficult without the added exposure.

For her part, Hailey wanted to do well, and so far this morning, she'd eaten four antacids. Leigh was exactly what she needed to calm down.

"I'm rather fond of the computer and the printer, now that you ask," Hailey said.

Leigh's expression turned downright mischievous. "How about my hunky brother? Gotten attached to him yet?"

Okay, so much for calming down. Just the mention of Nathan was enough to get her pulse racing. "He's very nice."

"Nice? So that's why you went with him for ice cream last night? Because he's nice?"

Hailey wasn't the least surprised that Leigh knew about their walk through town. Hailey figured that she'd met most of the population of Paxton during the stroll home. People had seemed to pop out from every direction. And Nathan had been charming to everyone they'd met. By the end of the evening, Hailey had to admit she'd been more than a little charmed herself. She wanted to believe it was the night and the companionship of an attractive man that had made her reluctant to see the evening end, but that was bunk.

The reason she'd hated for last night to end was that she'd had a terrific time with Nathan Barrett. But she'd rather dye her hair yellow with pink stripes than admit that to Leigh.

So to be on the safe side, all Hailey was willing to admit was, "Nathan was very nice to take me for ice cream. He thought I might be bored."

Leigh laughed. "Yeah, good old Nathan. He's a real sport to entertain a lonely lady."

"I appreciated it. I enjoyed finding out about Paxton." Deciding it was past time to turn this conversation around, Hailey said, "I heard you had a fun date last night."

Rather than looking contrite, Leigh's smile only grew. "That I did, as everyone in Paxton knows. Nothing like having your every move telegraphed around town."

"A lot of people did seem to know about your date."

Leigh shrugged. "Typical Paxton. Information capital of the world. If you sneeze, people two miles away say bless you."

Yesterday, Hailey would have thought Leigh was

exaggerating, but after the walk last night, she knew better. "I'll keep that in mind."

Leigh glanced around the office. "So other than the fax machine, are you getting settled in? I feel terrible for not getting up early this morning and coming into the office with you. Sorry I overslept."

"Leigh, Paxton only has four major streets. It wasn't like negotiating New York City."

"Well, there is that tricky bit on Pine Street where Rufus will chase after your car if you're not quick."

Hailey had to laugh at that one. "I met Rufus last night. All he did when I drove by this morning was woof at me. He didn't chase my car."

Leigh tapped her temple. "In his head he did. Rufus is more cerebral than physical, but we don't like to tell him that. We all pretend he chases us. Makes him feel he's important around here."

Hailey shook her head. "This place is insane."

"That's called charm," Nathan said.

Hailey glanced up to find him standing in the doorway to her office. He smiled at Hailey, then at his sister. "Hello, ladies. So Leigh, what brings you here?"

"I stopped by to see Hailey." Leigh looked at Hailey, then back at her brother. "Wanted to make certain that ice cream she had last night settled okay."

Nathan had a twinkle in his eyes when he looked at Hailey. He was so amazingly handsome in his dark blue suit, her breath caught in her throat. For several long seconds, he held Hailey's gaze. Then he turned his attention back to Leigh. "Sure you didn't stop by to talk about the movie you saw last night?"

Leigh snorted. "As if. I'm not telling you about my personal life, Nathan, so forget it."

"Just as well. My heart probably couldn't stand the details." He looked at Hailey and asked, "Are you getting settled?"

"Yes, thanks." And so far, everything was going just fine. A young woman from personnel had gotten her started, and the morning had flown by. With the exception of the temperamental fax machine, she'd had no problem figuring out the equipment. She'd even taken some time to organize a few of Nathan's files. Plus, she'd printed out his schedule. Despite her jittery nerves, everything was happening like clockwork. "No problems."

"Good." His gaze met hers again, and sure enough, her heart did a little thumpity-thump. What was it about this man that got to her so? She wasn't the type to let hormones cloud her judgment, but boy did they ever when he was around.

Hailey scrambled to think of something to say to him, anything at all, but she simply couldn't get her mind in gear. Finally he solved her problem by saying, "If you have any questions, just let me know."

"I have a question," Leigh said. "Why haven't you tossed this old fax into the garbage? It's junk, Nathan."

Nathan glanced at the machine in question, then

looked at Hailey. "You can swap it with the one in my office if it's giving you too many problems."

"No, I'm sure I'll be able to figure it out," she said. At his mention of his office she remembered his visitor. "By the way, your ten o'clock appointment is waiting in your office."

Nathan glanced at the closed door to his office, then returned his attention to Hailey. "And who would that be?"

Hailey glanced at his schedule. "The Paxton Ladies' Society. Actually the representative is the woman I met last night at the ice-cream shop—Caitlin Estes."

"Caitlin?" Nathan frowned. "She's not with the—" He stopped when the elevator door opened and a middle-aged woman exited. "Hailey, this is Amanda Newman. She heads up the Paxton Ladies' Society."

Amanda walked forward, her gaze moving from Hailey to Leigh to Nathan. "Am I late?"

Leigh laughed. "From what I can tell, Amanda, you're right on time. Seems Caitlin pretended to be from the Ladies' Society and is waiting in Nathan's office."

Amanda frowned. "I wish they'd stop doing this."

Truly baffled, Hailey had to ask, "Doing what?"

Nathan glanced at his closed door. "It's kind of a joke around town. Some of the single ladies occasionally try to...trick their way into seeing me. I'm busy and like to keep personal callers off my calendar, unless it's for charity. Which is why Amanda is here.''

Hailey studied the closed door. What had she done? "So Ms. Estes isn't with the Ladies' Society?"

Laughter sputtered from Leigh. "Not even close. Caitlin just wanted to get in to see Nathan and snagged this opportunity. Hailey, don't feel badly. Lots of the local ladies do this kind of thing to him all the time. They're trying to find ways to get his attention. They do things like delivering pies here or sending him truckloads of flowers." She slapped Nathan on the back. "My brother is one hot property."

Amanda sighed. "I shouldn't have mentioned that I was coming to see Nathan to so many people. I'll talk to Caitlin."

Before she could move, Leigh held up one hand. "No way, Mrs. Newman. Caitlin went to a lot of trouble. Let's not spoil it."

A feeling of dread settled low in Hailey's stomach. She felt terrible that she'd let this woman into Nathan's office. And since she'd caused the problem, she'd also be the one to solve it.

"I'll ask her to leave since she misled me." Hailey took a step forward, but Leigh skirted around her.

"I want to see what Caitlin's cooked up." Practically skipping, Leigh threw open the door.

Loud, pulsating music immediately started. Leigh and Nathan were the first ones inside the office.

Hailey heard Leigh's laughter and what sounded like a groan from Nathan. When she and Amanda Newman reached the doorway, they both froze.

For her own part, all Hailey could do was stare. Caitlin Estes was dressed in what appeared to be a cheerleader's uniform. She was performing a variety of routines for Nathan, and Hailey would give her this—Caitlin Estes was one limber lady. She did flips. She did tumbles. She jumped and cheered and hooted.

"I guess the ladies in town have tried about everything now," Amanda murmured when Caitlin did an impressive handstand right in front of Nathan, her little skirt flipping up to display a big red heart tattooed on her left thigh.

Finally, with a hop, Caitlin stood and grinned at Nathan. "Let me know if you want to see my other tattoos," she said with a wink. Then as calmly as could be, Caitlin put her coat back on, shut off her boom box and left the office, wagging her fingers in a wave to the rest of the group as she went by.

"Well, that was different," Amanda said after Caitlin got in the elevator.

"I can't believe she did that," Nathan observed dryly, walking over to his desk.

Hailey looked at him, trying to gauge his reaction to what had just happened. Thankfully he didn't seem angry. He also didn't appear upset or flustered. And a small part of Hailey was thrilled to see he didn't seem the least bit intrigued by what had happened. Mostly he seemed amused.

Still, she felt terrible. Here she'd promised to be the perfect assistant and then she'd gone and let that woman in. She should have questioned Caitlin more carefully, but she'd assumed the young woman was being honest.

That would teach her to make assumptions. She'd let the small-town, laid-back atmosphere of Paxton fool her, and so far, her first day on the job was off to a dismal start.

"Could have been worse," Leigh pointed out. "At least Caitlin was wearing panties."

NATHAN PULLED INTO HIS driveway, put his car in Park, and let out a long sigh. Home. Finally. After what had to be one of the longest days of his life. EZBooks had more bugs than an ant farm. He'd spent most of his day helping with the testing and making suggestions on fixes.

He'd expected problems because a program as complicated as this one always had bugs. But BizExpo was only a few weeks away, and Barrett Software needed to make a big splash there if the company was going to keep supporting most of Paxton.

Normally he considered himself a fairly lucky guy, but not today. Today he figured he stood a pretty good chance of a house dropping on him, so it was with a great deal of caution that he opened his car door and climbed out. For one second, he held his breath, waiting for another catastrophe to bonk him on the head.

Thankfully, though, nothing happened.

Until he heard the thumping noise coming from over on the sports court. Before he could consider the wisdom of investigating, he glanced that way. Hailey was playing basketball on the court, and from the way she was pushing herself, she was working off the tension of her day.

For a heartbeat, he simply watched her, enjoying the enticing sight. And Hailey Montgomery was indeed a sight, with her long legs and curvy body.

Although he didn't make a sound, she must have sensed him watching her, because she turned and looked at him.

"Hi," she said, breathing fast.

"Hi." Nathan wandered over to the court and set his briefcase down on the bench. "You've been playing hard."

She dribbled the ball a few times. "Want to take your best shot?"

Although there was nothing sexual about her comment, his gaze snagged hers. He knew he should say no and head on inside the house, but his mind couldn't seem to get his body to respond.

"Sure," he said, shrugging out of his jacket and tossing it on top of his briefcase. She handed him the ball. He sized up his shot, then watched with satisfaction as the ball whooshed through the hoop.

"Nice shot," she said, picking up the ball.

"That's the first thing that's gone right today."

Hailey stopped a couple of feet from him, and her smile faded. "I am so sorry about what happened with Caitlin. I had no idea she intended on doing...what she did. She was wearing a nice coat when she arrived.''

Nathan laughed. ''Don't worry about that. Caitlin and her friends are always doing stuff to me. They've been doing it for years.''

Hailey slowly shook her head. ''How can that not bother you? And to think, I let her into your office. I'll be much more careful in the future.''

He admired Hailey's dedication to a job she'd just started. The woman was a hard worker and realized how important this program was to Barrett Software. Knowing a type-A personality like Hailey was going to let the Caitlin incident gnaw at her, Nathan decided a distraction was in order.

He snagged the basketball out of her arms and started to dribble it.

''Let's forget about work. First one to twenty points wins.'' Then before Hailey could say a word, he went by her and easily sunk the ball. ''Two points for me.''

''Hey, that's not fair. I didn't even agree to play.''

Nathan grinned. ''Too late. I'm winning. What are you going to do about it?''

Hailey opened her mouth, and for a second, he thought she was going to refuse to play. But then abruptly, she grinned right back at him. ''You're on.''

Although he wasn't dressed for a game of basketball, he managed to keep up with Hailey. But just barely. The woman was good. Very good. By the time they were tied at eighteen points each, Nathan was sweating and breathing hard.

"This is it," Hailey said, easily moving the ball from hand to hand. "Hold on Nathan Barrett, I'm going to wipe the court with you."

He laughed. "In your dreams."

Hailey started dribbling down the court, then veered left, but he moved with her. She tried to recover and go right, but he blocked her again. Finally she turned and went to scoot past him, but he was too quick for her. He knocked the ball out of her hands, and when he lunged for it, ended up bumping Hailey.

"Whoa." He wrapped his arms around her waist and barely kept her from falling over. At first, she teetered, and he almost lost his footing as well. But finally, they managed to steady themselves.

"Well, that was graceful," Hailey said with a laugh. She blew out a breath and ruffled her bangs.

"Want to call it a draw before we kill ourselves?"

She smiled. "Probably a smart idea."

For a second, he returned her smile. Then he realized he still had his arms around her waist. Her hands were on his shoulders. And her warm, soft body was pressed against him. Without meaning to, he glanced at her full lips.

Let her go, you idiot.

His hands didn't move, and neither did hers. He met her gaze. He could see the same fire of attraction in her eyes that he felt burning inside of him.

"I should—"

"We can't—"

He nodded. "Right. I know."

She nodded. "Absolutely. Not smart."

He looked at her again. Her hands still hadn't moved. Neither had his. He could feel his heart thumping wildly in his chest. He needed to be smart. He needed to exercise willpower.

Hailey's gaze dropped to his lips. Then slowly, she leaned toward him.

Ah, hell. He needed to get this situation under control before something happened they'd both regret.

Her lips brushed his.

And his good intentions dried up and blew away.

4

HAILEY HADN'T REALLY MEANT to kiss Nathan. Sure, she'd wanted to—very much so. But she hadn't *meant* to actually do it. Kissing him wasn't a bright thing to do. Kissing him could lead to all sorts of problems.

But now that she was actually wrapped in his arms and kissing him for all she was worth, she had to admit it was pretty darn terrific. Nathan Barrett kissed like he did everything else—well. Very, very well.

As he deepened the kiss, tingles danced over her sensitized skin. Yep, the man could kiss. Oh, boy and how. He kissed so well that she pushed aside all the annoying reasons why she shouldn't be doing this and simply enjoyed herself. Nathan, too, seemed to be caught up in the kiss.

Hailey had no idea how long they stood on the basketball court kissing, but it was a long, long time. Even so, when Nathan finally broke the kiss, she couldn't help feeling disappointed.

Her disappointment only increased when he slowly removed his arms from around her and took a step back. Now that they were no longer touching, the air between them crackled with a combination of lust and regret.

Nathan cleared his throat. "I didn't mean to do that."

His comment was completely expected and the last thing Hailey wanted to hear. But he was right. Now was the time to backpedal like crazy away from what had happened.

"Technically you didn't kiss me. I believe I was the one who started this." She scuffed the toe of her sneaker on the ground. "Sorry. I can't imagine why I did that."

Oh great. She sounded like an idiot. Plus, she was a liar. She knew *exactly* why she'd kissed him—the man was hotter than an August afternoon in Texas.

But Nathan didn't question her explanation. Instead he acted like the perfect gentleman he always seemed to be. He gave her a small smile. "This kiss was more my fault than yours, Hailey."

The intellectual side of her forced her to ask, "No offense, but how do you figure that? *I* was the one who kissed you first. How does that make it your fault?"

"I could have stopped you."

"Hardly."

"Of course I could have."

She was skeptical. "I think you'll need to come up with a better explanation. I still don't see how it's your fault."

He opened his mouth, then promptly shut it. Hailey couldn't help smiling as she watched him struggle for an answer—one he never did end up finding.

"See, I'm right," she said with a laugh when he still hadn't come up with a reason after a few seconds. "It *is* my fault, not yours."

He flashed a rueful grin, and Hailey was glad the atmosphere between them lightened.

"I haven't given up yet," he said. "I only need a couple more minutes, and I'll think of a reason."

She shook her head. "Nope. Time's up. You have to admit it was my fault."

Her teasing accomplished what she'd hoped it would. They were no longer awkward and uncomfortable with each other. Instead they were joking and laughing about the kiss. For her part, Hailey had never felt less like laughing in her life. That kiss had shaken her clear to her toes.

But Nathan had been right. The kiss never should have happened, and since she had to work with this man, self-preservation demanded they put what had happened behind them. Way far behind them.

Nathan raised one eyebrow. "Are you always so opinionated?"

She nodded. "Absolutely. And it's not that I'm opinionated. It's that I'm always right."

He laughed and scooped the ball up off the ground. "Why don't we agree that regardless of who started the whole kissing thing, we shouldn't have done it? We do have to work together."

"Exactly."

He dribbled the basketball a couple of times, then

added, "And I don't think either one of us is looking to start something."

"True. I'm only here for the summer." She shifted her weight from one foot to the other and tried to ignore the nervous bubbling in her stomach. This was becoming awkward again. Now seemed like a wonderful time to escape.

"I think I'll go shower," she said, grabbing the first excuse that popped into her mind.

Nathan dribbled the basketball. "Okay. I think I'll stay for a while longer and shoot a few hoops."

Ah. Always the gentleman. He was giving her time alone, some breathing room to regain her composure. No wonder everyone in this town acted like he'd hung the moon. The man constantly thought of others.

Darn him. How was she supposed to ignore him if he insisted on being such a good guy?

"Have fun." She turned and was heading toward the house when she found herself adding, "And thanks for the—"

Eek. She slammed her mouth shut. Good grief. What in the world had she been about to thank him for? He seemed curious about that as well since he stood watching her with an expression that could only be described as cautious and amused.

"Thanks for?" he prompted when she didn't say anything after a few seconds.

Hailey scanned her mind, searching for a suitable alternative to thanking him for the best kiss of her life. Finally she grabbed onto the obvious.

"Thanks for the job. I really appreciate it."

A slow smile crossed his lips, and Hailey felt her heart rate accelerate. He knew she hadn't intended on saying that, but he let it go.

"You're welcome," he said, his gaze tangled up with hers. He looked away first, turning slightly and tossing the basketball toward the hoop.

It missed. By several feet.

Looked like she wasn't the only one rattled by that kiss.

"I DON'T SEE HOW WE CAN have EZBooks ready in time," said Tim Rollins, Barrett Software's head of testing. "My team keeps finding errors."

"With the voice recognition software?" Nathan asked.

"Yes. Plus, the customizable database doesn't work," Tim explained.

"It works. It just needs some tweaking. We can take care of all of these problems." This came from Emily Isles, the head of development.

Nathan held back a sigh and studied the people in the room. They were his lead managers, and they were all looking to him for reassurance. Every single one of them.

"We have a little over five weeks until BizExpo. We need to work together to guarantee the product is done and the demo is flawless." He turned to Tim. "Have you had the developers sit in on your tests so they can see for themselves what's happening?"

Tim shook his head. "Not yet. But I will."

"Good." Now he looked at Emily. "That should speed things up."

She nodded. "I'll get with Tim after this meeting and work out a plan."

"Good." Nathan glanced around the room, his gaze lingering way too long on Hailey. With effort, he made himself look away. If he didn't watch out, instead of thinking about design problems and coding roadblocks, he'd spend all of his time thinking about how great it had been kissing her last night.

So he needed to stop thinking about her.

"Which is probably impossible."

Nathan froze. Had he said that out loud? He scanned the faces of the other people sitting at the conference table. Based on the frowns he was receiving, it looked as if he had.

Ah, jeez. *Way to go, Barrett. Convince the staff you're losing your mind. Should do a lot for employee morale.*

"What's impossible?" The question came from Tim. "I think having development sit in on the testing will help."

"That's not what I meant," Nathan assured him. When everyone kept waiting for him to explain his comment, he blurted, "It's impossible not to be excited about EZBooks."

Absolute silence fell over the room. Finally Nathan pulled himself together enough to flash his best smile. Thinking on his feet even while sitting down, he decided to use this opportunity for a little pep talk. "I know. Sounds corny and stupid at this point since we still have a lot of problems and obstacles to overcome before we attend BizExpo. But I can't help it. I'm excited. EZBooks is great, and it should really put Barrett Software on the map. I'm proud of how everyone has pulled together and is working as a team to make this happen.''

By now, several people at the table were smiling back at him. Whew. That had been close.

Nathan stood, anxious to end the meeting. Anxious to get his head examined. ''Okay, any more problems I should know about?''

When no one had anything, he headed toward the door. He should go back to his office, but that would require walking with Hailey. More importantly, it would require talking to Hailey. At the moment, he figured the less time he spent around Hailey, the better.

So when he left the conference room, he walked with Tim to the testing department. He might as well pitch in himself. He could do some testing and think about something other than Hailey and that kiss.

And one other thing he intended on doing was to clean out the garage apartment. The sooner he moved Hailey out of the house, the better.

He figured that when it came to Hailey Montgomery, he needed to avoid her the way a certain superhero avoids Kryptonite.

HAILEY PUT HER HANDS ON HER hips and glanced around the room. Boxes were piled everywhere in teetering towers. Cleaning this place out would take hours, but when it was done, she'd have a nice little apartment all to herself. As much as she liked that idea, she felt badly about putting Nathan out.

"You sure you don't mind having this stuff moved? I can see if I can rent a place in town," she offered.

Nathan glanced around the crowded living room and shook his head. "Nice try, but no deal. You're going to help me lug all of this junk over to the attic in the house. There's no welching."

"But you could just leave everything here if it weren't for me," she pointed out.

Nathan walked over and opened a large brown and white box. "I'm not even sure what most of this stuff is," he said, turning to look at her. As always, she felt a skitter of excitement dance across her skin when their gazes met. "Most of it is stuff my mother kept when I was growing up."

Stunned, she looked at the piles and piles of boxes. "This is all childhood memorabilia? What did she do? Save every paper you ever wrote in school."

Nathan chuckled. "Not exactly. These are awards and trophies."

Awards? Trophies? All of these boxes? He couldn't be serious. "You're joking, right?"

He shook his head and looked more than a trifle embarrassed. "Nope. Almost all of the boxes have school awards in them. That's why I think I'll move them to the attic in the house. Who knows? Someday I may be interested in looking through this stuff. I doubt it, but you never know.''

Hailey suspected that Nathan had a sentimental streak in him every bit as wide as the one his mother had had. Look at how much this town meant to him.

She walked over and glanced in one of the boxes. Inside were election posters. She pulled one out, studying the picture of a young Nathan.

''You ran for class president?'' Without waiting for his answer, she hurried on. ''Of course you did. And let me guess—you won, right?''

He shrugged. ''It was a long time ago.''

The casual way he answered her made her female antennae go up. ''Oh, no, wait a minute. You didn't just win, did you? You slaughtered the competition.''

''It was a long time ago,'' he repeated.

Hailey laughed. ''I'm right, aren't I?''

By small degrees, a smile appeared on his face. ''Something like that.''

Figured. It figured Nathan would not only win the election, but he'd win it by a landslide. She'd only known the man for a couple of days, and already she knew that whatever he decided to do, he accomplished.

She studied the picture. Even in his teens, Nathan had been gorgeous. There wasn't a trace of adolescent awkwardness in his picture. Hailey shuddered to think what her own school picture had looked like at this age. Braces. Bad hair. Bad skin.

Ick.

But Nathan had been cute. The kind of guy who would never have noticed her if they'd gone to high school together.

"Great poster," she said, feeling more than a little defeated. Before she could be tempted to keep the poster, she quickly tucked it back in the box. Moving into this apartment was a way to put some distance between herself and Nathan. The last thing she needed were any photographs of him.

Nathan picked up one of the larger boxes. "I'm going to start carrying these to the attic."

Hailey scurried over to open the door for him. "You need to be careful going down the stairs with something that big. You could fall."

Nathan smiled at her over the top of the box. "Thanks, Mom, for the warning. I also promise not to run with sharp objects."

She frowned. "Very cute. Just don't ask me for help if you tumble down those stairs and smash your head wide-open."

"How could I come to you for help if my head is smashed open? I'd sort of be committed to staying where I was, wouldn't I?" he teased.

"Fine. But if you do, just know there's nothing I can do for you. I only know CPR, the Heimlich, and how to treat burns. Beyond that, I barely know the basics of first aid, and certainly not how to put Humpty Dumpty together again."

He laughed. "Great. So there'd be nothing you could do for me? Not one thing?"

Kiss it and make it better?

The thought popped into Hailey's mind before she braced herself, and she found herself blushing. Really, really blushing. Just like that. One second she'd been standing there talking to Nathan; the next second, she'd turned bright red. She didn't have to see her face to know what she looked like. She could feel the heat of the blush, and wanted the floor to open up and swallow her.

Nathan looked concerned. "Hey, are you okay? You seem…overheated."

Overheated. Yeah. That pretty much described her condition.

Hailey willed herself to calm down. When she finally felt she had at least a little control, she said, "I'm fine. Just a little warm."

He looked dubious. "You sure?"

"Absolutely." She moved away from him before she did anything else stupid, and eventually, Nathan either decided to believe her or he lost interest in the subject, because he headed out the door and down the stairs.

"Way to go," she muttered to herself. "Act like a complete idiot in front of the man. Who blushes at your age?"

Things were already awkward between them since that blistering kiss they'd shared. She needed to improve the situation not make it worse by thinking lecherous thoughts about her boss. She needed to forget the kiss had ever happened. Wipe it from her mind. Thinking about that kiss could get her distracted, and at this point in her life, she needed to be distracted by a man about as much as she needed a bad case of warts.

Focus. She simply needed focus. For starters, she'd focus on getting this apartment emptied out. Heading toward the far corner of the room, she picked up a box and opened it. Trophies. As Nathan had promised, the box was filled with trophies. All sizes and shapes and colors.

She picked one up shaped like a basketball and read the plaque. "To the Paxton Rocket's MVP for Eighth Grade."

Nathan came back through the door. With a grin, he headed over to take the trophy from her hands. "I'd forgotten about this."

Hailey nodded toward the box. "I can understand why. It looks like you mugged a trophy salesman." Leaning down, she picked up another trophy. This one was a football player. "Another MVP trophy."

Nathan shrugged. "What can I say? I'm good at sports."

Without meaning to, Hailey's brain flashed once more on the kiss. Sports weren't all he was good at.

Good grief. There she went again. Thinking about the kiss. Focus, focus, focus.

Trying to be as casual as possible, she took a couple of steps away from him. Distance. That's what she needed. Lots and lots of distance. And plenty of focus. Focus and distance. Distance and focus.

"Um, Hailey?"

She turned and looked at Nathan. "Yes?"

"Are you okay?"

She thought she was, but based on his tone, she guessed not. Looking down, she realized the problem. She was strangling the trophy she held. Literally strangling the poor football player. ''Oops. Sorry.''

She carefully replaced the trophy in the box. ''Why don't you display these?'' she asked, hoping to get her thoughts back on track.

Nathan laughed. ''I'd feel like a jerk, to tell you the truth. These are from when I was a kid. A lot of them don't mean anything. Everyone got a trophy.''

''Everyone got an MVP trophy in eighth grade? I don't think so. I was in the eighth grade, and I didn't get anything except a broken leg jumping over hurdles in Mrs. Delamaggio's P.E. class.''

She'd been trying to lessen the sexual awareness crackling between them, but her plan backfired. At the mention of her injury, Nathan's gaze shifted to her legs. Just for a second. Maybe only a fraction of a second. But it was long enough for her heart to do a thumpy-thump dance. When his gaze returned to meet hers, she could clearly see desire in his blue eyes. He wanted to kiss her again.

Just as she wanted to kiss him again. For a split second, they stood still, looking at each other. Then, almost as if choreographed, they took giant steps away from each other.

Boy, this was awkward. She could sense Nathan looking at her, but she refused to meet his gaze.

Things between them were getting worse instead of better.

"Hey, anyone up there?"

Relieved to hear the sound of someone else, Hailey turned toward the open front door. Nathan crossed the room and looked down the stairs. "Yeah, get on up here and give us a hand."

From the thundering noise coming up the stairs, Hailey figured an army was approaching. But after a couple of seconds, a dark-haired man walked through the door.

He flashed a grin, and Hailey immediately recognized the man from the pictures she'd seen on the mantel.

"Hailey, this is my younger brother, Trent."

Trent crossed the room and shook her hand. "Nice to meet you. You're the friend Leigh brought back from Austin, right?"

Hailey nodded, instantly liking the youngest Barrett brother. "Right. I'm working for Nathan for a few weeks."

Trent turned to Nathan and raised one brow. "Is that a fact? Well, good luck to you then." After glancing around the apartment, he asked, "So what's he got you doing? Helping him move the Nathan Memorial Shrine?"

Nathan groaned. "Cut it out."

Trent's grin only grew bigger. Leaning toward Hailey, he said, "Don't let that pretend modesty fool you. Nathan loves each and every prize in this collection Mom assembled for him."

"Did she collect all of your awards as well?" Hailey asked. But even before she'd completely finished speaking, both brothers laughed. "What?"

Nathan recovered first. "Trent wasn't exactly what you'd call a model kid growing up."

That surprised Hailey. She studied Trent. He had on a police officer's uniform. "Then isn't being on the police force an interesting career choice?"

Trent shrugged. "I'm the chief now, and let's just say, I mended my ways."

From the devious nature of Trent's grin, Hailey wasn't one hundred percent certain he'd completely mended his ways. She had the feeling that a few mischievous holes still existed in the man's soul.

Turning back toward Nathan, Trent asked, "Man, you look like executive roadkill." He winked at Hailey. "Doesn't Nathan look like hell, Hailey? The man's a heart attack waiting to happen."

Nathan frowned at Trent. "Very funny. Why are you here?"

"You're such a charmer, Nathan. Well, since you asked so nicely, I'll nicely answer. I heard Leigh had brought a visitor home from college, so I wanted to stop by and meet her." Trent smiled again at Hailey.

Nathan was frowning at his brother. "Okay, you've met her. You going to help us or simply stand there using up oxygen?"

Hailey bit back a smile at Nathan's comment. Trent wasn't the least offended. He nudged the clos-

est box with his foot. "Are you sure you're ready
to put this shrine into storage?"

"More than sure," Nathan said dryly.

Hailey believed him. Although she knew Nathan
had worked hard for all these accolades, they
seemed to embarrass him.

"Well, if you're sure." Trent picked up one of
the boxes. "Where am I carrying this?"

"Attic. And for Hailey's sake, be careful not to
fall down the stairs. Me, I don't care one way or the
other."

Trent nodded, grinned again at Hailey, then
headed out the door. As he clumped down the stairs,
he started whistling. It took a moment for Hailey to
recognize the song, but when she did, she laughed.

Nathan glanced at her. "What?"

"Trent. He's whistling 'I'm Too Sexy.'"

Nathan made a snorting noise very reminiscent of
Leigh's. "In his own mind."

Hailey laughed again, then turned her attention
back to packing. Carefully she replaced the trophies,
her fingers lingering on Nathan's name carved on
one or two. The man certainly had collected more
than his share.

Her gaze drifted to the man in question. He was
busy packing and taping boxes closed. As he
worked, Hailey studied him. Now there was a man
who was way too sexy, at least he was too sexy for
her own peace of mind.

The thunderous sound of Trent bounding back up
the stairs pulled her attention away from Nathan.

"Hey, I forgot to ask you," Trent said as soon as he came through the open door. "Have you heard who Leigh is dating? I can't believe it. Two seconds after Chase leaves on his honeymoon, and she's running around with Jared Kendrick. Have you talked to her yet?"

Nathan shook his head. "No. Not yet."

"Well one of us needs to and soon." He picked up another box.

Hailey couldn't resist pointing out again, "I think you should let Leigh decide who she wants to date. She's an adult."

Both brothers turned to look at her, their expressions almost identical. They were obviously horrified by her suggestion.

"You don't know Jared," Nathan finally said.

"But I know Leigh. She's smart. And savvy. She wouldn't date this man if he were as terrible as you think. I'm sure he's very nice."

The brothers laughed. "Nice? Jared? Um, not exactly the term I'd use," Nathan said. "The man makes Trent here look like a homebody."

Trent moved over and picked up the box Hailey had just finished packing. "I have an idea. I'm taking Sue Ann to the rodeo on Friday night. Hailey, why don't you and Nathan come along, and you can meet Jared yourself? I think you'll have a better idea why Nathan and I aren't too pleased about this."

"Who's Sue Ann?" Nathan asked.

Trent groaned. "Sue Ann. You know, the woman I'm dating."

Nathan looked puzzled. "Since when?"

"Nathan, you should be ashamed of yourself. I've been dating Sue Ann for almost a lifetime, and you don't even know her name?"

It did seem kind of remiss to Hailey. "I'd love to come to the rodeo. I've never been to one."

"Oh, you'll like it. Lots of fun." Trent headed back toward the door, but Nathan stepped in his way.

"Define a lifetime," Nathan said.

Trent shook his head. "Man, you work too hard. You're not even up-to-date on what's happening with your family. No wonder Leigh's taken up with Jared."

"Define a lifetime," Nathan repeated.

"I've been dating Sue Ann for almost two weeks." Trent nudged by his brother. "You need to get out more."

With that, Trent headed down the stairs.

"He considers two weeks a lifetime?" Hailey couldn't help asking.

"Yes. Trent's dating life runs on hyperdrive. He doesn't date any one woman for very long. The last I knew, he was dating a woman named Wendy."

"I guess we'll both get to meet Sue Ann at the same time," Hailey said.

Nathan shook his head. "Don't count on it. Friday's a long way away. Trent may be dating someone else by then."

"Those poor women."

"No, they know what Trent's like. None of them

take him seriously. He's a flirt, good for a few laughs, a little fun. But he's not the type to settle down. The ladies in this town know what kind of guy he is.''

For one split second, Hailey almost asked Nathan what kind of guy he was. But then she realized she already knew. Nathan was the forever kind. When he fell in love, he'd always stay in love. He'd settle in this town that adored him and live happily ever after with a no-doubt absolutely perfect wife who would be gorgeous and smart and funny and didn't need to constantly eat antacids to keep the bubbling in her stomach under control just because she was trying her darnedest to work on a doctoral thesis that didn't want to cooperate no matter what she tried and—

"You okay?" Nathan asked yet once again.

Hailey blinked. Good grief. Where had all that come from? She looked at Nathan. He was frowning at her.

Apparently she wasn't okay. Apparently she harbored a great deal of dislike for a woman Nathan hadn't even met yet. How weird was that? It wasn't like she was jealous. The last thing she wanted to do was fall for a man who had roots in a small town like this one. She had her own plans. Her own goals. She didn't want to live happily-ever-after with Nathan, even if he was a fantastic kisser.

Nathan moved toward her. "Really, are you okay?"

"Um, yeah. I'm fine," she finally managed to say once she remembered how to speak.

Oh, yeah, she was fine all right. Losing her mind. But other than that, right as rain.

Nathan was obviously unconvinced. "Are you sure?"

She could hardly tell him what she'd been thinking, so she settled for saying, "I was worrying about my dissertation."

"Ah." For a moment, he simply studied her and looked as if he might challenge her response. Then, thankfully, he turned and went back to work.

Hailey released the breath she'd been holding. Fumbling in her pocket, she pulled out an antacid and chewed it slowly.

Good thing she wasn't sticking around this town for much longer. Paxton was starting to get to her. If she didn't watch herself, pretty soon she'd be gossiping about Leigh and stepping over dogs that looked like they hadn't moved in a couple of years and sneaking into Nathan's office to do cheers.

Yep, it was a really good thing she was leaving in a few weeks. A really good thing.

5

"HEY, WHERE ARE YOU HIDING Hailey?" Leigh asked, waltzing into the family room like it wasn't almost two in the morning.

Nathan nodded toward the grandfather clock in the corner. "Kinda late, isn't it?"

Leigh flopped onto the sofa. "You're too young to be so old."

"Ha, very funny." Turning his options over in his mind, Nathan chose his words carefully. Yelling at Leigh won't do any good. As Hailey kept pointing out, his sister was an adult. A wild adult, but still an adult. So all he said was, "I worry about you, Leigh. I don't want you to get hurt."

She groaned. "I'm a grown woman. You and Trent and Chase have to accept it."

His gut instinct was to argue with her, but Leigh was right. He had to let her make her own choices in life even if those choices made him crazy.

It was so damn difficult not to worry about Leigh. She might be an adult, but she also attracted trouble like a picnic attracted ants.

"I'll butt out if you promise me you'll be careful," he finally said.

Leigh flashed him a grin. "Wow, Nathan, that's quite a concession from you. I can't believe it."

"Yeah, well, just so you know, I'm not too happy about it, either. Don't make me regret this, okay? That means, I'm not going to step in and save you, either, so be very careful what you do."

She drew an imaginary *X* on her chest. "I promise. I won't get in trouble."

"Why don't I believe that?"

"Because you're a cynic."

No, it was because he knew his sister. But as difficult as it was going to be, Nathan vowed he'd stand by his agreement. He'd butt out of her life, even if it drove him insane.

Leigh settled back on the couch, looking way too pleased with herself. "So you never told me what you did with Hailey."

"She moved into the garage apartment," he said. "And Trent and I really appreciate all the help you gave us."

Leigh laughed. "You're cute when you're snotty. Seriously, I would have helped. If I'd known."

"I told you twice that Hailey and I were cleaning out the apartment after work."

Leigh pretended to consider what he said. "Oh, you mean when you called this afternoon and said 'Leigh, we're cleaning out the apartment after work' you meant you were—"

"Cleaning out the apartment after work," he said dryly.

"Ah. Well, that explains why I got confused. You

need to be clearer when you tell me these things, Nathan. Jeez, I'm not a mind reader.''

''Funny. Very funny. Seriously you should spend at least a little time with Hailey. You did convince her to come to Paxton.''

Leigh narrowed her eyes. ''Are you getting tired of her company?''

His sister was being annoying, and she knew it. ''I don't think you're being a very good friend, that's all.''

''Ouch. Got me with that one. Okay, I'll spend more time with Hailey.'' Her expression brightened. ''I know, I'll ask her to come to the rodeo with me.''

''Trent already did,'' Nathan pointed out.

Leigh blinked. ''Excuse me?''

''He's taking his latest girlfriend to the rodeo on Friday and asked Hailey to come along.''

''Trent's taking Hailey along on one of his dates?'' Leigh's laughter bubbled out. ''Now that I'd like to see. Hailey, playing chaperone.''

''I'm coming with them, so it won't be like Hailey's a third wheel.''

The grin on Leigh's face turned downright mischievous. ''Oh, really? You're going along? What, as Hailey's date?''

Nathan frowned, not appreciating his sister's sense of humor in the least. ''Of course not.''

''Why not? I know you like Hailey.''

''She works for me, in case you've forgotten,'' Nathan said pointedly, hoping Leigh would get the hint and drop the subject. But true to form, the more sensitive the topic, the more it interested Leigh.

"Is that the best excuse you can come up with?" Leigh said with a snort. "If you like Hailey, you should go ahead and date her."

"I have no interest in dating Hailey," Nathan maintained, knowing that he was lying like a rug. Lying badly, too. But the last person he wanted to discuss Hailey with was Leigh. "I simply thought she might be more comfortable going to the rodeo if I came along, too."

Leigh clearly didn't buy his excuse for a second. "Seriously, why don't you go out with Hailey? I think the two of you would be perfect together."

Suspicion slammed into Nathan. He hadn't been born yesterday, and he could smell one of Leigh's plots a mile away. Not that this one was proving to be much of a challenge. His sister's intentions had been fairly obvious all along.

"Leigh, I know your plan is to try to fix me up with Hailey."

She fluttered her eyelashes. "Who me? Never."

Nathan ignored her denial and continued, "It isn't going to work. Hailey and I are too different, and we both have our own agendas and things we want to achieve. It would never work out between us, so stop being a pest."

"That's a nice little speech. Who are you trying to convince—you or me?"

Nathan sighed. Today had been a really long day, and the last thing he wanted to do was discuss

Hailey with Leigh. Hell, he didn't want to think about Hailey at all. He'd done way too much of that today as it was.

"Why don't we spend a little time talking about you and Jared? Seems to me you two are spending way too much time together."

Leigh laughed. "Oh, touché, big brother. Nice way to turn the tables. So okay, if you want to talk about Jared, we will. He and I have gone out on a couple of dates. Nothing serious and it's no big deal."

It took every ounce of Nathan's self-control not to point out to his sister that Jared was hardly the right sort of man for her to be dating. Leigh knew very well what sort Jared was, and he'd promised to back off. But promising and doing were two very different things.

"You know I'm worried about you?" was all he finally said.

Leigh crossed the room and gave him a big hug. "Yes. And you're sweet to be that way. A total pain in the rear, of course. But sweet."

Nathan chuckled. "Thanks. I think."

"So here's the deal. I'll butt out of your love life, and you'll butt out of mine. That way we'll both have only ourselves to blame no matter how things turn out."

Since Nathan would give anything to keep Leigh from meddling in his love life, he accepted the agreement. He wasn't happy about it because he really felt she was making a huge mistake by going out with Jared. But he accepted it.

"Deal," he reluctantly said.

Leigh hugged him again and gave him a loud, smacking kiss on his cheek. "Did I ever tell you that you're my favorite brother?"

"You're a natural born con artist, kiddo."

"It's a talent, what can I say?"

Nathan couldn't help laughing. His sister drove him nuts and worried him sick. She also made his life a lot of fun. He wanted the very best for her.

"Promise you'll be careful," he said.

Leigh sighed. "You know, I'm not the only one who should be worried about winding up with a broken heart. You could be in trouble and not even know it."

Nathan wanted to argue but couldn't. When the lady had a point, she had a point.

"ARE ALL RODEOS THIS NOISY?" Hailey asked, leaning closer to Nathan.

He grinned. "If they're done right they are. Why, is it getting to you?"

Hailey shook her head. No. The noise wasn't bothering her. Not really. In fact, for the most part, she found the experience exhilarating. It was hard to believe she'd lived in Texas so long and hadn't once gone to a rodeo. But up until tonight, she'd never imagined she'd have fun at a rodeo.

Of course, she'd never been to one with Nathan before.

"The man on the horse is Jared," Nathan said, indicating a tall rider in the main arena. "That means Leigh's probably around somewhere nearby."

Hailey scanned the crowd, finally spotting Leigh on the far side. "She's right there."

Nathan nodded. "See. I knew she'd be nearby. She can no more resist Jared than a bird can resist a freshly washed car."

His tone was resigned, but Hailey didn't buy Nathan's act for a minute. He didn't like Leigh dating this Jared person, but he was trying to be civilized about the situation. On her other side, Trent had no such reluctance. He'd kept up a running soliloquy for the past half hour about how his sister was involved with the wrong guy.

Not that Trent's date seemed to be his soul mate. As far as Hailey could tell, Sue Ann Finely had ogled every man in the place. Twice. The petite redhead wasn't exactly subtle, either. She'd even oohed and aahed a couple of times and once leaned over Trent to nudge Hailey and say, "Check out the guy in the white Stetson."

No, Trent and Sue Ann weren't a love match. Trent was equally unfocused on his date. If he wasn't complaining about Jared, he was smiling at the women who stopped by to say hi to one or both of the Barrett brothers.

Hailey was finding the show in the stands much more interesting than anything happening in the arena. Six women had already stopped by specifically to say hello to Nathan. Caitlin Estes had stopped by twice. And each time, Hailey made herself ignore any inappropriate feelings she might have toward the women flirting with Nathan. It wasn't any of her business, and she certainly wasn't jealous. Nathan was her boss, and hopefully, her friend. But that was all.

And she reminded herself of that each and every time one of those hussies…er, um *ladies* stopped by to say hello.

Trent hollered across Hailey to get his brother's attention. "Hey, Nathan, maybe we'll luck out and Jared will disappear like he did before, then our problems are solved."

"Don't be a meanie," Sue Ann said. "Jared's a great guy."

Both Trent and Nathan snorted in unison, and Hailey bit back a smile. These Barretts certainly weren't shy about letting the world know their opinions.

"*Great* is a relative term, Sue Ann," Nathan muttered.

Sue Ann frowned. "He's not my relative. I just like him."

"That's not what I meant," Nathan started. "I meant that not everyone thinks he's great."

Sue Ann turned in her seat so she could half-face Nathan. The movement made her oversize silver earrings sway and bob, and Hailey once more found herself wondering why a woman as tiny as Sue Ann would want to wear earrings the size of grapefruit.

They kept clinking and clanking. Just like the rodeo, Sue Ann's earrings were making a lot of noise.

"Well, whatever you meant, you're wrong about Jared. He is great. And trust me, I should know. I used to date a rodeo clown," Sue Ann announced. Then she settled back in her seat as if she'd somehow ended the argument.

Nathan glanced at Hailey, a baffled expression on his face. "What?"

Hailey shrugged. "Beats me."

Before any of them could ask Sue Ann to explain, she stood, straightened her T-shirt that read Everything Is Bigger In Texas, and said "Y'all please excuse me while I go to the little girls' room."

Nathan had a definite twinkle in his eyes when after Sue Ann left, he leaned toward Hailey and asked, "You want to ask about the rodeo clown or should I?"

"You ask." Hailey took a sip of her soda. "I'm happy pretending I know what's she's talking about."

Nathan sighed with exaggerated dramatic flare. "Fine. I'll ask." He looked at his brother. "I don't suppose you know what Sue Ann meant. I mean, you have been dating the woman for a lifetime."

Trent shook his head. "Haven't a clue. But Sue Ann is like that. Full of mystery. I prefer to remain unenlightened most of the time."

Hailey turned to look at him. "Trent, how can you build a relationship with someone when you don't make an effort to understand them?"

Trent scratched the side of his face. "Relationship? Let me think here for a second." He snapped his fingers and grinned. "That's right. I'm not worried about my relationship with Sue Ann because we don't have a relationship. We're just dating."

A loud cheer went up from the crowd, momentarily distracting Hailey. Jared must have done something good in the rodeo world, but Hailey hadn't a clue what it was, so she turned her attention back to Trent just as Sue Ann returned from the restroom.

"Still, I think when two people are dating, they should understand each other. Know how the other one feels about a lot of subjects. It's not enough to simply share common interests. You should know a great deal about the other person."

Sue Ann settled back into her seat, gave Trent a loud, smacking kiss, then looked at Hailey. "What sort of things should you know?"

Hailey shrugged. "Well, for starters, there's the usual. Where each of you went to school. Your birthday. Things about your family. Your goals and dreams. Then you should also learn each other's philosophies and ideologies."

Sue Ann blinked. Twice. "Why would I need to know all that? We're just dating."

Hailey couldn't believe they were having this conversation. It seemed to her this was obvious. "Aren't you curious about the person you're dating?"

Sue Ann grinned. "Oh, honey. I know plenty

about Trent. Plenty.'' Then she proceeded to give Trent a couple more smacky kisses.

Hailey was all set to continue her debate with Sue Ann and Trent as soon as they came up for air, but Nathan patted her on the arm. ''You might as well let it go. They're not going to see this your way. Trent doesn't do relationships, and he doesn't date women who do relationships.''

With a sigh, Hailey settled back in her seat. ''I just don't understand. How can they not know at least the fundamentals, like each other's birthday?''

''Different approaches to life, I guess.''

''It's not like the two of you know each other's birthdays, either,'' Trent said, draping an arm around Sue Ann.

''Hailey and I aren't dating—''

''September 7,'' Hailey said without thinking.

Nathan turned and looked at her, surprise evident on his handsome face. ''You know when my birthday is? Why?''

''Your previous assistant had it marked on the calendar,'' Hailey confessed, feeling like a fool for offering up the information. Now both Trent and Sue Ann were grinning at her as if she'd let slip some great state secret.

''So Nathan,'' Trent said slowly. ''I don't suppose there's any chance you know when Hailey's birthday is?''

''That really doesn't prove anything, so wipe that stupid smirk off your face,'' Nathan said.

Sue Ann looked from Hailey to Nathan then back at Hailey. "Does that mean he knows?"

Truthfully Hailey wasn't sure. She also wasn't sure that she wanted to know if he knew.

"It doesn't matter," she hurriedly said, wanting to direct the conversation in a new—and hopefully not so dangerous—direction. "All I was trying to say was that it seems to me that people who are dating would want to share information about themselves."

Sue Ann leaned across Trent and yelled to Nathan, "Hey, do you know when her birthday is or not? You never did answer my question."

Nathan frowned. "Hailey's point is that—"

"I think he knows," Sue Ann announced in a singsong voice. "I think he knows." She looked at Trent. "Seems to me, these two sure talk a lot about being honest and up-front with people, but then they sure are sneaky about some things."

Trent grinned at his brother. "I couldn't agree with you more, Sue Ann. And usually Nathan is such a trustworthy, forthright person. I can't imagine what's gotten into him tonight."

Nathan groaned. "I don't know what I did to deserve you as a brother."

"Stood in the right place at the right time. Seriously, you need me in your life, Nathan. I keep you on your toes. So now, tell me. When's Hailey's birthday?"

For a second, Nathan remained silent. Then he said, "November 11."

That was the last thing Hailey had expected. Stunned, she turned to look at him. "How in the world did you know? I never told you when my birthday was."

"It was on your application. I'm good at remembering numbers."

For several long moments, Hailey simply looked at Nathan. She was surprised by his revelation. Truly surprised. Next to her, Trent and Sue Ann laughed and teased, but Hailey couldn't focus on their nonsense. All she could focus on was Nathan.

Then another cheer from the crowd broke the spell that had settled over her. She blinked and looked away from Nathan.

"I knew you'd know when her birthday was. You can't fool me," Trent said.

Nathan gave his brother a narrow-eyed look. "Just because I know when her birthday is doesn't mean anything."

"Sure it does."

Hailey had to jump in on this one. "No, Trent, it doesn't. As Nathan explained, he's good at remembering numbers and happens to remember when my birthday is. It doesn't mean anything."

"Then why doesn't Trent remember when my birthday is?" Sue Ann asked with a pout. "I've told him a couple of times but he keeps forgetting."

"Trent has the manners of a warthog," Nathan explained.

Rather than being offended, Trent laughed again.

"Not true. It's just that while you're good with numbers, I'm the brother who's good with his hands."

"I can swear to that," Sue Ann said with a giggle.

For one stupid nanosecond, Hailey wanted to point out that Trent wasn't the only talented Barrett brother. Nathan had fogged her windows when he'd kissed her. But thankfully, before she could say something that would embarrass both her and Nathan, common sense returned and she kept her mouth shut. The last thing she wanted to do was fuel any errant speculation.

But boy-oh-boy, was she tempted.

"DID YOU ENJOY THE RODEO?" Nathan asked on the drive home. So far, Hailey had been pretty silent. Not that he'd set any records for conversation himself, but still, the silence in the car was starting to be awkward.

Of course, that wasn't what was bothering him the most. What bothered him more was the reason that the silence was awkward. He was way too aware of Hailey sitting next to him. All evening, he'd been at war with himself, wanting to kiss her, to touch her again.

How stupid could he be?

Apparently very stupid since despite his best efforts, he couldn't stop thinking about kissing her. So now he was hoping if he could get Hailey talking, it would take his mind off of all the other things he had no damn business thinking about. Like how great it felt to hold her. And touch her. And kiss her.

"The rodeo was interesting," she said. "But I wish I'd had a chance to talk to Leigh. I haven't seen much of her since I came to Paxton. But she obviously had a great time. She seemed so excited tonight at the rodeo."

"When the words *Leigh* and *excited* end up in a sentence together, bad things usually happen," Nathan said dryly.

Hailey laughed. "Oh come on, your sister isn't that bad."

Nathan couldn't help asking, "Are you certain you've actually met my sister? Because if you have, I can't believe you'd say that."

"I'll admit, she has a different approach to life. But she's smart and fun and determined."

Nathan pulled the car into the driveway and parked it inside the garage. "It's the determined part that worries me. You didn't have a chance to meet Jared tonight, but trust me, he isn't the type to settle down and raise two-point-five children."

"Don't take this the wrong way, because I know Leigh's your sister, but I don't think she's looking for a guy to settle down with."

Hailey shifted in her seat so she was turned toward him. In the bright light in the garage, Nathan could clearly see her face. She smiled slowly, and lust slammed into him. She was so pretty, so sweet and smart. No matter what his brain told him about not being attracted to her, his body had tuned him out.

Almost against his will, he reached out and brushed a couple of strands of hair away from her eyes. Hailey seemed surprised by his action, but she didn't pull back.

"What about you? Are you looking for two-point-five children?" he asked, then wanted to hit himself in the head with a laptop computer when he did. What was wrong with him? He shouldn't be touching Hailey's soft hair. Nor should he be flirting with her.

Hailey opened her car door and climbed out. Nathan reluctantly did the same.

"I'm too busy right now to think about things like that," she said, shutting her car door. The metallic click the door made seemed to add an auditory emphasis to her statement. "After all these years, I'm finally going to get my doctorate. I'm also going to have a chance to spend time with my father. My future is mapped out."

Nathan nodded and waited for her to precede him out of the garage. "I wasn't talking about right now. I know you've got plans. I meant later."

Hailey stopped at the bottom of the stairs leading to the garage apartment. She turned her head to look at him. "I haven't really thought about it. I was an only child who was raised to act more like an adult than like a child. I don't know much about children. I don't even know if I'd make a good mother."

"Of course you would." He moved closer to her. "Look at how patient you are with Leigh."

Hailey laughed softly, the sound enticing in the still night air. "You love your sister, and you know it."

"Yeah, I do," he admitted. He nodded toward the top of the stairs. "My mother raised me too well not to walk you to your door."

"You're kidding, right? I'm what? Fifteen steps from the top?"

"If you'd known my mom, you'd understand why I have to do this."

Hailey rolled her eyes, but her smile made it clear she didn't object. "Fine. Far be it from me to undo a mother's training."

She preceded him up the steps, stopping once or twice to glance around and say, "See any monsters yet? Any robbers?"

Nathan simply sighed and continued to follow her. But when they reached the landing and Hailey opened the door, he realized immediately that he'd had an ulterior motive all along. Because the second she opened that door, he followed her inside the apartment without once considering the consequences.

"See, I'm safely home," she said, turning on the small lamp by the door. "Thanks again for taking me to the rodeo. It was fun."

The atmosphere between them seemed to crackle. He should never have followed her up the stairs. He should have stayed downstairs, far away from her.

Far away from temptation. But all of the IQ tests he'd taken in school were dead wrong about him— he wasn't smart. He wasn't even marginally bright.

He was the stupidest man to ever draw a breath because even knowing he shouldn't, he leaned forward and kissed Hailey.

6
_____

HAILEY DIDN'T EVEN THINK about pulling away. She'd wanted Nathan to kiss her since the last time on the basketball court. So here she was, getting her wish.

Without questioning her good fortune, when Nathan slid his tongue across her bottom lip, Hailey opened her mouth, rose up on her toes and slipped her arms around his neck. He instantly accepted the offer she made, wrapping his strong arms around her and settling her body intimately against him. Then his tongue met hers in a slow, seductive dance.

Yahoo.

Instinctively Hailey pressed harder against him. He sure could kiss. She felt him everywhere, heat flooding through her. Maybe someday she'd be embarrassed that she'd acted this way, but not tonight. Tonight, she wanted this kiss to go on forever.

He turned her slightly and backed her against the door. Then, he cupped her upturned face as he deepened the kiss. Hailey was lost in the wonder of his embrace when the sound of a car engine coming up the driveway finally seeped through her lust-fogged brain.

Nathan heard it, too, and he ended the kiss and leaned his forehead against hers.

"Leigh," he said finally, his voice husky.

It took a minute for his meaning to dawn on Hailey, but when it did, she slipped out of his embrace and hurriedly put the distance of the small living room between them. Leigh was home from her date, and the last thing Hailey wanted was for her friend to find her kissing Nathan.

Truthfully, calling what they'd just been doing kissing was like calling a tornado a gentle breeze. They'd been on fire, and it was going to take some doing for her to get her pulse rate under control.

Nathan didn't seem to be doing much better. Unfulfilled desire still heated his gaze and his breathing was rapid and ragged.

"I should leave," he said.

Hailey nodded. "Probably the best idea."

But he didn't leave. He stood looking at her. He seemed as consumed by indecision as she was. They both knew the right thing for him to do was to leave. But a part of Hailey, a really nosy, annoying part, couldn't help wishing he'd forget about doing the smart thing and instead cross the room and kiss her crazy once more.

But Nathan didn't move. Instead he remained across the room from her and said, "We need to stop kissing like that."

Before Hailey could stop herself, she asked, "How would you like to kiss?"

Nathan tipped his head and gave her a mischievous look. "You know what I mean."

Yes, she did. Unfortunately.

"What do you suggest? I mean, we both already agreed not to kiss again, and yet we did," she pointed out. "And we're both equally guilty, since I kissed you the first time, but you kissed me this second time."

"True." Nathan leaned against the door, obviously lost in thought. Hailey waited patiently for any suggestion he might have. She certainly didn't have one of her own to offer. She wanted Nathan. A lot. And even though getting involved with him would mess up her plans, she couldn't seem to get her brain to win the war it was fighting with her traitorous body.

"I know," Nathan finally said. "We'll penalize ourselves."

"How?"

"The next person to kiss the other could forfeit a hundred dollars."

Hailey wrinkled her nose. "Unfair. You have a lot more money than I do. Think of something else."

"I can't. Do you have any suggestions?"

Give in to temptation?

Okay, bad idea. "Let me think." But the longer she thought, the fewer ideas came to her. She couldn't afford to lose any money, and she also wasn't completely sure that she wouldn't kiss Nathan again. So that meant that whatever punishment they thought of couldn't be too terrible. Just on the off chance she lost the wager, of course.

An idea eventually occurred to her. "How about the loser washes the winner's car?"

"Which one is considered the loser and which one is considered the winner?

She frowned. "Whoever kisses the other first has to wash the other person's car."

Nathan looked openly dubious. "You think that's a strong enough incentive to keep us from kissing?"

"It's the best I can think of. Unless you have a better idea."

"No," he said. "Okay, that will be our penalty." He opened the door. "Leigh's already inside, so I'm going to head on home. Talk to you tomorrow."

"See you."

Right before he shut the door he said, "For the record, I have a feeling that before this summer is over, we'll both end up with really clean cars."

Funny, she had the exact same feeling.

"YOUNG MAN, DO YOU HAVE any idea how late it is?" Leigh teased the second Nathan walked into the kitchen. "Have you been hanging out with floo-zies and ne'er-do-wells?"

Great. Just great. He should have expected his sister to ambush him.

"You haven't been home long yourself," he pointed out.

She laughed. "True, but then, I was with a ne'er-do-well, which means you must have been with a floozy."

"Very funny."

"Seriously, didn't you just leave Hailey's apartment?" She gave him a wicked grin. "Anything happen I should know about? Do I need to clear my calendar and make room for another wedding?"

Although Nathan knew Leigh was only kidding, he couldn't stop himself from glaring at her.

"For your information, I walked Hailey to her apartment door when we got home from the rodeo. It's that simple, so don't make a big deal out of this." He walked past her and got a soda out of the refrigerator. Even though it was after midnight, he needed something to help him cool off. The kiss he'd shared with Hailey still had his blood simmering.

Leigh leaned against the counter and crossed her arms over her chest. Nathan could almost see the gears grinding in her devious mind, and he decided to head her off before she started plotting and planning.

"How about you? Should I start dusting off my tux for a wedding between you and Jared?"

Leigh laughed. "As if. And you know it. So is this your way of telling me to mind my own business?"

"Yes," he admitted.

For a couple of seconds, Leigh studied him. Just when Nathan had given up hope, she shrugged.

"Fine by me. Don't tell me what's up between

you and Hailey. I won't pry. But you were the one who pointed out to me that Hailey is a woman who's got her life mapped out, and is probably not the right woman for you. I'm only reminding you because I don't want to see you get hurt when she leaves.''

The warning seemed ridiculous coming from Leigh. She was the one in danger of getting hurt, not him. Still, he appreciated the thought behind her concern.

''I have nothing to worry about, Leigh. I already told you, I'm not getting involved with Hailey.''

''Whatever you say,'' she said. ''But for the record, I look best in bridesmaid gowns that are burgundy, blue, or green. Whatever happens, I do *not* want to be stuck in a yellow gown. I look like a giant French fry. Got it?''

Nathan frowned. ''Go to bed, Leigh.''

''Okey dokey.'' Laughing, his sister headed up the back stairs. But long after she went to bed, Nathan sat in his study, wondering what in the world he was going to do about this attraction he felt for Hailey. Not only were they all wrong for each other, but now wasn't the time to let himself get distracted. He couldn't get involved with a woman right now. Maybe after BizExpo. Maybe after EZBooks became a success.

But not now.

And besides, it wasn't like he could build a future with Hailey. In a few weeks, she was returning to Austin and then moving to Massachusetts after that. The best they could hope for was a fling. Is that really what he wanted at this point in his life? He was too old not to think about the future.

And much too old to be acting like a lust-crazed teenager. So the best approach would be to only see Hailey at work. He'd make certain he didn't spend time with her outside the office. That way he wouldn't be tempted to touch her or kiss her again.

Okay, maybe he'd be tempted, but he wouldn't be able to act on that temptation. And at this point, he'd settle for what he could get.

Avoidance. That was the key. He had to avoid Hailey at all costs. He wouldn't get caught within twenty feet of the woman.

"IT'S REALLY NICE OF YOU to invite me to your brother's house for dinner," Hailey said two days later as she sat in the passenger's seat of Nathan's luxury sedan.

"Ha, like he had a choice," Leigh said with a snort from the back seat. "Megan and Chase want to meet you. He was told to bring us both to dinner. No arguments."

Hailey turned and looked at her friend. "Still, it's nice of Nathan to drive."

Again, Leigh snorted. "You're thanking him for nothing. He's one of those guys who always drives. Always. He's got that have-to-be-in-control thing that prevents him from letting someone else take over." She tapped her brother on the shoulder. "Isn't that right, Nathan?"

"Huh? Are you talking to me? I thought you were

going to just talk *about* me the whole drive without once acknowledging that I'm sitting right here. I was worried for a second that I'd gone invisible.''

Leigh laughed, and Hailey couldn't help smiling at Nathan's good-natured teasing.

''You're such a jerk,'' Leigh said, laughter still tinting her voice. ''Seriously, tell Hailey how you always like to be in charge.''

''I only like to be in charge, Leigh, because I'm always right about things.''

Hailey had to laugh now. ''Oh, please. No one is always right. Everyone is occasionally wrong.''

''Not Nathan,'' Leigh said from the back seat. ''I can't think of a single time when he's been wrong. It really fries my hush puppies, but it's true.''

That was ridiculous and couldn't possibly be accurate. ''He wouldn't be human if he didn't make mistakes,'' Hailey said. And she of all people knew that Nathan was human. Boy-oh-boy, did she ever. The man was definitely flesh and blood and kisses hot enough to make her toes curl.

Just the thought of the last kiss they'd shared distracted her to the point where it took a couple of seconds for her to realize Leigh was talking to her.

''…so when the weather people said it wasn't going to rain, Daddy told Nathan he was about to be proven wrong. But it didn't rain. It poured. It deluged. Just like Nathan said it would. So even as a kid, he was never wrong.''

Although Hailey had missed the first part of

Leigh's story, she'd heard enough to get the gist of it.

"That's an educated guess," Hailey said. She shifted in her seat to look at Nathan. He seemed highly amused by the entire conversation. No doubt his ego was feeling pretty well fed with his sister singing his praises this way.

But come on! Never wrong? It was impossible.

And blatantly untrue. Two nights ago, when he'd kissed her, he'd been wrong. They both had agreed not to kiss anymore, and yet Nathan had broken that promise. He'd been the one to kiss her. This time it hadn't been the other way around.

But that was an example she couldn't share with Leigh.

"And then there's Rufus," Leigh went on. "Last year, everyone said there was no way to get that dog into a car and take him to the vet. His owner, Steve Myerson, was frantic. Paxton doesn't have its own vet, so Rufus has to be driven to where there is one. Nathan finally got involved and solved the problem."

Despite herself, Hailey had to know. "What did you do?" she asked Nathan.

"Nothing special." Nathan turned the car down a long, narrow driveway leading to what looked like a pretty, white house.

"Double ha," Leigh said. "He knew right away what would work. And he was right. The dog has a thing for bright pink tennis balls. Not white or yellow. The ball has to be pink. But if you throw one, he will follow. Well, sort of. As much as Rufus follows anything. Somehow Nathan knew it would work.''

''You're able to read the minds of dogs?'' Hailey teased. ''Wow, now there's a skill that could come in handy. Met any talking horses? Chickens with a lot on their minds? Interesting cows?''

Nathan chuckled, the sound was rich and deep. Without trying, she could remember every detail of his last kiss. The way he'd held her in his arms. The way his mouth had felt against her own. The way—

Stop it!

Hailey mentally kicked herself. Enough of that. She was not going to think about kissing Nathan again. Thinking about him was bad for her health. At least for her mental health. He should come with a big warning label slapped on his side that said: Contact With Lonely Women Can Result In A Loss Of Intelligence.

Because that was the problem with kissing Nathan—it confused her. A lot. Every time she kissed him, she lost all sense of priority. Up until meeting Nathan, she'd always thought she had the willpower of three people. Now she knew that when really tempted, she caved quicker than a sand castle hit by a wave.

Not that it was entirely her fault, though. The man was gorgeous and smart and nice and one heck of a kisser. Plus, when he took off his shirt to play basketball, the sun gleamed across his strong muscles and—

"Yoo-hoo, Hailey?" Leigh said from behind her. "You still with us or have you been secretly kidnapped by aliens who left your body behind? If it's the aliens thing, dibs on selling the story to the tabloids."

Hailey blew out a shaky breath. Wow. She really needed to get herself under control. Finally she managed to ask, "What did you want, Leigh?"

"You're not listening to us. Nathan asked you a question, and you've been sitting there like a zombie," Leigh said.

She had? She was? Good grief. With effort, Hailey turned her head and looked at Leigh, her mind still struggling to banish the image she'd conjured up of Nathan without a shirt. Um. What were they talking about? Oh, right. Her losing her mind.

"I'm still here," she said. "Sorry. I was thinking about—" Words failed her. What could she say? She'd been thinking about...

Nathan.

She shook her head and tried again. "Work."

Leigh frowned. "Work? You mean your dissertation?"

Relief flowed through Hailey, and she lunged for the excuse. "Exactly. My dissertation. I was thinking about my dissertation."

Leigh snorted. "As if."

Hailey made a snorting noise right back. "It's the truth."

"Yeah right, and I'm the Tooth Fairy."

"Leave her alone," Nathan told his sister, pulling his car up in front of a two-story house.

Leigh held up her hands. "Fine. I won't bother Hailey." She opened her door and right before she stepped out, she said to her brother, "But I mean it—no yellow."

"What is she talking about? No yellow what?" Hailey looked at Nathan, hoping her errant thoughts had calmed down enough that she wouldn't keep having erotic images of him.

Wrong. One smile from him and her heart took off like a thoroughbred in an open field. This dinner with Nathan's family was going to be much more difficult than she'd anticipated if she couldn't get her libido under control.

"Are you okay?" Nathan asked.

Oh, no. Not that again. Hailey forced a smile across her face, but she knew desire still flickered in her gaze. She could see the answering attraction on Nathan's face. For countless seconds, they simply looked at each other. Then Hailey finally managed to say in a way-too-raspy voice, "I'm fine. Truly fine."

Nathan grinned. "Yeah. I know."

"WHAT'S TAKING YOU SO LONG? Hurry up," Trent yelled at Nathan.

Nathan headed down the porch steps and crossed over to Chase's garage. As usual following a Sunday dinner, he and Trent were admiring the classic 1956 Pontiac Star Chief Chase was restoring. But this ritual was all that was usual about today. Not a single other thing was the way it normally was. Chase had spent the past two hours flirting and kissing with his new wife, Megan. And Trent had brought yet another new girlfriend to dinner. What was her name? Amber? Autumn? Azalea?

"What's your date's name?" he asked Trent when he rejoined his brothers.

Trent shot a narrowed-eyed look at Nathan. "Azure. Her name is Azure."

"Right. Azure." Nathan watched as Trent ran one hand over the new chrome fender Chase had added in the past week.

"This car is a beauty, Chase," Trent said.

Nathan had to ask, "Trent, what happened to Sue Ann? You seemed pretty happy at the rodeo two nights ago."

Chase turned to look at Trent. "You've changed girlfriends in the past two days? When are you going to learn that the grass isn't greener?"

Trent grinned. "When the grass stops being greener."

"You've got the wrong attitude toward love," Chase said.

"Who's talking about love? I thought we were talking about dating." Trent laughed at his own joke.

"He's going to die alone because he's never going to grow up and become an adult," Chase said to Nathan. "A man needs to settle down at some point in his life."

Nathan couldn't help laughing. "That's what you say now that you're in love with Megan. But if memory serves me, you were kicking and screaming about not falling in love just a few months ago, Chase. You drove Trent and me crazy telling us you didn't believe in love and there was no way you were in love with Megan."

"I was a fool," Chase said, then he said to Trent, "Hey, stop touching the chrome."

"Jeez, I'm not three, Chase."

Chase looked at Nathan. "He does a pretty good imitation, doesn't he?"

"Funny. Very funny." Trent went back to admiring the car.

Chase moved over to stand next to Trent. "Seriously, marriage is wonderful. A man needs to find a special woman and build a life with her."

Both Nathan and Trent dissolved into laughter.

"What?" Chase asked, looking affronted. "It's true."

"You sound like a greeting card," Trent said.

Chase snorted. "You two are just jealous because I've found someone great, and you'll be lucky to have a buzzard give you a second look."

Boy, Chase's tune sure had changed since he'd married Megan. If ever there'd been a man who was convinced love didn't exist, it had been Chase.

But Megan had changed his mind.

Just thinking about his brother's happy marriage made Nathan wish things were different with Hailey. She was unlike any woman he'd ever met. Not only was he attracted to her, but he also loved spending time with her, listening to her, joking with her.

She was one special lady.

"Yo, Nathan. Are you having a stroke or something?" Trent trotted over and slapped him on the back, knocking most of the air right out of Nathan's lungs. "You look weird."

Nathan struggled to regain his breath. "Hey, Trent, you almost killed me."

"I did not," Trent maintained. He turned toward Chase, seeking confirmation. "I was trying to help. He looked weird, didn't he Chase?"

"Yeah, you looked weird." Chase adjusted the side mirror. "You looked even weirder than usual."

"Very funny." Nathan finally recovered his balance and shifted away from Trent. "Don't hit me anymore, okay?"

"Fine, but don't look weird then," Trent said.

"Any chance that weird expression on your face had something to do with your date, Hailey Montgomery?" Chase asked.

"She's not my date."

Chase nodded. "Okay. Then any chance that weird expression on your face had something to do with your not-date, Hailey Montgomery?"

Nathan groaned. "No. Hailey and I are just friends."

"Megan and Chase were just friends until they started having wild and wicked sex," Trent pointed out. "Maybe you and Hailey are that kind of friends."

"No, we're not."

Trent grinned. "Too bad. Personally I'm looking for a female friend like that. Sounds like a heck of a deal to me."

"You're an idiot, Trent. No woman is ever going to want to marry you," Chase said.

Trent's grin only grew wider. "That's the general idea."

After Trent went back to admiring the car, Chase looked at Nathan. "Seriously. Are you okay?"

"Yes. Just thinking about work."

"How's the program coming along?"

"It has problems," Nathan admitted. "I'm not sure it will be ready in time for BizExpo."

"Sure it will," Trent said. "You always pull the fat out of the fire, Nathan. You will this time, too."

Nathan wished he shared his brother's confidence, but he didn't. He wasn't sure this time he could make a minor miracle happen.

But he sure hoped he could.

The back door opened, and Megan stepped out onto the porch. "Chase, honey, are you boys going to stay out here all night?"

As soon as Megan appeared, Chase's face lit up. Nathan couldn't help feeling a little jealous of the happiness his brother had found. Unlike Trent, he'd like to find someone special and build a life together in Paxton.

Too bad that woman couldn't be Hailey.

"We're done," Chase said, trotting over to join Megan.

"Ah, jeez," Trent said when Chase kissed his new wife. "There they go again. Hey, Chase, is this how it's going to be from now on? Whenever Megan calls, you come running?"

Chase grinned. "Oh, yeah. You bet. As fast as I can." Then he kissed his wife again, and they went inside the house.

"Face it, Trent. Chase is in love."

Trent hung his head. "It's a sad day when a man walks away from his brothers for a woman."

Nathan laughed and headed toward the house. "You really aren't ever going to find anyone to marry you, Trent."

"Amen to that," Trent said. "Amen to that."

7

HAILEY TURNED WHEN SHE HEARD the back door open. As soon as Nathan entered the kitchen, his gaze met hers. As always, she felt a thrill of excitement dance through her.

Good grief. She didn't want to be so attracted to this man. He had roots so deep in this town they could strike oil. And his family was like one, big meddlesome mob. Although she liked them, she couldn't get used to how easily they delved into each other's lives.

"Good, the men are here," Leigh said, setting the last of the dirty dinner plates on the kitchen counter. "We women are officially off duty now. Let's go sprawl in the family room, watch some sports thingee on TV and scratch ourselves in impolite places while the guys take care of the dishes."

Hailey laughed. "Um, Leigh, I'm not sure doing the dishes doesn't sound a whole lot better than what you've suggested."

"Oh, okay," Leigh said with a huff. She turned to Azure and Megan. "I suppose you two want to do something gentile and ladylike as well."

Megan was laughing, but Azure frowned. "Why do we have to scratch?"

Leigh snorted and rolled her eyes at Trent. Then she said to Azure, "Don't worry about it, hon. Just come on along."

Still muttering about not wanting to scratch anything, Azure followed Leigh, her stiletto heals clacking loudly on the wooden floor. At a little over twenty years old, Azure was the youngest person at the dinner. She also seemed the most baffled. She didn't seem to follow any of the conversations. Hailey figured Azure and Trent wouldn't be dating too long. At least she hoped not for both of their sakes.

"I'm so glad I had the chance to meet you," Megan said as she fell into step with Hailey. "Leigh mentioned she was bringing a friend home from college, but with Leigh, you never know if you should anticipate something wonderful or run for cover."

Hailey smiled at Megan. She really liked Chase's wife. She was smart, nice and levelheaded. "I know what you mean about Leigh. She's something else."

"Who's something else?" Leigh asked when they reached the family room.

"You," Hailey explained, settling on the over-stuffed couch.

Azure frowned again. "What else are you, Leigh?"

Leigh snorted again, but Megan leaned over and

patted Azure's hand. "Don't worry about it. Hailey simply meant that Leigh is a bit…"

Leigh leaned forward in her chair. "Yeah, I'd like to hear this, too. I'm a bit?"

"Crazy," Hailey supplied at the same time Megan said, "Wild."

Leigh laughed. "Yeah, I can be both of those things sometimes. But come on? Who can blame me? You've seen the guys I grew up with. It's a miracle I'm not in jail somewhere."

Megan and Hailey both nodded.

"That's true, Leigh," Megan said. "Although I dearly love Chase, you're a model citizen compared to what you could have become after being raised by those Barrett brothers."

Azure tipped her head. "You don't like your brothers, Leigh?"

"Oh, I like them, I even love them. But they drive me up a wall sometimes."

Azure glanced around. "Which wall?"

Hailey bit back a laugh, but Leigh groaned.

"It's a *saying*, Azure," Leigh explained.

Azure sighed. "I've never heard any of these sayings before. They must be things you old people like to say, like 'Bless my boots.'"

"Hey, I'm only a tiny bit older than you," Leigh said. "I am not old. And I have never in my life said 'Bless my boots.'"

Azure didn't seem impressed. She studied Leigh, then said, "You look so much older than me."

Leigh turned toward Hailey and Megan. "Remind me to whack Trent on the head when he comes in."

Azure frowned once again. "Why?"

Deciding to step in before a war broke out, Hailey turned to Megan. "So, have you lived in Paxton all of your life?"

"Most of it. How about you? You're from Austin, right?"

"That's where I live now. Growing up, my mother and I moved around the country a lot. She liked to go on what she called adventures. She'd pick a new town, and we'd move there."

"Did you enjoy moving around that much?" Megan asked.

Azure sighed loudly and stood. "I'm bored."

As she tottered out of the room on her high heels, Leigh rolled her eyes.

"Whoever said that the young are the hope for tomorrow has never met Azure," Leigh said dryly.

Hailey hated to be mean, but Leigh definitely had a point.

A few seconds after Azure entered the kitchen, Nathan and Chase came into the family room.

"We thought we'd leave Trent alone with his date," Nathan said, coming to sit by Hailey.

Chase sat next to Megan, who kissed him on the cheek.

"If you ask me, Trent should charge Azure's parents for baby-sitting," Chase said.

Megan tapped his arm. "Don't be mean."

"Hey, she called me old," he said in his defense.

"She called all of us old. She came into the kitchen and told Trent she's tired of hanging around all of us old folks and wants to go dancing."

Leigh turned to Megan and Hailey. "See? This is exactly what I'm talking about. How could I possibly turn out normal with Chase, Nathan and Trent raising me."

"Hey," Chase said. "Trent I'll give you, but there's nothing wrong with Nathan and me."

"Oh, pulease." Leigh leaned toward Hailey. "Consider yourself lucky that you're an only child."

Truthfully Hailey hadn't given much thought to not having a family before arriving in Paxton. Sure, she'd been looking forward to her new job and teaching with her father. But now she was looking forward to reestablishing family in her life, to spending time with her father and getting to know him.

Of course, part of the reason she was looking forward to it was that her father was nothing like Leigh's brothers. Even though she hadn't spent much time with him, there was no way he could be like Leigh's brothers.

"You're lucky to have us," Nathan said. "Several circuses offered us good money for you, but we never once considered selling."

"Ha, ha." She turned to Hailey. "How do you stand working for this man? If it were me, I'd rather take out my own appendix using a rusty butter knife and salad tongs."

Hailey laughed. "He's not so bad."

Nathan turned to look at her, and she found her gaze held by his. Desire washed over her. Holy cow, did this man get to her. She felt tingles straight down to her toes, and she was very glad no one in the room could read her mind.

"Thanks for the faint praise," Nathan said. Even though his words weren't seductive, the way he said them was. Hailey's gaze dropped to his lips. She wanted to kiss him again. No matter how much she tried to resist him, she kept failing. Miserably.

"Hello, earth to Hailey and Nathan," Leigh said.

Hailey blinked and looked at her friend. Leigh had a knowing, smug expression on her face.

Hailey frowned. "What?"

"Not a thing," Leigh said in a singsong voice. "Not a thing. Not a single thing."

"Stop it, Leigh," Nathan said.

She grinned at him. "You love me, and you know it. Like I've said, if it weren't for me, your life would be boring."

Trent and Azure walked in at that moment. "I'm bored, too," Azure said. "I want to go."

Leigh laughed and asked the group, "Quick, what do you call a seesaw with nothing to do?" When they all shrugged, she said, "Board."

Azure frowned. "I don't get it. Is this another of those old people sayings?"

Hailey bit back a laugh, and glanced at Nathan. He winked at her, and she felt her heart do a little flippy-flop.

Yep, no matter how much she tried, she was finding it impossible to resist Nathan Barrett.

NATHAN EYED THE NEWSPAPER on top of the roof. Damn. How come it always ended up there? He wasn't expecting his newspaper to be resting on the doorstep when he came out each morning, but was it really too much to expect it to be on the ground? Muttering, he tossed his basketball up on the roof and watched as it bounced and rolled to the edge, thankfully knocking the paper down on its way.

"Danny, you have the worse aim of any person on this planet," he muttered as he picked up the basketball and newspaper.

"Who's Danny?" Hailey asked from behind him.

He hadn't heard her walk up. "My paperboy," Nathan explained. "He always tosses my paper up on the roof."

Hailey glanced at the roof and whistled. "Wow, that's quite a feat. You should have the local baseball coach put him on the team."

"I would except Danny's aiming for the porch."

She smiled. "Oh. That would be a problem." Moving up the walkway a few steps, she said, "You're awake earlier than usual."

"Couldn't sleep." Man, that was an understatement. He'd been wired when they'd gotten home from Chase's house last night, and after several restless hours, he'd finally given up and come outside to get the paper.

"What about you?" he asked.

"I get up this early every morning so I can jog before work," Hailey said.

For the first time, Nathan noticed she was wearing shorts, a T-shirt and running shoes. Her outfit was hardly racy, but it definitely got his blood pumping.

"Want to come along?" she asked with an inviting smile.

"Sure," Nathan found himself saying before his mind had a chance to override his hormones. Damn. What a stupid thing to agree to. Here he was trying his hardest to fight the attraction he felt for this woman and he'd just agreed to jog with her.

Had he completely lost his mind?

Apparently. And since he'd agreed, Hailey was smiling at him like he'd invented electricity. He certainly couldn't back out now.

"Give me a second to put on running shoes," he said, since he already had on shorts and a T-shirt.

He brought the basketball and paper inside and set them in the foyer. It took him only a couple of minutes to put on his running shoes, and then he was back outside.

"You pick the direction," he said. "But remember, I don't jog every morning so I may have trouble keeping up with you."

"Now why don't I believe that?" She headed down the driveway at a modest pace. Nathan had no trouble keeping up with her. He worked out regularly on a treadmill. The terrain around Paxton was flatter than a stagnant stock market, so jogging here was easy.

"I've never seen you out running," Nathan said when he drew near Hailey.

"I always run early," she said. "Before you leave for work."

"You know what time I leave for work?"

"Sure. Seven-thirty. On the dot. Except on Saturdays. Then you go in at eight."

They headed toward town, and Nathan came to a couple of conclusions. First, he liked that Hailey had paid so much attention to his schedule. And second, he realized he was the most boring man alive. He always went to work at the same time every day? He gave a rut a bad name.

"I had no idea I was so structured," he admitted, none too happy to find out that he was.

Hailey glanced at him. "What's wrong with structure? It's a good thing. It gives life a framework." She smiled slightly. "I like structure. It's not something I had growing up and now I find it comforting."

Hailey found structure comforting? For a split second, Nathan felt good about that. Until, of course, he realized that the last thing he wanted Hailey Montgomery to feel around him was comforted.

"Maybe Azure's right. Maybe I am old and boring," he said.

Hailey bumped her arm against his. "Trust me, you are neither old nor boring."

He grinned. "Damned by faint praise."

"Fishing for a compliment?" she teased. "I

would have thought all those trophies would have fulfilled your need for praise.''

Nathan chuckled. ''We all need an attaboy now and then.''

''Or an attagirl.''

''Or an attagirl,'' he agreed, keeping his pace even with hers. ''You've done a lot in your life to deserve praise. Was your mom the type to cheer you on?''

''Oh, yeah. Big time.''

Nathan glanced at Hailey. She sounded wistful, and he couldn't help wondering how long it had been since she'd had that kind of encouragement. ''And your dad? Is he big on cheering for you?''

Hailey smiled and shook her head. ''No. He's very proper. But he's kind, and always does the right thing. That's very important, too.''

''I think so.''

She slowed her pace, and when Nathan shot her a questioning look, she said, ''In a way, you're like him.''

Nathan groaned. ''I remind you of your father?''

With a laugh, Hailey explained, ''No. Not like that. I only meant you're kind. You think of other people. You try to do the right thing even if it isn't easy. I admire you.''

''I admire you, too,'' he said.

''Why? For mooching a job and a place to stay from you?''

He chuckled. ''No. For working hard. For throwing yourself into a project and pitching in.''

This time, when Hailey smiled, he could tell how pleased she was by what he'd said. But he meant it. He really admired Hailey. He was all set to discuss this some more when he noticed Steve Myerson up ahead on the sidewalk tugging on Rufus's leash.

"Hey, Steve," Nathan said, wishing he and Hailey hadn't been interrupted just when the conversation was getting interesting, but unable to ignore an old family friend.

"Hey, Nathan. Mind giving me a hand with Rufus? You did so well last time that I'm glad you came along. He has an appointment with the vet, but for some odd reason, I can't get him to move."

Might be because Rufus hasn't moved since his last vet appointment over a year ago.

Nathan looked at the dog, then looked at Steve's minivan. Finally he looked at Hailey.

"Didn't a pink tennis ball work last time?" she asked. "Why don't you do what you did last year?"

Nathan looked at Steve, who scratched his bald head. "Don't have any of those left. The last one I cut a hole in and put it on my antenna so I could find my van when I go to Food Factory." He explained to Hailey, "That warehouse store is gargantuan, and the parking lot is huge and filled with minivans the same color as mine. I could never figure out where I'd parked. Now I just look for the pink tennis ball on the antenna."

Nathan doubted that anyone could miss Steve's minivan. It was purple. The older man always maintained it wasn't purple but rather deep plum.

Nathan, like the rest of Paxton, simply agreed. None of them had the heart to point out to Steve that his minivan was not only purple, it was singing dinosaur purple.

Putting a pink tennis ball on the antenna of that van was about as necessary as tossing a lit match on the sun. There was no way anyone could ever miss Steve's minivan.

"So what do you think, Nathan?" Steve asked.

Nathan knelt next to Rufus and patted the old dog. "Feel like going for a ride?"

"Rufus doesn't much care what he does," Steve said. "Got any ideas?"

At Steve's question, Nathan turned his head—and found himself looking directly at Hailey's tempting legs. Oh, yeah, he had a few ideas. None of them had a thing to do with the dog, of course. But he had ideas all right.

"Maybe I can help." Hailey knelt on Rufus's other side, and Nathan cursed losing his great view of her legs. Of course, at this angle, he now had a great view of her pretty face. She was flushed from running and looked tousled and sexy.

"Are you thinking what I'm thinking?" Hailey asked.

He certainly hoped so. He smiled. She smiled back.

"Enticement. That's the key," she said softly.

Oh, yeah. That worked for him. He was one hundred percent behind the idea of enticement. He barely managed not to groan when Hailey wet her lips.

"Enticement," Nathan said.

"Exactly," she said.

"Liver," Steve said.

And Nathan felt like a bucket of ice water was poured over his head. He looked over his shoulder at Steve. "Excuse me?"

"Liver. Rufus loves liver. And I've got some in the fridge. Had it for dinner last night. Hold on."

As Steve headed into the house, Nathan slowly stood.

"Liver," Hailey said.

Nathan nodded. "Liver." She'd also stood, and he found himself unable to look away from her. "Was that the sort of enticement you had in mind?"

"Um, sure."

Nathan watched with fascination as a faint blush colored Hailey's cheeks. He kept his gaze fixed on her face and watched her become increasingly flustered.

"I've got the liver," Steve yelled coming back out the front door.

Hailey looked at Nathan. "What else would I have meant?"

"I'd give anything to know," he said, unable to stop himself from smiling. "Anything."

A smile haunted Hailey's lips but she didn't say anything because Steve reached them with the piece of liver. Rufus barely raised his head, which for a normal dog would have been showing no interest at all. But for Rufus it was practically dancing the tango.

"See, I told you he liked liver," Steve said, giving some to the pooch.

Hailey patted the dog, which remained firmly tacked to the sidewalk. "I still don't see how we're going to get him into the minivan."

"Oh, it won't be hard now that he's so excited," Steve said. He looked at Nathan. "You take the dangerous end and let the young lady here grab the safe end."

Nathan examined the dog, baffled as to which end was safe. From what he could tell the front end drooled a lot. But the back end of a dog like Rufus was…well, frankly unpredictable.

He looked at Hailey and raised one eyebrow. She bit back a giggle.

"Come on, let's get him loaded before he realizes what you two are up to," Steve said. "I'd help, but my back hasn't been the same since the seventies."

Nathan gave him a questioning look, and Steve explained with a laugh, "You know, disco."

This time, Nathan couldn't prevent himself from laughing as well. Hailey laughed, too. Even Rufus seemed amused.

"Those were the days," Steve said. "Now what say we put Rufus in the minivan?"

Since there was no way to avoid the inevitable, Nathan tried to lift Rufus. Although the dog didn't seem to mind in the least, he also weighed more than a truckload of macrocomputers.

Despite considering himself a fairly strong guy, Nathan had one hell of a time getting a grip on the dog. If he held Rufus around the waist, both ends sagged dangerously low. Hailey moved forward and held up Rufus's head, so Nathan reluctantly supported the back end.

"The van's over here," Steve said.

Like they could miss a huge, purple minivan.

"Boy, this dog weighs a ton," Hailey said, huffing.

Nathan shifted his hands forward a little so he could carry more of the weight. "He's a big dog, but I think the main problem is he's so relaxed."

"If he were any more relaxed he'd be dead," she said.

Finally they reached the van and carefully set Rufus in the back.

Nathan looked at Steve. "Can someone help you get him out at the vet's? You won't be able to do it alone, especially not with your back problems."

"Oh, don't worry about that. Doc Williams comes out to the car to give Rufus his yearly shots. Seems easier." He again scratched his shiny head. "But I will need some help when I get home. Don't suppose you could stop by this afternoon?"

Hailey looked horrified by the idea, so Nathan said, "We'll be at work. But I'll make sure Trent and Leigh stop by to give you a hand."

Steve grinned. "Thanks. I appreciate it."

After the older man climbed in his van and drove off, Nathan looked at Hailey.

"I smell like lazy dog," he said.

With a strangled sound, she sat on the curb, her hands covering her face. Concerned, Nathan sat next to her. "Are you crying?"

When she lifted her head, he saw she was laughing. "No. I've never worked so hard in my life not to smile."

"Yeah, Rufus is something else."

"I can't remember ever having so much fun." She laughed again. "The dangerous end? Which end is that?"

Nathan grinned. "It was a toss-up, I'll tell you. I wasn't sure what to do for a minute there."

"This town is unique, I'll give you that."

He liked to think so. "Yeah, Paxton's a fun place. Sort of the entertainment capital of the middle of nowhere."

She grinned back at him. "I don't know about you, but I really need a shower. Badly. I also smell like lazy dog."

Nathan stood and helped her up. "Come on. Let's go become human again."

Rather than jog, they walked on the return trip, laughing repeatedly about Rufus. When they finally got back to his house, Hailey waved, then dashed upstairs to her apartment to clean up.

Nathan headed inside his house, wondering at

what point he'd become so attracted to Hailey that even covered with dog fur and smelling like Rufus, she was the most compelling woman he'd ever met.

8

"HI...UM, DAD," HAILEY SAID two weeks later when she called her father. As always, she stumbled when calling him Dad. Prior to recently, she'd only spoken to her father a few times a year. Now she called him a couple of times a month, but even with the extra communication, their conversations were often stilted. She only hoped that would change once she moved to Wyneheart.

"Hailey, dear, how are you? How is that job in Peyton working out?" As always, her father sounded distracted. She could hear papers rustling in the background. No doubt he was working while at the same time talking to her.

She had a perfect image of him in her mind from her last visit to Wyneheart. He probably was sitting behind his huge desk, his papers systematically organized, a clock prominently displayed so he kept on schedule at all times. Unlike her own desk, on Benjamin Montgomery's desk, there were no papers slipping off the sides like lemmings plunging into the sea, no reference books teetering in Leaning Tower of Pisa piles, no half-consumed rolls of antacids scattered around.

No, Benjamin Montgomery's desk was neat, organized and efficient. Hailey couldn't help wondering what he was going to think once she finally moved to Massachusetts, and he saw how disorganized she could be at times.

He would probably have an embolism.

"Paxton. The job is in Paxton, Dad, not Peyton."

"Ah, so it is. Sorry, dear. Anyway, how is Paxton? I know you anticipated the place being dreadful."

"Paxton is great. I've met a lot of very friendly people here. And Barrett Software is a terrific place to work. Very advanced."

"If it's so advanced, why don't they locate their headquarters where the industry is growing? Someplace like Silicon Valley or on the East coast."

"Because the owner, Nathan Barrett, is very loyal to Paxton. He was born here and knows the town depends on him."

"Hmm," was all her father said, so she knew he wasn't listening to her again. The workings of small-town Paxton didn't interest him.

"So how are you?" she asked.

"Wonderful. Busy. Yesterday, I was struck by a brilliant idea for a new book, examining symbolism in Whitman. Not the same old, same old. But a really new approach. I've already roughed out the outline and can't wait to start writing. And how are you?"

How was she? She wasn't sure what to say to that. She was…confused. Confused by the feelings she had for Nathan. Confused as to what would happen to her if she acted on those feelings. Over the past couple of weeks, she and Nathan had both worked hard at being friends. But the memory of the kisses they'd shared danced between them like an annoying ghost. Whenever she was in the room with Nathan, she became confused about so many things.

Like how was she going to feel ten years from now if she *didn't* act on the feelings she had for him. And she had deep feelings for the man. She admired him. She wanted him. She liked him. And he confused her.

But her father wasn't the person to discuss those feelings with. He was trying. He really was. But he didn't have a clue how to be a father, and he certainly didn't know what to do with a female offspring. If she poured her heart out to her dad, she'd end up embarrassing both of them.

Instead she settled for the simple answer, "I'm fine."

"And your dissertation? Are you almost done?"

Um, if one considered almost done to be roughly a third of the way through it.

"Not quite," she admitted, feeling ridiculously like an errant child.

"Hailey, goals don't achieve themselves," her father said. "You must pursue them relentlessly. Victory belongs to those who claim it. A winner is the one who never relaxes. Always keep your eye on the horizon, your focus on the achievement, and your hand on the helm."

Oh, great. Just what she needed. Cross-stitch adages. "I know, Dad."

"Seriously, what seems to be the problem? You should be done by now."

Hailey couldn't tell him the problem was Nathan. The man got to her. Every time she was near him, she felt as if she'd just gotten off a Loop-D-Loop ride at a carnival. He confused her to the point that whenever she sat down to work on her dissertation, she ended up thinking about him instead.

She'd called her father hoping to refocus her energies. Now that she thought about it, his sayings were exactly what she needed. She should write them down and slap them on the wall next to her desk. She needed to pursue her dreams like a fox hot on a rabbit's tail. She needed to keep her eye on the goal and her hand on the...no wait, had it been her hand on the goal and her eye on the helm? She frowned. That didn't sound right.

Well, whatever he'd said, she agreed with it. She needed to keep her hormones under lock-and-key and her lips to herself.

Maybe that's what she needed to put on the wall next to her computer.

"I'm making progress," she told her father. "And I'm going to make even more over the next couple of weeks."

"That's my girl," her father said, and unexpected warmth flowed through Hailey. Yes, she was his girl. Even though they didn't know each other very well, they were both working hard to make up for the past. She wasn't alone in this world. She had family.

Okay, maybe not family in the way Nathan had family, but she wasn't sure she could take having a family like his. The Barretts had good intentions, but they were a crazy bunch.

She'd take her organized, practical father any day. Together, they formed a sane, rational family.

"READY FOR SOME GOOD NEWS?"

Nathan glanced up as Hailey entered his office carrying a stack of papers. During the past few weeks, she'd worked long hours helping Barrett Software flatten the problems with EZBooks. She'd done whatever anyone asked—pitched in on the testing, run reports, and even wrote some of the online helps. She was a smart, dedicated lady.

"I love good news." Nathan stood and crossed the room to take the papers from her. He hadn't meant to touch her, but his hands brushed hers when he took the report. They both felt the contact, and for a minute, simply stared at each other. Then Hailey took a step back from him.

"Those are the results from the latest batch of tests. Tim dropped the report off on his way home," she said, with a slightly breathless hitch to her voice.

Nathan forced himself to ignore the attraction he felt to Hailey and studied the papers instead. When he read the information, he let out a hoot. "Hot damn. The latest tests went great. Almost every function works flawlessly."

Hailey grinned. "I know. Congratulations."

"Congratulations to all of us. You included. You've really been a big help."

He could tell she was pleased by his compliment. A light flush colored her pretty face. "Thanks for saying that."

"I mean it." And he did. He really appreciated all of the help she'd given the team. He also appreciated the help she'd given him. She'd helped keep him on schedule. But more than that, he liked having her around. Being with Hailey made him happy.

"I'm having fun," she said softly, her gaze locking with his. "I'm glad I came to work here."

"I'm glad you're here, too." He found himself taking a step closer to her. Desire slammed into him like a fist.

Don't kiss her, you idiot.

Hailey tipped her head slightly. Her gaze moved from his eyes to his lips. He could easily tell she was thinking what he was thinking.

Do not kiss her!

Nathan struggled to remember all the reasons why he shouldn't kiss Hailey. He knew there were reasons. Lots of them. Too bad he couldn't think of a single one at the moment, and since he couldn't, he did the next best thing.

He went ahead and kissed her.

As ALWAYS, NATHAN'S KISS made Hailey wild with desire. But now, there was more. Much more. Kissing Nathan felt right. Felt perfect. She felt as if she'd finally found where she belonged.

So she kept on kissing him, and kissing him, and kissing him until the sound of the elevator in the distance made them both realize where they were and what they were doing.

"The cleaning crew," Nathan said when they stopped kissing and reluctantly stepped apart.

"Yes," was all Hailey could think to say.

"Guess we should head home," he said.

"Yes."

Nathan smiled slowly. "Are you going to agree to whatever I suggest?"

Hailey knew he was teasing her, but she wasn't when she answered, "Yes."

Nathan looked at her. Hailey felt her heart beating like a hummingbird's wings as she waited for his reaction.

Please don't say no.

Finally he asked, "Does that yes mean—"

"It means yes." She gave him a slow, seductive smile and she watched understanding dawn on him. "The next move is up to you, hotshot. You know where to find me."

With that, she headed out of his office, stopping by her desk on the way to get her purse. At the elevator, she ended up having to wait for the cleaning crew to exit, then she got in and took it to the lobby. As she walked across the parking lot, she kept hoping against hope that she'd hear Nathan running to catch up with her.

But the night remained silent except for the sound of distant traffic. Oh well. He'd no doubt leave in a few minutes and meet her back at the house. He probably wanted to think this over. She only hoped he came to the right conclusion.

Leigh maintained Nathan was never wrong. Well, Hailey hoped he didn't make the wrong decision this time. The right decision was to become her lover. She was tired of playing this game of cat and mouse. He wanted her. She wanted him. They should be together.

As she drove to Nathan's house, she kept checking her rearview mirror, looking for signs that he might be following her. But he wasn't. No headlights appeared behind her, and she couldn't help being disappointed. Had she really misread Nathan? It didn't seem possible. The man had just kissed her silly.

But he hadn't followed her home. So after parking her car, she headed up the steps to her apartment, cursing men in general and Nathan Barrett in particular. How could he not want her, too? She knew he wanted her. She was positive he wanted her.

"Darn him," she muttered, unlocking her door.

"Darn who?"

Hailey squeaked and spun around. Nathan stood at the bottom of the steps.

"I thought you weren't interested," she said breathlessly, thrilled to see him.

He chuckled and bounded up the stairs. "You

can't be serious. Me? Not be interested? Not possible."

"But I didn't hear you leave your office. And you didn't follow me home," she said, glancing around, looking for his car. "Hey, I didn't hear you pull up, either."

Nathan reached the top of the stairs and slipped his arms around her waist, tugging her close. "That's because I got here ahead of you."

"How? I left before you."

Nathan's grin was pure devil. "No, you didn't. The second you walked out, I sprinted down the stairs. No way was I going to give you a chance to change your mind." He reached over her shoulder and pushed open the door to her apartment.

Hailey laughed as he backed her through the doorway, his arms never moving from around her waist.

"You're sure about this, right?" he asked after they were inside and he'd shut the door.

"Yes," she leaned up and kissed him deeply. "I'm very, very sure. We both know this isn't about being together for a lifetime. But why should we waste what time we do have?"

"I like the way you think, Ms. Montgomery."

She laughed. "Why, thank you, Mr. Barrett. I'm pleased you agree with me."

He slowly undid the topmost button on her blouse. "I do have one question."

Deciding two could play at this game, Hailey

started unbuttoning his shirt. "And what would that be?"

Step by step, he undid all of the buttons on her blouse, then tugged it free of her skirt. Hailey mirrored his actions, unbuttoning his shirt and tugging it out of his pants.

"What is your question?" she asked again.

"Hmmm?" Nathan had been trailing the fingers of one hand over the tops of her breasts. Now he looked at her. "Oh, right. My question is if we have to wash each other's car each time we kiss, what's tonight going to cost us?"

THEY WERE ALMOST TO HAILEY'S bed before reality managed to seep through the lust clouding Nathan's brain.

"Hold on a sec," he said between kisses. "We're not ready."

She laughed, the sound low and sexy. "Oh, yes, we are. We're more than ready. We've been ready since you kissed me on the basketball court."

"Um, Hailey, that's not what I meant. I meant I don't have anything with me, so we aren't ready."

She continued undressing him, her small hands playing havoc with his blood pressure. "It seems to me you have everything you need with you already."

He started to laugh, but the sound came out as a moan of pleasure when she slid one hand down his chest. He barely managed to say, "I don't have condoms."

"Oh. Right. Condoms. Glad you remembered." She headed toward the small bathroom. "I have some."

When she came back out, she handed him a few packs.

Nathan glanced at the condoms. "They're green."

"I know. Some friends gave them to me last year when I got to go to Ireland with a group from the English Department. The theory was the green condoms would bring me luck."

"Did they?"

She shook her head. "Not a bit. But they are now."

"Hailey, I'm not sure about green condoms," he admitted.

"I'm positive you'll look wonderful in green."

He smiled, loving being with Hailey, loving touching her this way. The woman made him feel as if he could climb mountains, face dragons, solve any problem.

"Please don't tell me that those condoms glow in the dark," he said, dropping a string of kisses across her closest shoulder.

Her smile was more of a smirk. "Okay. I won't tell you. But don't be surprised."

Nathan groaned. "I don't believe this."

"Think of it this way, green glowing condoms beat no condoms at all."

She was right. And it wasn't as if he could go home and get some normal condoms. He hadn't been involved in a relationship in a long time, so he didn't have a thing in the house.

Besides, he didn't want to leave Hailey, even for a couple of minutes. She was the most amazing woman he'd ever known, and he didn't intend on leaving her tonight.

Hailey leaned up and kissed one corner of his mouth. "Don't tell me you're going to disappoint a lady."

Nathan pulled her close. Slowly he slipped his hands upward from her waist until they rested directly beneath her breasts. "I'd never think of it."

"Oh, goody," she said on a sigh as he slipped his hands even higher and cupped her gently.

He chuckled and released her long enough to open her bra and slip it off her arms. "You are so beautiful."

"Oh, really? Well what do you plan on doing about it?" she teased.

"Lots of things. Lots of wild things." Without preamble, he kissed her, coaxing lips apart and thrusting his tongue inside. His chest rumbled with a satisfied growl as she met his ardor with her own.

Kissing Hailey was the most amazing experience. He'd never believed in fireworks going off during a kiss, but they sure did with Hailey. Hailey obviously agreed. Rising on her toes, she brushed her body against his, her mouth closing around his tongue and keeping it prisoner.

Finally, with a shudder, Nathan tore his mouth free. "Hailey." His voice was a raspy caress.

Stepping back, he studied her and continued caressing her breasts. When she practically purred with pleasure, he dropped his hands to her waist, then tumbled them both to the bed.

"How am I doing, sweetheart? Are you happy?" His tongue dipped into her navel. A half-sob, half-moan escaped her lips as his tongue continued to caress her skin.

"I'll take that as a yes." He left the cove of her navel and moved his mouth first to one hip and then to the other. After that, he trailed kisses up to her breasts.

"Nathan," she sighed after a few moments. "You're driving me crazy."

"That's the general idca."

"Then it's my turn." She shoved him back on the bed and proceeded to show him just how wild lovemaking could be. He'd known being with Hailey would be like this—amazing and earth-shattering. When he couldn't take anymore, he tugged her into his arms.

"I think it's time we used one of those green condoms," he murmured, kissing her.

"Sounds like a great idea." Her voice was heavy with passion. "No wonder everyonc says you're so smart."

His heart pounded in his chest. Hailey felt like heaven in his arms, so soft and sexy and amazing. With her murmured encouragement, he helped her out of her clothes, then quickly got rid of his own. Turning to the nightstand, he grabbed one of the green condoms. At that point, he no longer cared what color they were or if they glowed in the dark. Hell, they could have played the theme from *Jaws* for all he cared by then. He was on fire for Hailey.

Slowly he joined them, then for one moment, held her gaze. Emotions he couldn't name flooded through him, mingling with the desire he felt.

"Hailey," he murmured, uncertain how to tell her that she meant the world to him.

She smiled and said softly, "I know."

And he knew she did. For that one moment, he knew they were as close as two people could be.

Then she teased, "Hey, hotshot, is this the best you can do?"

He grinned. "Sweetheart, you ain't seen nothing yet."

She groaned and ran her hands down his back. "Is that any way for an intelligent businessman to talk?"

"It is when he's about to do this," he said as he drove them both to distraction.

When he finally pushed them over the edge to ecstasy, he knew letting this woman leave him would be almost impossible. Their lovemaking had been everything he knew it would be.

Afterward, as he held her in his arms, he couldn't help feeling a sense of rightness. Of completeness. And he knew why he felt that way. As much as he hated to admit it, even to himself, he was in love with Hailey. He'd probably been in love with her for a long time.

But he knew telling her would be a mistake. Plus, it wouldn't do any good. Hailey didn't want to build a life with him in Paxton, and he cared about her too much to ask her to give up her plans for him.

Meanwhile, there was no way he could leave Paxton. Too many people depended on him.

"I knew green was your color," she said, snuggling against his chest.

Nathan smiled, happier than he could ever remember being. Even though loving Hailey was useless, he loved her all the same.

9

HAILEY WAS LOST IN THOUGHT when she entered Nathan's office and went to place some papers on his desk. She'd hardly seen him since they'd become lovers. EZBooks was keeping everyone running. But they were making progress at last, and Hailey knew that if anyone could pull this off, it would be Nathan. The man was amazing.

And she missed being with him. Their lovemaking had been wonderful, truly wonderful. As she'd expected, he was a tender, thoughtful, exciting lover.

She started to set the papers down, then froze when she saw what was on his desk.

"I don't believe it," she muttered. Caitlin Estes had sent a full sheet cake to Nathan with her picture on it. And not just any old picture. In the shot, she was in her cheerleading uniform. Again. Good grief. Apparently Caitlin had had a lot of success in that uniform because she obviously thought it would do the trick with Nathan.

A not-so tiny part of Hailey took satisfaction in the knowledge that Nathan was no longer available. At least, he wasn't at the moment. At the moment, he was hers. All hers.

Of course, he was just a loaner. She had no ownership rights where Nathan was concerned. All too soon, she'd be gone from Paxton. Then maybe Caitlin would succeed in her plan to catch his attention.

Hailey sighed. Darn. She hated that thought. She hated the thought of Nathan with anyone but her. But the reality of her relationship with Nathan was that he had to stay here. And she had to leave. She had a job waiting for her in Massachusetts.

As simple as that. She pulled her roll of antacids out of her pocket. Boy, life really stunk sometimes.

"Are you nervous about EZBooks?" Nathan asked, walking up to stand next to her and nodding at the antacids in her hand.

Hailey grabbed the excuse he offered. "Yes. Do you think it will be ready in time for the show?"

"Yes." He took the roll of antacids from her, then shut his office door. "You don't seem to get as nervous as you used to. I rarely see you using these things anymore. Any reason why you need them today?"

Hailey took the antacids from him and slipped them back into her pocket. "I've been more relaxed this summer, but today, I've been thinking about my dissertation a lot."

He grinned. "So you're relaxed this summer? I wonder why?"

She had to laugh at that. "I'm going back to work. The boss is a real dragon and I don't want him yelling at me."

Nathan continued to grin at her. "Fine. Run away. See if I care."

"Oh, you care all right. I know you do." She nodded toward his desk. "By the way, Caitlin struck again."

Nathan walked over to his desk and studied the cake. "Will this woman ever get the idea that I'm not interested in her?"

"You have to give her points for perseverance," Hailey said. "She knows what she wants and isn't going to give up."

"It's not going to do her any good. Sometimes you have to accept reality. If something isn't going to work, it isn't going to work."

Hailey nodded. Yep. He was right. Sometimes you had to accept reality, even if it stunk.

"I'm going back to work," she said, heading for the door before she did something foolish like kiss him. Or cry. She definitely didn't want to cry.

"Hailey."

She turned and looked at him. "Yes?"

"I'm sorry I've been stuck at work so much. I'd like to spend time with you."

She nodded again. She definitely wanted to spend time with him as well. Feeling a tightening in her throat, she quickly headed out the door. Blast it all. She wasn't going to cry. She absolutely wasn't. She rarely cried, and she certainly wasn't going to today.

And she wasn't going to do anything really stupid like fall for Nathan. She was way too smart for that. The last thing she wanted to take with her when she left Paxton was a broken heart.

NATHAN HAD JUST GOTTEN HOME from work when he bumped into Leigh in the foyer. She was sitting on a suitcase, obviously waiting for him. "What's up?"

"I'm going to stay with Trent," she said.

That didn't make any sense. Leigh and Trent were too much alike to get along. Their fights were the stuff of local legend. "Why?"

She shrugged. "I want to spend some time with him."

"But he lives in Paxton. You see him all the time. More than once a day at least."

Leigh looked Nathan dead in the eye. "I'm going, which means that your house will be empty. You will be the only person here, so it's not like anyone will know anything that happens in this house while no one is here."

Nathan chuckled. "I have no idea what you just said."

"Jeez, you're dense. Nathan, think. You will be alone in the house," she said slowly.

Nathan knew what she was telling him. He and Hailey would be without their chaperone. He just hadn't realized that Leigh knew the two of them wanted to be alone. He also hadn't realized Leigh knew why they wanted to be alone.

Then again, he wasn't sure why he was surprised. Everyone in this town always knew everything. Probably people at the grocery store were talking about his relationship with Hailey.

"This is unnecessary," he said. "You don't have

to leave. I'm spending almost all of my time at the office. In fact, I'm heading back tonight. You can stay here.''

Leigh snorted. ''You won't always be at the office. And I don't want you to have to sneak into your own house at four in the morning every day. You're really bad at it and make way too much noise.''

''How did you know I—'' He skittered to a verbal stop when a new and scary thought occurred to him. ''Why were you awake at four in the morning?''

She frowned. ''Hey, I'm actively not interfering in your life. The least you can do is actively not interfere in mine.''

She had a point, so Nathan nodded. ''Okay. Consider the question withdrawn.''

Leigh made a big production out of grabbing her suitcase. ''Good. Now I've got to run. Trent doesn't know I'm coming. I want to scare him.''

''Leigh, you can't simply barge in on Trent. Maybe he has a reason he'd like to be alone in his house, too.''

She laughed. ''Trent and Azure broke up right after the dinner at Chase's house. You need to keep up with what's going on around you, Nathan. Jeez, you'd think you were focusing on your own life or something.''

''You don't have to do this,'' he said one last time.

She winked. ''Yes, I do. And seriously, have fun. But don't break Hailey's heart.''

"I would never do that," he said.

"Yeah, yeah, that's what all guys say. Right up until the moment when they break our hearts."

With that, she headed out the front door. A couple of minutes later, there was a knock on the back door. Nathan wasn't a bit surprised to find Hailey standing there.

She looked confused. "Leigh just stopped by and said you wanted to see me."

Nathan came over and slipped his arms around her waist. "Leigh has decided to go stay with Trent for a while. Apparently she thinks there's some reason why I need my privacy."

Hailey fluttered her eyelashes. "Gee, Mr. Barrett, I can't imagine what reason that would be."

He feathered kisses on her face. "I don't know, Ms. Montgomery. Do you think if the two of us think really hard, we can come up with a reason?"

"Um, I'm pretty sure a reason has come up already."

Nathan laughed. "Then why don't we go upstairs and—"

"Wait."

Nathan blinked. "And wait?"

"No," she said with a laugh. "Well, yes. I mean you need to wait here."

With that, she pulled free of his arms and dashed out the back door.

"Guess I must have lost my touch," Nathan muttered. He knew he shouldn't be fooling around with Hailey. What he should be doing was changing his clothes and heading back into the office. But he couldn't bring himself to do it tonight. Not when he had the chance to be with Hailey.

Before he had time to get lonely, Hailey was back. In her hand, she had a box, which she tossed to him.

"Here you go, hotshot. I bought these today."

Nathan looked at the box, then back at Hailey. "You bought neon-colored condoms?"

"I figured we did so well with the green ones that we could have a lot of fun if we had a whole box of colors to choose from."

Nathan laughed and hugged her again. "You're crazy."

"Maybe," she said with a sexy smile. "But I'm positive my theory is correct. So let's go test it out, okay?"

"Sounds like a great idea."

HAILEY RUBBED THE TENSION from her neck and tried to refocus on the computer in front of her. Boy, she was tired. Really, really tired. For the past week, she and Nathan had practically lived at the office. She'd even started missing her morning jogs so she could come to work early with him.

And when they were home, well they weren't getting a lot of sleep. She was way too aware of how few hours she had left with Nathan to waste many of them sleeping.

All of which meant she was tired but very, very happy.

"I think we may pull this off after all," Nathan said, walking into her small office.

She smiled at him. "Really?"

"Yes. The testing group said they've pounded on the remaining code and haven't found any more problems. And trust me, those people are relentless. If the code was going to break, they'd make it happen."

"Nathan, that's wonderful." As much as she wanted to walk over and kiss him, she wouldn't at work. She had made a point of keeping their personal relationship out of the office when other people were around. Still, she was tempted.

"What's wonderful?" Leigh asked, wandering in. She flopped into the chair across the desk from Hailey and glanced from her brother to Hailey. "Are you two keeping secrets from me?" She laughed. "Oh, right, I forgot. This is Paxton. No one has any secrets."

"Unfortunately you're right. So if you must know, I was telling Hailey that it looks like EZ-Books is ready to go."

"Wow, not a moment too soon," Leigh pointed out.

"Yes, so now you can understand why I think it's wonderful that the program works," Hailey said to her friend.

Leigh looked at Hailey, a questioning expression on her face. "I can understand why this is great. But I kind of thought there were some other wonderful things going on in your life right now, too. I'm interested in those things as well.''

Hailey felt the warmth of a blush color her cheeks, but she refused to be embarrassed. ''This is Paxton, the land of no secrets.''

Leigh laughed and looked from Hailey to Nathan then back to Hailey. ''So now that things with the program have worked out, you two think there's any chance other things will work out?''

Hailey found her gaze drifting to Nathan. ''Things will turn out the way they're supposed to turn out.''

Nathan gave her a small, resigned smile. ''True.''

Leigh groaned. ''Great. Just great. You two are going to give up without a fight. I cannot believe this.''

Turning his attention to his sister, Nathan asked, ''And how are things with Jared? Did they work out?''

''Real cute, Nathan. You know the rodeo people have all left. But just because things didn't work out for me doesn't mean they can't work out for the two of you.''

''Why do you care, Leigh?'' Nathan asked.

''Because I like you guys. I want to see you happy. You're really disappointing me.''

Nathan looked at Hailey. ''She's disappointed because she likes that I'm too busy with my own life to butt into hers.''

Leigh pressed one hand against her chest. ''*Moi?* Have ulterior motives? Not possible.''

Both Nathan and Hailey laughed.

"It's true," Leigh protested but without a lot of conviction.

"I'm pretty sure you've had ulterior motives from the day you were born," Nathan said.

Leigh shrugged, a smile on her face. "Could be. But you know, this time, I'm right. You two should consider putting up a little more fight, you know. Things don't always have to turn out the way things are meant to, you know. Sometimes, you can force them to go your way. Like that old fax machine. Give it a good whack and it will work."

Hailey wished Leigh were right. But what her friend wasn't taking into consideration was all that either she or Nathan would have to give up to be together. Nathan would have to walk away from the town he loved and the people who depended on him.

And she would miss out on the chance to finally get to connect with her father. Not only that, but she would also lose a job that was perfect for her, one she'd spent years working toward.

Those weren't exactly easy things to overcome.

When Hailey glanced at Nathan, he was watching her. No doubt he was thinking the same thing she was. If there were a way, they both would probably find it. Because they cared about each other. A lot.

But was this love? And if it was, would it last? Was what they felt worth giving up everything for?

Tough, tough questions.

Leigh slapped her hands against the arms of her chair. "Well, I can tell you two have absolutely nothing to say to me, so I'm going to leave now. I haven't bothered Trent in at least four hours, so it's about time I go drive him crazy.''

She grinned at Nathan and Hailey. ''You two have fun now. And remember what I said. There are always options if you just know how to hunt them down. Don't give up without a fight.''

NATHAN GLANCED OVER at Hailey. He was glad he'd talked her into riding with him to Dallas for the computer show. Over the past couple of days, he'd thought about what Leigh had said. Although he rarely took his sister's advice, for obvious reasons, he couldn't help thinking she was right this time. Maybe he and Hailey should try a little harder to make their relationship work.

For starters, there were a lot of things they needed to discuss, and they were running out of time. This drive was the perfect opportunity.

''Hi,'' she said, waking up from a nap. She gave him a sweet, sleepy smile, and he wrapped his hands tighter around the steering wheel.

Tell her, you coward.

''Did you say something?'' she asked.

He certainly hoped not. He cleared his throat. ''No. But there is something I want to tell you.''

''What? Is it about the program?''

''No.'' He refocused his attention on the road, trying to decide whether this was a smart move or emotional suicide. Maybe he should just leave things as they were. He didn't have to tell Hailey how he felt. He could just leave it alone.

But he'd hate himself if he did that.

He glanced at her again. She raised one eyebrow.

"Is this some big secret or something? What, are you really an alien from another planet and now that we've made love, I may give birth to a part human, part squid child?"

He laughed. "Uh, no. That wasn't what I was going to say."

She grinned. "Good, because there is no way I'm changing the diapers on a half-squid baby."

Leave it to Hailey to make him laugh. He looked back at the road. He'd never told a woman he was in love with her before and frankly wasn't sure what was the right approach.

"I..."

"Yes? Nathan, you're killing me with the suspense. At least tell me if this is a good thing or a bad thing."

"A good thing. At least, I think so."

A semitruck was passing him, so he waited until it went by before continuing.

She reached over and patted his leg. "Then tell me. This isn't like you to act so shy."

That got him. "I'm not being shy."

"Okay, then coy."

"Hey, I'm a guy. I'm never coy," he maintained.

"Oops. Sorry. Didn't mean to offend you. So okay, what is it? Just blurt it out in a manly fashion."

He frowned. "Hailey, I'm in...what I mean is that I'm..."

Damn. Why was this so difficult to say?

"Nathan, what in the world are you trying to say?"

He drew in a deep breath, then went for broke.

"I love you."

He wasn't sure what response he expected from her, but it sure wasn't the absolute silence that greeted him. Complete, absolute silence.

Way to go, Barrett. Now she'll probably never talk to you again. Guaranteed way to send the lady running for the hills.

"I'm not expecting anything of you, Hailey," he assured her. "I know you have plans, and I know you can't stay in Paxton. I just wanted to let you know how I feel about you."

He heard her draw in a shaky breath. "I'm not sure what to say," she admitted.

Although he hadn't expected her to say she also loved him, it still smarted when she didn't reciprocate his feelings.

He cleared his throat. "I just wanted you to know. You don't need to say anything."

And she didn't. Say anything. She didn't say she loved him. She didn't say she liked him. Heck, at this point he would have settled for a "Can't we just be friends?" remark.

But Hailey took him at his word.

She didn't say a thing. Not one damn thing.

Not a good sign at all.

"CAN YOU BELIEVE THIS CROWD?" Tim said to Hailey as they stood at the Barrett Software booth watching Nathan do yet another demo of EZBooks.

"It's amazing. He's already been interviewed by a couple of newspapers and three magazines," Hailey said, thrilled the product was doing so well. "The voice recognition component is a big hit."

"This will make Barrett Software huge," Tim said.

Hailey agreed. The booth had been constantly surrounded over the past two days, and even now, Nathan was still running a demo of the product to a large group of interested buyers. She was thrilled for him and for everyone else at Barrett Software.

She grabbed a stack of the info cards and along with Tim, handed them out to the crowd. Once she was done, she indulged herself and watched Nathan for a few minutes. She had to admit, he was a charmer. Everyone loved him.

Of course, it helped that EZBooks worked flawlessly. But in a swamped place like this, the attendees had a couple of hundred different displays they could go to, but huge groups stopped at their booth because Nathan pulled them in. She couldn't help noticing that a lot of the visitors to their booth were female. Not that she could blame them. He was smart. He was witty. He was handsome. He was wonderful. And...

And she loved him. The realization hit her like a tidal wave. Wow. As she stood there, watching him, Hailey drew in a shaky breath. She really was in love with Nathan. Hopelessly, stupidly, blindly in love with a man who was all wrong for her.

Why hadn't she done something easy, like fall for a guy who lived on Mars? Because when it came right down to it, Paxton was almost as far away from the life she planned on building in Massachusetts.

How had she let this happen? What was she going to do now?

"This is going great," Nathan said after he finished the presentation.

Hailey nodded. "Yes. Great."

He leaned closer and inspected her face. "I know I ask this a lot, but are you okay?"

With effort, Hailey forced herself to smile. "Yes. I'm fine."

"Are you tired?"

"A little." She kept staring at him, stunned by her own feelings. She loved him. Really, truly, deeply loved him. The emotion was so intense and startling that she almost blurted it out to him in the middle of the demo booth.

Good grief.

Nathan glanced around. "Tim and the others can handle the crowds for a while. Why don't we take a break? I'll buy you a soda."

She hesitated. Was being alone with Nathan right now a good idea?

He leaned closer and murmured, "I'll flirt with you."

Unable to stop herself, she smiled. "Oh, okay."

As Hailey followed him to the small café and got

a soda, she debated whether she should tell him how she felt. But the more she thought about not telling him, the more she mentally kicked herself for being a wimp. Nathan had been honest with her. She needed to be honest in return.

Drat!

But was being a coward really such a bad thing? Lots of famous people had been cowards. Plus, what good would come from him knowing? In fact, he might think that since they both loved each other that she was willing to give up her dreams to stay with him, which wouldn't happen. So why tell him?

"Do you want to sit in here or outside?" Nathan asked.

She sighed. She couldn't chicken out, darn it, no matter how tempting the idea might be. The man deserved to know he was loved in return.

But why did it seem as if doing the right thing was never easy? You'd think just once in a while, life would give you a break. But she wasn't getting one today, that was for sure.

She glanced around the cramped room. "Outside."

"It's hot out there," he said.

Hailey figured they wouldn't be out there long. How much time did it take to tell someone you loved them, but wanted to stop seeing them? Five minutes? Ten?

Ought to go pretty quickly.

"Okay." Nathan carried the sodas and waited for Hailey to precede him. When she walked outside, a blast of hot air hit her. Figured. She literally would be in a hot seat this afternoon.

Heading to the table in the farthest corner, Hailey sat and took her soda from Nathan.

Nathan glanced around, then teased, "If you'd picked a table any farther away, we'd be back home in Paxton."

Nodding, Hailey fumbled in her pocket and pulled out an antacid.

"Oh, no. Something's wrong," Nathan said, his attitude now serious. "What happened?"

Hailey chewed the chalky tablet and debated how to word this conversation. She needed to phrase her confession delicately. She needed to draw on her skills as an English major to handle this well. "Nathan, we need to talk."

"That doesn't sound good. Not good at all. Can I have one of those antacids?" he asked.

Hailey smiled. "I think you'll be fine."

"I'm not so sure. You look pretty serious." He took a sip of his soda, then said, "Okay. I'm set. What's wrong?"

"You're not facing a firing squad."

"Feels that way," he said, his gaze locked with hers.

Yes, it did. Especially since as much as she loved Nathan, after she told him about her feelings, she also planned to tell him what he didn't want to hear. She had to tell him that as soon as they got back to Paxton, she planned on packing and returning to Austin.

Love or no love, they didn't have a future together, and it would be better in the long run if they stopped seeing each other right now. She needed to end this quickly, efficiently. Her heart was going to break, sure. But she needed to put Nathan and Paxton, Texas, behind her if she was ever going to get on with her life.

Of course, she didn't need a crystal ball to know Nathan wasn't going to like that she was leaving. But he had to know. She couldn't let him think they were going to live happily-ever-after.

She cleared her throat. He sat watching her closely. "Um, Nathan, do you remember how on the drive here you told me you love me?"

He pretended to consider her question, but there was a definite twinkle in his eyes. "Let me think. We talked about the weather. We talked about BizExpo and EZBooks. But love? Did we discuss love? Let me think for a second."

She sighed and drummed her fingers on the table. "You know very well what you told me on the drive. You said you loved me."

He gave her a gentle smile, but she could tell he was expecting more from this conversation than she was going to deliver. "Okay, yes. I remember I told you I love you. I also remember you didn't say anything back. Not one single word."

"Well, I'm saying something now. Nathan Barrett, I love you, too."

10

HAILEY WAITED ANXIOUSLY for his reaction. Thankfully he grinned and indicated the nearby crowd.

"You picked a heck of a time to tell me," he said. "But I'm very happy to hear you feel that way. I think the first thing we should do is—"

"No."

He raised one eyebrow. "No?"

"That's right. No." Before he could misunderstand, Hailey added, "We can't have a life together. And even though I love you, I believe we should stop seeing each other."

She'd obviously stunned him. He leaned forward and said, "That wasn't exactly what I had in mind."

"I know. But just because we love each other doesn't mean we're meant to be together. We want different things. Have different plans."

Nathan leaned back in his chair. "You have to give me a minute here. The woman I love just told me she loves me, too. I need to enjoy that for a while."

Hailey sighed. "Nathan, I think we should—"

He held up one hand. "Wait. I'm not through enjoying it yet."

Despite the seriousness of the topic, Hailey laughed. "You nut."

He grinned. "Hailey, I know what you're going to say, but I still can't help being thrilled that you love me, too. Even if we both want different things out of life. And even if we can never make this work, I'm blown away that you love me."

Before she could answer, he stood and circled to her side of the table. Then he kissed her, long and deep. "I've never been in love before. It's an amazing feeling."

"Yes, it is." Hailey patted the side of his face. "And you're an amazing man. But—"

Nathan chuckled and leaned away from her. "Nope. No buts. Not yet. Let's enjoy the being in love part for a while."

"But after we get home, I need to pack up and head to Austin," she said. "It doesn't matter that we love each other."

Nathan walked over and sat back down. "Oh, yes, it does. It matters very much."

"You know what I mean. What difference does it make if we love each other? We can't make this relationship work."

For the longest time, Nathan simply looked at her. Happiness practically radiated off of him. Finally he said, "I know we can't last forever. But we love each other. That has to count for something."

She'd expected this discussion to be difficult. She just hadn't planned on impossible. "We both want different things out of life."

"Couldn't we change what we want? I vote that we develop new plans," he said. "I vote that we don't throw away what we feel for each other."

Hailey twisted her hands in her lap, wondering what was the best way to make him understand.

"Nathan, although I love you, I can't tear my life apart. For all either one of us knows, this love we feel won't even last. It could be simply really strong lust."

"It will last," he said firmly. "It isn't just lust."

"You don't know that."

"Yes, I do. You need to have faith in us."

She sighed and fought back the urge to cry. Crying wouldn't help anything. Instead she tried to formulate another approach.

"Okay, let's say we decide to be together. Which one of us gives up everything? Do you leave Barrett Software? And if you do, what happens to Paxton? Or do I miss out on the chance to finally get to know my father, something both he and I have been looking forward to for a long, long time? So which should it be, Nathan? You hurt the people of Paxton or I hurt my father?"

"Dammit all, Hailey, there's got to be a way," he muttered.

"I don't know what it would be."

He looked determined. "I'll think of something. Solving problems is one of my best talents. I'll solve this one, too."

She wanted to believe him. Oh boy, she wanted to believe him. But she sure didn't see how to make this work. Still, she couldn't help holding on to the glimmer of hope he offered.

"I guess we'd better get back to the booth," she said, standing.

Nathan stood as well. "I will solve this," he said.

She doubted it. But she gave him a small smile. Then together, they headed back to the booth in silence, each of them lost in their own thoughts but both of them wishing life could be different.

HAILEY GATHERED THE LAST of her clothes and struggled to fit them into her one remaining suitcase. Why was it that clothes that came out of a suitcase never seemed to fit back in it right? She hadn't bought anything while in Paxton. No *I Survived Paxton* T-shirts. No cowboy clothes at the rodeo. So why wouldn't the stupid things fit?

After repeated attempts, she resorted to banging on the suitcase. She wasn't in the mood to fight with her clothes right now. She just wanted to go back to Austin and start working on fixing her broken heart.

She was banging so hard on the suitcase that it took her a minute to realize someone was knocking on her door. She fought back the thrill of excitement she felt. It wouldn't be Nathan. He had avoided her as much as she'd avoided him since they'd gotten back from Dallas yesterday.

When she opened her door, Leigh stood outside. "Hi."

"Hi."

Leigh frowned. "You look like hell."

Hailey imagined she did. "I've been packing to go back to Austin."

"I thought you weren't leaving for another three days?"

Hailey shrugged. "I decided there was nothing left for me to do here, so I might as well head on home."

With a snort, Leigh said, "No offense, but you're a terrible liar."

"What? I'm not lying. I'm—"

Cutting Hailey off, Leigh continued, "You're lying to me and you're lying to yourself. You love Nathan and you know it. Everyone in town knows it."

"We don't love each other," Hailey said, but rather than a stern protest, the words came out as almost a sigh.

Leigh snorted again. "Don't throw away happiness, Hailey."

"Leigh, even if we did love each other, it could never work. I have to think of my father. He and I have plans."

"Have you asked him what he thinks you should do?"

"No," Hailey admitted.

"You should," Leigh said. Then she turned and headed down the stairs. "Talk to you later. I just thought of something I need to do. But before you leave, Hailey, call your father. Tell him what's happening."

Hailey stood at the top of the stairs to her apartment, staring after Leigh. Her friend was wrong. Dead wrong. Asking her father what he thought was unfair. She'd made promises to him. Promises she couldn't break.

Shutting the door, Hailey glared at her suitcase.

Shirts and jeans hung out the sides like the arms of an octopus. Maybe she could find a box or a bag around here and put some of the clothes into it. She went over to the closet and poked around, finally finding an old box in the back. After snagging the box, she was all set to toss her errant clothes inside when she realized the box wasn't empty. It contained several framed pictures.

Despite herself, Hailey sat on the sofa and took out a few of the pictures. They were of Nathan and his brothers and sister. In each shot, the four of them were clowning and joking and laughing. The Barrett siblings might fuss, but they really loved each other a lot.

"They're so lucky." She rooted through the box and brought out the remaining two pictures. One was a school portrait of Leigh. Hailey figured her friend was in first or second grade in the picture. She had a big green and blue bow on the top of her head and looked ready to kill the photographer.

Hailey laughed, then looked at the last picture. It was of Nathan at approximately the same age. He was missing his two front teeth, but that didn't stop him from flashing a killer smile at the photographer.

Always the charmer. Even in grade school.

Hailey traced her thumb across his face, and felt the warmth of tears on her cheeks. Drat. She'd promised herself she wouldn't cry. Crying was silly and useless. She'd made the right decision. She had. Leaving was the right thing to do.

"Stop it right now," she said. "I mean it. Stop

crying right now, or I won't buy any fudge ripple ice cream for a month."

Despite her threat, the tears kept falling.

"This is ridiculous," she said, sniffling. She headed toward the kitchen and grabbed a tissue. Blotting the tears didn't seem to help, either. Nothing seemed to help.

Without thinking, she grabbed the phone and dialed. Her father answered on the first ring.

"Hailey, dear, it's so good to hear from you. I was talking to Marge Adler today. She teaches American Literature and like the rest of the English Department, can't wait for you to arrive."

Hailey sniffed. Oh terrific. More waterworks. "That's great," she said, hoping her overly cheerful voice would cover up the sounds of her crying.

A long, long, *long* silence greeted her. Finally her father asked, "Hailey, are you crying?"

The way he said the word *crying* made it clear he hadn't a clue what to do with a daughter in tears.

"Um, a little. I'm really looking forward to moving to Wyneheart and spending time with you, but I'm also going to miss Paxton."

"I see. Do you always cry when you move?"

"No." She never cried. Ever. Well, hardly ever. The only other time she could remember crying was when her mother passed away. But moving never made her cry. It mostly filled her with anticipation, not with sorrow.

"So this Paxton is a special town?"

She thought about that. Yes, Paxton was special;

at least it was to her. She'd met a lot of terrific people here, many of whom she considered friends.

And she was definitely going to miss Rufus. Saying hi to him on the way by each morning while she was jogging was one of the bright spots of her day. In fact, she was almost convinced that sooner of later, Rufus would actually wag his tail for her. It could be wishful thinking, of course, but she couldn't shake the feeling that it was a possibility.

"Hailey, are you still there?" her father asked.

"Yes. And yes, Paxton is special."

"I see. Well, Wynchcart is a special town as well. Filled with very charming people."

Hailey sighed. Charming. Yes, she was sure Wyneheart had charming residents. But they weren't charming in the way that Nathan was. The man could charm the snow out of the sky on an August afternoon.

"I sense there's more to your sadness than missing Paxton. Want to tell me what's really wrong?"

Despite Leigh's suggestion, Hailey hadn't intended on pouring her heart out to her father, but the next thing she knew, she blurted, "I'm in love with Nathan Barrett."

"I see."

"And his company is the only reason the town of Paxton is still thriving. If he were to move his business, the town would be reduced to tumbleweeds."

"I see."

"So he can't possibly follow me."

"I see."

"And if I stay here, then I don't get to teach at Wyneheart or spend time with you."

"I see."

Hailey sighed. "But even though I know leaving here is the right decision, I can't seem to stop crying."

"I see."

Despite how upset she was, Hailey sighed. Her father was trying, but she had to admit, he was really bad at this comforting thing.

"Anyway, Dad, that's why I'm crying. But I guess in time I'll feel better," she admitted. "I'm just down right now."

"Nonsense."

Okay, she'd accepted that he wasn't good at comforting, but calling her emotions nonsense seemed a trifle harsh.

"I'm not usually so weepy about things," she said in her own defense.

"No, I didn't mean how you felt was nonsense, I meant your plan."

Hailey frowned. "Dad, I think maybe I should just call back later."

"No. I need to tell you something that will make you feel much better. I love you, Hailey."

Well, that did make her feel somewhat better. She liked knowing she had her father's love. "I love you, too, Dad."

"Good. Then there's something you can do for me."

"What?"

"Stay in Paxton with Nathan."

She blinked. "But, Dad, what about you and the job and my future?"

"I never got the chance to be much of a father to you when you were growing up, Hailey. I've always regretted that. But today, I'm getting my chance. The most important thing in the world to me is that you're happy. And dear, love is too precious to walk away from. If you really love Nathan, you should be with him. Now I'll finally have a reason to use those frequent flyer miles I've been accruing, I'll come visit, quite often as a matter of fact. And you have to promise to come visit me as well."

"But what about the job you had lined up for me?"

"You're very smart. You can find another one at the University of Texas or any of the other colleges around. I'll help you in any way I can."

Hailey felt more tears trickle down her cheeks. She couldn't believe how sweet her father was. How had she been so blessed to have two great men in her life?

"Hailey, dear, are you crying again?"

"I love you, Dad."

"I love you, too. Now go find Nathan, ask him to marry you, then get on a flight to Massachusetts and introduce me to him. I never got to play the part of a stern father interrogating his daughter's beau. I don't want to miss my chance."

Hailey laughed, knowing her father was going to love Nathan as much as she did.

"Thank you," she said softly.

"Just don't be surprised if I also find myself a

teaching position in Texas. I want to be around when the grandchildren arrive.''

Hailey felt more tears come and this time she didn't even try to stop them. Her life had suddenly become too wonderful for words.

"YOU'RE AN IDIOT," Leigh said the second she walked into Nathan's office.

"If I agree, will you go home?"

She rolled her eyes. "As if. Now what are you going to do about this?"

Nathan held onto the slim hope that his sister wasn't talking about his relationship with Hailey. "What am I going to do about what?"

"You know good and well about what. Hailey. You. The fact that even Rufus is smart enough to know the two of you belong together. So why are you letting her leave?"

Nathan had asked himself the same question a million times even though he knew the answer.

"Not that it's any of your business, but I can't ask Hailey to give up her future and stay here. And I can't very well go with her since that would mean the end of Barrett Software."

Leigh sighed. "Jeez, Nathan, you have the most complicated problems. Okay, I'll admit you'd be a real jerk if you asked her to stay. But would the company really fold if you lived someplace else?"

Unfortunately the past few weeks had shown him what a vital part he was to the company. When EZ-Books had run into problems, he'd done everything from some coding to helping with design problems and finally pitching in on the testing.

"Yes. Barrett Software needs me."

"Can't the company come with you? Can't you relocate?"

Nathan gave his sister a pointed look. "And what would this town do for revenue? A large portion of the town works for me."

"Okay. Okay. But what if you sell the company to someone else?"

"What if that someone else moves the company?"

Leigh groaned and slapped his desk. "Stop finding negatives. Look for positives."

He felt compelled to point out, "There aren't a lot of positives, Leigh."

"There's the most important positive—you and Hailey love each other."

"You seem awfully certain of that."

Leigh nodded. "I am."

Nathan smiled at his sister's confidence. "You sure you're not just trying to get me so distracted that I'll leave you alone?"

She grinned. "I'll admit, it's a definite upside. But seriously, I'm glad you found someone perfect for you. Now stop being such an idiot and work this out. You're a smart guy. You solve big problems every day. You need to solve this one, too. Don't let her get away, Nathan. You know you'll never find someone like her again." Finally she added softly, "She's really leaving, Nathan. You can't let that happen."

Nathan knew his sister was right. He couldn't let Hailey leave, at least not alone. He needed her in his life. As much as it seemed selfish to sell the company just so he could be with the woman he loved, he also knew he'd regret it forever if he didn't do everything in his power to make things work with Hailey.

He'd just have to make absolutely certain that whatever company he sold Barrett Software to would treat the employees right and leave the headquarters here in Paxton. If he handled this correctly, he could have Hailey in his life without destroying the town or the lives of the people who worked for him. Sure, he'd miss Barrett Software. He'd miss it a lot.

But not as much as he'd miss Hailey if he let her leave.

"I'll find a buyer for the company," he announced to his sister. "Of course, they'll have to promise to keep it based here in Paxton, so it may take me a little while. But you're right. I can't let Hailey out of my life."

"Now you're talking," Leigh said with a grin. "So go tell Hailey before she heads back to Austin."

By the time Leigh finished speaking, Nathan was already halfway to the door.

HAILEY WAS ALL SET TO GO find Nathan when there was a knock at her door. A thrill of excitement danced through her, and she knew before she even opened the door that this time, it was Nathan.

"Hi," she said, after opening the door.

He grinned and leaned against the doorjamb. "Hi yourself. Guess what?"

"Wait. I have something to tell you," she said, anticipation bubbling inside of her.

"Nope, sorry, but this time I'm not doing ladies first. I need to tell you my news before you can tell me your news."

She couldn't keep herself from smiling. "I thought you were raised better than that?"

"No. That's just a rumor." He glanced beyond her. "May I come inside?"

"You own the place." She pushed the door open wider. "Make yourself at home."

He walked past her and sat on the couch. Hailey barely kept from hugging him on the way by. But she'd let him tell her his news first. It wouldn't be easy to wait, but she'd do it.

She settled next to him and smiled. "So what do you want to tell me?"

"I've decided to sell Barrett Software."

Hailey couldn't believe what she was hearing. "But what about the employees? What about Paxton?"

"I'll find a company to buy me out that will promise not to move the headquarters."

"You can make such stipulations?"

He nodded. "Pretty much."

"You don't sound very positive."

"Hailey, don't you see? This way we can be together."

She couldn't believe how much he loved her. He

was willing to sell Barrett Software and move away from Paxton just to be with her. "You'd really do all that? For me?"

He leaned over and kissed her deeply. "You mean everything to me. I'll do whatever is necessary to keep you in my life."

Hailey blinked back tears of joy. "Really? Because I feel the same way. And as much as I appreciate your willingness to sell your company, it won't be necessary. One of the things I love about you is how loyal you are to your family and to Paxton."

"I'll make certain they're both fine before I leave for Massachusetts," he assured her. "I want to be with you."

"Nathan, you can't take the risk that your employees would have to move. Even if you got promises in writing from the buyer, something could go wrong."

He took one of her hands in his own. "I'll make certain nothing goes wrong. I promise."

She shook her head. "That's not good enough. If the new owners decided to move, you couldn't stop them. Then what would happen to Paxton? To the employees? To Rufus? Let's face it, we know it's almost impossible to move him."

"That won't happen," he assured her again. "And not just because it would be impossible to move Rufus. Because I'd never let anything bad happen to this town."

She placed one hand on the side of his face, loving him, loving being able to touch him like this. "That's exactly why we're not going to Massachusetts. I spoke to my father and he agrees with me. I can find another job at a university close to Paxton. And we can visit Dad often, and he'll visit us. But…''

He raised one eyebrow. ''But?''

''I can never find another man as wonderful as you.''

Again, he leaned over and kissed her. This time, the kiss caught fire, and Hailey suggested, ''Want to move to the bed and continue this discussion?''

Nathan pretended to be shocked. ''Ms. Montgomery, what sort of man do you think I am?''

''A wonderful, terrific, magnificent, fantastic man who I hope to spend the rest of my life with.''

He brushed her lips with his. ''And you're the most amazing, fascinating, exciting woman I've ever met. Will you marry me?''

''Yes,'' she said on a sigh.

He kissed her hand. ''I promise you, Hailey, that I'll do whatever it takes to make all of your dreams come true. I won't let you down.''

''Same back at you, hotshot,'' she said, knowing their life together was going to be filled with love and hope and promise. They would work together to make certain they both got what they wanted and needed from life.

This time when he kissed her, she wrapped her arms around him and held him tight, unable to believe how lucky she was.

''Wow,'' Nathan said when they finally ended the kiss. ''That was something else.''

''Honey, you ain't seen nothing yet,'' she teased.

Nathan had a definite twinkle in his eyes. "Hey, is that any way for an English major to talk?"

"It's perfectly acceptable if she's an English major in love," Hailey said. "And I am most definitely an English major in love."

*   *   *   *   *

Hold onto your seats...
'cause we're not done with
The Barretts of Paxton, Texas just yet!
Liz's next Double Duets will feature
Trent's story and Leigh's...
Look for MEANT FOR TRENT
and LEIGH'S FOR ME
in the fall of 2002!

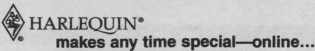

Meet the Randall brothers...four sexy bachelor brothers
who are about to find four beautiful brides!

WYOMING WINTER

by bestselling author

Judy Christenberry

In preparation for the long, cold Wyoming winter, the
eldest Randall brother seeks to find wives for his four
single rancher brothers...and the resulting matchmaking is
full of surprises! Containing the first two full-length novels
in Judy's famous *4 Brides for 4 Brothers* miniseries,
this collection will bring you into the lives, and loves,
of the delightfully engaging Randall family.

Look for WYOMING WINTER in March 2002.

And in May 2002 look for SUMMER SKIES,
containing the last two Randall stories.

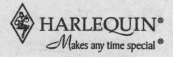

HARLEQUIN®
Makes any time special ®

Visit us at www.eHarlequin.com   PHWW

Every day is

A Mother's Day

**in this heartwarming anthology
celebrating motherhood and romance!**

Featuring the classic story "Nobody's Child" by Emilie Richards
He had come to a child's rescue, and now Officer Farrell Riley was
suddenly sharing parenthood with beautiful Gemma Hancock.
But would their ready-made family last forever?

Plus two brand-new romances:

"Baby on the Way" by Marie Ferrarella
Single and pregnant, Madeline Reed found the perfect husband in the
handsome cop who helped bring her infant son into the world. But did his
dutiful role in the surprise delivery make J. T. Walker a daddy?

"A Daddy for Her Daughters" by Elizabeth Bevarly
When confronted with spirited Naomi Carmichael and her brood of girls,
bachelor Sloan Sullivan realized he had a lot to learn about women!
Especially if he hoped to win this sexy single mom's heart....

Available this April from Silhouette Books!

Where love comes alive™

Visit Silhouette at www.eHarlequin.com   PSAMD

These New York Times *bestselling authors*
have created stories to capture the hearts and minds
of women everywhere.
Here are three classic tales about the power of love—
and the wonder of discovering the place
where you belong....

FINDING HOME

DUNCAN'S BRIDE
by
LINDA HOWARD

CHAIN LIGHTNING
by
ELIZABETH LOWELL

POPCORN AND KISSES
by
KASEY MICHAELS

Available only from Silhouette
at your favorite retail outlet.

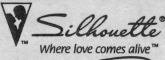

Where love comes alive™

Visit Silhouette at www.eHarlequin.com

MONTANA *Born*

From the bestselling series

MONTANA MAVERICKS

Wed in Whitehorn

Two tales that capture living and loving
beneath the Big Sky.

THE MARRIAGE MAKER by Christie Ridgway

Successful businessman Ethan Redford never proposed a deal he
couldn't close—and that included marriage to Cleo Kincaid Monroe!

AND THE WINNER...WEDS! by Robin Wells

Prim and proper Frannie Hannon yearned for Austin Parker, but
her pearls and sweater sets couldn't catch his boots and jeans—or
could they?

And don't miss

MONTANA *Bred*

Featuring

JUST PRETENDING by Myrna Mackenzie

&

STORMING WHITEHORN by Christine Scott

Available in May 2002
Available only from Silhouette at your favorite retail outlet.

Silhouette

Where love comes alive™

If you enjoyed what you just read,
then we've got an offer you can't resist!

Take 2 bestselling love stories FREE!

Plus get a FREE surprise gift!

Clip this page and mail it to Harlequin Reader Service®

IN U.S.A.	IN CANADA
3010 Walden Ave.	P.O. Box 609
P.O. Box 1867	Fort Erie, Ontario
Buffalo, N.Y. 14240-1867	L2A 5X3

YES! Please send me 2 free Harlequin Duets™ novels and my free surprise gift. After receiving them, if I don't wish to receive anymore, I can return the shipping statement marked cancel. If I don't cancel, I will receive 2 brand-new novels every month, before they're available in stores! In the U.S.A., bill me at the bargain price of $5.14 plus 50¢ shipping & handling per book and applicable sales tax, if any*. In Canada, bill me at the bargain price of $6.14 plus 50¢ shipping & handling per book and applicable taxes**. That's the complete price—what a great deal! I understand that accepting the 2 free books and gift places me under no obligation ever to buy any books. I can always return a shipment and cancel at any time. Even if I never buy another book from Harlequin, the 2 free books and gift are mine to keep forever.

111 HEN DC7P
311 HEN DC7Q

Name	(PLEASE PRINT)	
Address	Apt.#	
City	State/Prov.	Zip/Postal Code

 * Terms and prices subject to change without notice. Sales tax applicable in N.Y.
** Canadian residents will be charged applicable provincial taxes and GST.
   All orders subject to approval. Offer limited to one per household and not valid to
   current Harlequin Duets™ subscribers.
   ® and ™ are registered trademarks of Harlequin Enterprises Limited.   DUETS01

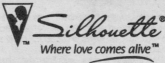